FIRES OF THE ATESI

A HUNTINGTON ADVENTURE

Books by Thom Reese

Huntington Adventures
Dead Man's Fire
Chasing Kelvin
A Savage Distance
Fires of the Atesi

The Dracula Journals
Dark Decades
Ravaged Souls
Eternal Midnight

Novels
The Demon Baqash
The Empty
13 Bodies: Seven Tales of Murder & Madness
The Infusion of Archie Lambert

COMING SOON!
The Voyage of the Amethyst Castle

FIRES OF THE ATESI

A HUNTINGTON ADVENTURE

Thom Reese

SPEAKING VOLUMES, LLC
NAPLES, FLORIDA
2021

Fires of the Atesi

Cover design by Hannah Linder

ISBN 978-1-64540-547-4

For Kathy

Acknowledgments

As with all my novels, I have many people to thank. I sit alone in a room coming up with fantastical ideas, some of which become part of a story others just don't fly or are too absurd even for my fictional realities. I need objective viewpoints to help me stay on the right path. And none of my novels would be as good without these indispensable people by my side. As always, my number one supporter is my wife, Kathy. I never would have accomplished any of this without her. My loyal beta readers Jeff Granstrom and Crystal Rosenblatt gave me invaluable advice which made this novel richer and more fulfilling to you, the reader. A warm thank you Kurt and Erica Mueller from Speaking Volumes for their continued faith in my writing and encouragement. You are much appreciated. As always, my daughters Trista, Amy, and Brittany inspire me daily. Many thanks to Amy Densham and Stephen Degnim for their grassroots efforts in getting the word out about my novels, to Doug Norris, Topher Barnes, Ken Chapman, Mike Chapman, and Greg Van Houten for their moral support. And of course, thank you to each of you, my readers. None of this would have purpose without you. Thank you all.

Seven months ago, Marc Huntington acquired an ancient amulet with peculiar and disturbing properties. And though the amulet was used to save his life, the very thought of the relic causes nightmares and terror. Yet, he has never since let it leave his presence.

Chapter One

Columbia

Marc (Hunt) Huntington laid on his belly, propped on his elbows, gazing through night vision binoculars. The building was more a fortress than a dwelling. The sheer tan walls glowed nearly golden beneath the full moon, guards patrolled the grounds, electric fences reinforced the perimeter. Hunt wiped perspiration from his brow with the back of his hand and then slapped at a mosquito. It was late, past midnight, the temperature only hovering around fifty degrees Fahrenheit, but it was humid and Hunt's adrenaline was pumping. "You up to the climb?" asked Hunt.

His partner/estranged wife Dana glared. "That's bloody insulting. I'm as capable as you."

Hunt grinned saying, "Yeah. I knew that. Just trying to be courteous."

"I think the term you're looking for is chauvinistic. Courtesy has nothing to do with it."

"Which of course is why I have a female partner. We going to do this spat thing or get on with the job?"

Dana tossed a saucy grin in Hunt's direction. "That's it. Just hide behind the mission."

"I'll take what I can get," quipped Hunt, returning the grin. Bathed in the brilliant moonlight, Dana looked like an Asian princess, maybe even a goddess. Hunt couldn't help but stare.

"What?" asked Dana, her eyes twinkling with mirth.

"Nothing. Just . . . nothing." Now wasn't the time to talk about their tenuous relationship.

He glanced about the brush. They were on a tree covered rise overlooking the home of Paulo Gomez, an up-and-coming drug lord specializing in modified cocaine with significantly higher potency than that currently on the market. This compound housed labs used to experiment on the new drugs. Gomez kept at least fifty caged resus monkeys he used as test subjects. The animals were located on the east side of the compound and Hunt had had an opportunity to observe these creatures during his reconnaissance. They were highly agitated and aggressive. He'd seen one handler savagely attacked, possibly losing an eye during the encounter. Whatever Gomez was pumping into these beasts hopped them up like a meth addict on a nuclear adrenaline rush. He hoped it never hit the streets. The result would be horrifying.

The grounds were well guarded, but the Huntingtons had already managed to breech the fence undetected and deactivate the security system. Hunt had memorized the security routines. The next patrol on this side of the building wasn't due for another ten minutes. Still, it didn't hurt to check their six. Unexpected things happened. It was part of the gig. Overconfidence was often paid for in body bags.

Gomez had kidnapped the teenage daughter of an American A.T.F.E. (Alcohol, Tobacco, Firearms, & Explosives) agent, threatening to kill her if the man didn't allow certain shipments to fly under the radar. One U.S. special ops team had already made a failed attempt at rescuing the girl and so she'd been relocated to this more remote location. The girl's father had offered a reward of fifty thousand dollars for her safe return. Not a huge payday, considering the risks, but a girl's life was threatened. Hunt planned on gaining that reward money while simultaneously giving a big screw-you to the cartel. The job wouldn't be easy but, as rescue and recovery specialists, he and Dana did this stuff for a living. They'd put together a solid plan with contingency options. He felt their chances were on the upside of seventy percent.

Dana gave Hunt a signal. He nodded and, rising to a crouch, moved forward following his wife. Slipping through the shadows, they made the wall in less than five minutes. There was only one guard on this, the western wall, and Hunt dispatched him with a tranquilizer dart. Pulling the unconscious man deeper into the shadows, Dana said, "Remember, there will be a guard nearing the corridor as we enter. We'll likely need to fight as soon as we clear the wall."

Hunt nodded. He'd known of this complication, of course. There was simply no better option. For at any other time there would have been more opposition than a single guard to overcome.

The grappling hook caught on the second attempt and Dana, going first, began scaling the wall nearly as a monkey might a tree. Chuckling, Hunt followed suit. In truth, he had trouble keeping up with her. Dana had always been fit, but in recent months she'd made it nearly an obsession to train harder than most Olympic athletes ever had. She'd been subdued several months ago. Viciously attacked. She was determined that she'd never again be helpless.

By the time he made his target, Dana had already slipped out of sight.

Climbing through an upper window and into a narrow corridor, Hunt found that Dana had already dispatched with the guard who leaned unconscious against the wall. Helping Dana to pull him into a shadowy corner, Hunt went over the plan mentally. If their intelligence was correct, the girl was being held one level down and on the eastern side. There would be at least two additional guards in this wing, but once they made the chamber, they should be secure. If the guards kept with their established pattern of the past week, the Huntingtons would have nearly seven minutes before the first guard should be noticed missing. At that point, the remaining seven would be mobilized.

Dana moved around the nearest corner, heading to the eastern side of the building and forcing Hunt to follow. It took less than four minutes to make the bedroom which, in theory, held the girl. They had encountered no other guards along the way. This troubled Hunt. He'd studied this place for over a week using a drone and other electronic surveillance equipment. He knew the number of the staff and where each should be at any given moment. Sure, interruptions happened, unexpected events broke routines. But where were the two additional guards? It wasn't that he missed the opposition, but it meant his intelligence was now invalid. Something had changed. Maybe simply by chance or more possibly because of their presence. Hunt knew when the guards were generally at each position, but he had no way of knowing if there were radio protocols. If one of the two incapacitated men had failed to place a check-in call it might have alerted the team to a potential threat.

Hunt held up his hand signaling for Dana to hold position. Leaning forward, he pressed an ear against the thick wooden door and listened intently for more than a minute. He made eye contact with Dana, nodding. She returned the nod and signaled that she would enter first. Maybe Hunt was a bit of a chauvinist after all. He hated letting Dana take the lead into dangerous situations. But she'd been a British intelligence agent, and while her experience had been less physical than Hunt's Delta Force background, she was a very capable operative.

But he loved her. And wanted to keep her safe. Well, as safe as this line of work would allow. Did that really make him a bad guy? Attaching a small explosive charge at the door handle, Hunt stepped away, shielding his face. The charge offered a sharp pop accompanied by a flash and a hiss.

Dana immediately moved into the room. "Three hostiles," shouted Dana even as Hunt entered on her heals and caught sight of the two guards he'd expected to encounter in the corridors plus one bonus baddie.

Dana stabbed upward into the closest man's belly with a Taser. The man gasped and shuddered before falling sideways jittering and gasping as electricity shot through his body.

Hunt pivoted left, taking a fighting stance. The man before him was perhaps a full head taller than Hunt, broad shouldered, and well-muscled. He held an AK-47 and was swinging it around to fire when Hunt stepped into the man's space preventing him from utilizing the weapon. Despite his size, the man was quick, jabbing the butt of the rifle into Hunt's left shoulder. But it was a glancing blow as, anticipating the move, Hunt feinted right. A step back and a stutter left gave Hunt the needed room to maneuver. He jabbed at the man's solar plexus, but the move was deflected. They grappled with one other, Hunt doing his best to keep the AK-47 out of the game. Hunt pushed with all his might but advanced only by two steps. The man's strength and bulk was far greater than his own, while the skill belonged to Hunt. Still, he would need to finish this quickly. The man had the strength of an elephant.

A savage fist aimed at the face. Hunt was barely able to deflect. Hunt was backed against a wall, dislodging several pictures which tumbled to the floor. Ducking to avoid the next jab, Hunt pulled a knife free of its sheath and slashed his opponent across the right calf, cutting through muscle and tendons. The larger man fought to remain upright, but his leg would not support him. Nearly before the man connected with the floor, Hunt kicked him hard in the head with his booted foot. The man was out before Hunt kicked his weapon free of his hands.

Turning to survey the room, he saw that Dana had also dispatched her opponent and was now advancing toward the terrified girl who had sat cowering on a bed throughout the battle. "It's okay," said Dana. "You're Ashley, is that right?" The girl nodded while still gawking at the three unconscious thugs. "Good, good. Your father sent us to rescue you. You're going to need to trust us."

Hunt was at the door looking for additional hostiles. "Ashley, why were those guards in this room? Is that normal or had they come in because they knew we were coming?"

The girl just shook her head. She was slight, no more than five feet in height, with a butterfly tattoo on her neck and lips that seemed designed for a perpetual pout.

"Ashley," said Dana. "You need to help us."

She shook her head as if clearing a fog. "They come in sometimes to threaten me. I think they wanted to do . . . bad things." Here, she looked down, avoiding eye contact.

Hunt saw Dana stiffen but she stayed on task. "Did they give any indication that something unusual was happening tonight?"

"No. I don't know. I was scared. I didn't know what they wanted." She then leaned forward and spit on the nearest unconscious man and then nodded with a grin. "He deserved that."

"Yep. Sure did," said Hunt. "Now, we've got to move. Ashley, I know this is nuts, but you've got to do everything we say, you understand? We know what we're doing." To Dana he said, "Assuming this was a fluke and they haven't called in the cavalry, we've got just under three minutes before the first guard is found missing. We need to move."

Nodding, Dana guided Ashley off the bed and positioned the suddenly wide-eyed girl between her and Hunt. There was hesitation but not outright resistance. The girl was certainly confused, but not stupid. She understood what was happening. Hunt could see her attempting to muster some of that teenage bravado as she sneered at the fallen guards. He had a feeling the girl could be a handful.

Hunt had memorized the layout of the place and led them down a back staircase that landed just outside the kitchen, which at this time of night should be unoccupied.

It was, and they moved quickly through the cooking space and then out onto the rear lawn.

They were midway across the space when spotlights lit the grounds. Shouting and cursing erupted from the rear. Stealth was no longer an option.

A voice came across a loudspeaker. "*Suelta los monos.*"

"What was that?" asked Dana.

"They're releasing the monkeys on us like attack dogs," said Hunt, who spoke fluent Spanish.

"Monkeys?" asked Ashley. Apparently, she was unaware of what went on here.

"Test subjects. Hopped up on some crazy turbo-powered cocaine," said Hunt. "Hurry." The girl looked at him like she thought he was a lunatic, but still, she moved with them, offering no argument.

But it was too late. The air was already filled with screeching howls. Dozens of frantic shapes appeared from the shadows, eyes unnaturally wide, jaws clamping. Hunt pulled Ashley between he and Dana as they fended off the swarm of primates while still racing across the grounds. Both Huntingtons were armed, but though they took several of the beasts out with well-placed shots, there were simply too many of them. These were not normal monkeys. Whatever concoction they'd been given had caused them to become frantically aggressive.

Racing through the trees, their hoots and screeches bombarded the small party. And soon snarling primates were climbing all over them, teeth bared and limbs pummeling. Hunt pulled three of the things off Ashley, who had fallen to her knees screaming in terror, before a half dozen of the beasts landed on Hunt, pulling him to the ground. As he fought the biting, scratching primates, he saw Dana wrestle free of several monkey's and pull Ashley to her feet to race toward the fence. Ashley stumbled, Dana righted her as a monkey landed atop her head, clawing at her face. Dana fired a shot directly into the thing's head, sending it hurling behind her. Hunt and Dana both loved animals, but there was no room for sympathy here. This was kill or be killed.

Hunt rolled, pulling a monkey free by its neck and hurling it at a tree. He bashed another with the butt of his gun, and then smacked two others together, head-to-head, before rising and racing after Dana. A monkey clung to Hunt's leg, biting into his thigh and Hunt batted at it continuously, but the thing would not release. Finally, he shot it at point-blank range.

In preparation for their escape, Hunt had already cut an opening in the nearby fence and the trio now raced toward the slender opening. "Hurry. This way," shouted Dana as she led the terrified girl through the narrow gap in the once electrified chain link. She batted away a wildly snapping monkey and then slipped through after Ashley.

"There's a steep grade just before us," said Hunt as he raced to catch up with the others. "It leads to the water. We've got a boat waiting." Two monkeys rode his shoulders. Angling, he propelled himself at a nearby tree, back first, smashing the chattering beasts between himself and the tree. One of the monkeys fell free, the other maintained its grip.

There were now shouts from the rear. Automatic weapons fired about them.

Dana pulled Ashley forward through the brush as Hunt returned fire. The girl was crying and stumbled as she attempted to keep up with Dana. They were less than two minutes from the water and Hunt had prepared a surprise for any followers who got too close.

Bounding down the grade, smacking at the clinging monkey, and firing off random shots, Hunt felt several bullets wiz by connecting with a nearby tree and nearly cutting it in half. Crouching, Hunt nearly tumbled down the uneven grade but managed to right himself just as another volley of bullets ripped past. The monkey scampered away, apparently retaining just enough sense to fear weapons fire.

Dana and Ashley were already in the boat when Hunt raced onto the narrow beach an unknown number of pursuers close behind. "Go!" shouted Hunt. "Go!" as he entered the shallow water and rolled into the boat. "Keep down!" he shouted to Ashley as the engine whined and Dana twisted the throttle. The small craft lurched and surged as Dana tossed the final two screeching primates into the frothing water.

Glancing back at the beach, Hunt removed a small remote control from his breast pocket and depressed a button. There were three boats along the water's edge. Each exploded in a whoosh of flames. Gasping for breath, Hunt said. "That'll slow them down."

"But they'll catch us," screamed Ashley. "We're just in a little boat. They'll catch us!" Whatever composure the girl had maintained had now evaporated. Tears were flowing freely and she shook like a nudist at the North Pole.

Hunt attempted to offer a soothing tone. "Nah, nah, nah. We're meeting up with an amphibious plane about a mile out and around the bend. We'll be out of the country before your pals back there can figure out their next move."

Attempting to calm the frantic girl, Hunt smiled and said, "Hi, I'm Marc. And this stunning beauty is my wife, Dana. Sorry, but we're offering no meals on this cruise."

His attempt at humor fell flat. Ashley crossed her arms, attempting to contain her shivers and glared at Hunt with a disdain that only teenage girls have in their arsenal. She probably didn't know what to believe. Dana placed a palm on her back. "You'll be okay now. We're taking you home."

As planned, it took nearly ten minutes to reach the plane. It was exactly where Hunt had instructed the pilot to place it. He'd used the man before and found him to be reliable. But the reliability came at a cost. The pilot's fees were outrageous.

As they neared the floating Cessna, Dana's satellite phone chimed. "Who is it?" asked Hunt as Dana pulled it from a pocket.

"Jonathan," said Dana.

"Don't answer that now," said Hunt, suddenly irritated.

Dana offered a saucy grin. "Why? It's my ex-husband."

"Exactly my point," groused Hunt.

To his irritation, she accepted the call, went through a bit of chit-chat, but then hurried Jonathan Thorpe to the point. When she disconnected, she said, "We're going to Turkey."

"What? Why?"

Dana smiled. "Jonathan found a job for us. One hundred thousand up front. Another one hundred thousand at completion."

Great. He'd have to deal with Thorpe again. The guy always found a way to weasel his way close to Dana. "What's the gig?" he asked with no enthusiasm.

"I have absolutely no idea."

Hunt glared. He hated this almost as much as the rabies shots he'd be forced to endure because of the multiple monkey bites.

Chapter Two

Somewhere in Turkey

He'd been known by many names through the centuries. Ates Iyesi, Od Iyesi, Od Kahn. Recently he'd simply been known as the Atesi—the flame. His followers thought of him in different ways. As the fire father, the flame spirit, the fire god. The concepts were all the same, simply different aspects of his being. And the name didn't matter in the least. What mattered was devotion. There had been a time when his human followers were plentiful, where he was broadly respected and worshiped by the local shamans and their devotees. But time moved forward, new ideas were preached to the humans. The old religions were forgotten. Ates Iyesi was nearly forgotten.

But there remained the faithful few. Those that rejected the ways of the masses. Those that desired to be set apart. The Atesi held no illusion that their devotion was solely centered on him. He knew humankind too well to believe such a thing. What these people truly worshiped was their own rebellion against established religion, the religion of the state.

Still, this was something the Atesi could work with. Something he could manipulate. Their devotion might currently be marginal and fueled by simple rebellion at the status quo, but soon they would understand that they were in the presence of a true deity and that only absolute commitment would be tolerated.

The Atesi scanned the small assembly. Less than twenty devotees cluttered the shabby would-be temple. In truth, it was an abandoned grocery mart. Folding chairs had been set in seven rather uneven rows. Boxes of merchandise from the building's former purpose lined the walls. The Atesi's objective was to recruit willing soldiers, not to impress the masses with elaborate cathedrals. In truth, the ramshackle setting was quite purposeful. The Atesi desired to attract people that lived on the fringe, social outcasts, those dissatisfied with the establishment. This dilapidated structure brought with it a sense of rebellion, of admission into a recalcitrant underground movement. The Atesi intended to mold these misfits to his needs.

That said, most of the attendees were talking and joking amongst themselves as if this was simply a social gathering.

Well, that wouldn't do, would it?

The Atesi twisted his neck, causing a series of popping sounds. He stepped to before the assembly. His movements were disjointed, shaky, his left arm flopped up and then down involuntarily. He drooled. The Atesi despised the flesh, the necessity of inhabiting a human form in order to appear before his followers. The body was difficult to manipulate, the muscles slow to respond to his mental commands. But even in this corruptible form, he could demonstrate his great power.

Gazing out over the assembly, he said, "Well, well. What have we here? A band of mutts, it would seem."

The crowd quieted. The Atesi heard someone mutter, "What did he just say?"

The Atesi chuckled. "I called you mutts. Does anyone care to challenge me on the assessment?"

Blank stares, a few awkward shuffles, some averted eyes.

Ah, they were a pathetic lot, but they were his to mold. In truth, their role in his ascension would be minimal. Helpful, but minimal.

"So," he said. "You answered my call and so dare to break with Allah. You wish to worship the old god, Ates Iyesi. I applaud your impudence. Certainly, you will experience rifts within family groups and a decline in social status. But this is the least you should suffer for the privilege of serving a living deity."

At this point, his pathetic human body shuddered, both arms jerked.

Someone chuckled.

"Who was that?" asked the Atesi.

Silence.

"I said, who dared to laugh at me?"

More silence.

And then, "I did." A young human, perhaps thirty years in age stood. He was a bit paunchy and his hair was an unruly bush. He had a sly grin on his smug round face.

Perfect.

The Atesi had desired an example.

"Ah!" said the Atesi. "Ah-ha! It appears you find me humorous. Perfect! Wonderful! Would you care to share with us what you find so amusing?"

The chuckler said nothing.

"Oh, come now. Please. If you laughed, you must have found something humorous."

The Atesi stepped forward. His movements were jerky, uncoordinated. At one point he nearly stumbled. Damn the flesh!

"You laugh," said the Atesi. "Because you see only the imperfect human instrument I'm forced to inhabit in order for you to see me through those near useless eyes of flesh. And yes, it is a pathetic thing, this body. Much like your own frail form." Here, the Atesi pinched the young man's cheek. "Soft. Insubstantial. How do you people endure such an existence?"

No response.

The Atesi grinned. "Ha! I see, I see. To you—to all of you—the flesh seems sufficient. This is only because you've never experienced the glory of divinity. You are mortal. You are temporary. Would you care to see what a true spirit of the ages can do?"

He leaned in close to the chuckler. "Do you?"

The young man nodded nervously.

"Good. Good! Ha! This should be fun. Fun! Do you hear me?" The Atesi turned slowly, assessing the curious eyes of each person. These people had simply responded to an online notice claiming that Ates Iyesi had returned and that he summoned the faithful. The Atesi knew human nature. There was no question that those on the fringe, those dissatisfied with their lot, would come. Not out of devotion, but out of curiosity, out of a longing to belong to something bigger than themselves. But the reason they came did not matter. It was that they came that was significant.

"I am known as the fire father, the flame spirit. Would anyone care to see how I came to bear such a moniker?"

A few scattered nods.

"How about you?" he said to the chuckler. "Would you like to witness the great and terrible truth?"

The young man stood silently. The Atesi saw him tremble.

"Of course, you would like to see. You would all like to see. That is why you are here—all of you. You want to learn if I am what I claim to be. To know if there truly is something miraculous in this wretched world, to seek some value to your pathetic existence. Well, allow me to assure you, I most certainly am exactly what I claim to be."

There was a young woman seated next to the chuckler. The Atesi took her hand, instructed her to rise. Nervously, she stood before him as, grinning, he spit on both of his palms, rubbed them together, and then smeared the spittle on her cheeks. Smiling, the Atesi addressed the crowd. "You see? You see!"

As expected, no one could fathom what he expected them to see.

"Ah! Oh-ho!" exclaimed the Atesi. "You do not see. For I have yet to give you anything to witness." Turning to the chuckler, the Atesi said, "Blow on her."

"What?"

"Blow on her face. As if you were extinguishing a match. I'm sure you're capable of the petty deed."

The chuckler looked at the Atesi and then at the girl. Shrugging, he said, "Sure. But this is pretty stupid."

The Atesi laughed. "Of course, it is. That is why we're all here. Because I'm stupid. Blow!"

With a nervous chuckle, the young man did as instructed.

The woman's cheeks immediately burst into flames. She screamed, batting at the flames as they spread to her hair and then down her form as if she'd been doused with gasoline.

There were shouts of hysteria and panic as the Atesi turned to the chuckler and said, "You've served your purpose. Join her."

The chuckler burst into flames, spinning about in a panicked twirl before tumbling to the ground to squirm and scream.

The room was now in chaos. People were rushing toward the doorway at the far end of the hall.

"No!" cried the Atesi, and the double doors slammed shut. "Listen to me well," said the Atesi, having to shout over the diminishing screams of the dying humans. "I have done this seemingly horrific deed for a purpose. You will come to learn that everything I do has a purpose." He paused, scrutinizing the crowd. "I am fully aware that most of you were here on a lark. You may have believed, however imperfectly, or you may have simply wanted some small excitement in your pathetic lives. But none of that matters. For you are here and you now belong to me." He glanced down. The girl was now motionless, the chuckler still squirming, but only just.

"I offer you a role in what is to be the great and final chapter of this age. But I will not tolerate doubt or subversion. Does anyone doubt my resolve?"

There were scattered murmurs, "No, Lord." "I am willing, great Atesi." "We are faithful, fire father."

"Good, good. Enough of that cowering." He paused and glanced at the two still forms at his feet. "Now, clean up this mess. This is no place for refuse. And when you are done with that, we will discuss the end of the age and your part in it."

Chapter Three

Turkey

Hunt glanced to his right, addressing Dana. "I still don't see why we had to bring Thorpe."

"Because," said Jonathan Thorpe, who was seated to Dana's right in the back seat of the ancient Volkswagen van. "I am the one who made the connection. That would make me, I suppose you would call it, the facilitator. You should thank me, for, as we both know, this could be a quite profitable venture. You do appreciate profit, I assume."

"Yeah," said Hunt. "About that. You said these guys were looking for me specifically. But you were vague about the reason. I remember you saying you'd tell us when we got closer." Hunt pointed to the structure barely visible over the next rise. "Well, we're about as close as we can get. Spill it, Thorpe."

"Yes, well, always the gentleman, Marc. Though, I do suppose the time is upon us." Thorpe's tone was, as always, very upper crust British, just shy of haughty.

After several moments of silence, Hunt prodded him again. "Thorpe, what is it you don't want to tell me?"

Thorpe shrugged. "It has to do with your amulet."

"My amulet?" Hunt's heart jumped and he unconsciously gripped the thing through his shirt.

"Yes. You do only have the one, I presume."

Dana turned to Thorpe saying, "Jonathan, what is this about?" Hunt could hear a twinge of her cockney accent peeking through. Normally, she hid her upbringing well, affecting a proper tone more akin to

Thorpe's, but when she was excited or nervous her east-end roots tended to creep through. Mention of this bizarre amulet obviously unnerved her nearly as much as it did him.

"That, dear, is beyond the scope of my knowledge. I suppose need-to-know and all that whatnot. But here's the crux of it. The people of the monastery put word out that they were looking for the person in possession of an amber amulet containing a locust from the Biblical plagues on Egypt. Quite a curious request in that, well, that is a rather specific artifact, and one which I know you to possess. How they knew of the amulet or even that someone was now in possession of it, I couldn't say."

Hunt felt as if the air rushed from his lungs. A bead of perspiration tickled his brow. Still clutching the stone through his shirt, he asked, "Why do they want the amulet?"

"I don't believe they want the amulet per se. I believe it is the person in possession of the amulet they wish to see. Again, they were not quite forthcoming with the information. I am, after all, simply the intermediary."

"Nah. No go. We can turn around right here." Everything having to do with the amulet was shrouded in supernatural weirdness, and though he quite literally owed his life to the thing, everything about it made him cringe. Gripping the amber even tighter through his shirt, Hunt turned to gaze at the jutting cliffs. He felt his fingers quiver and willed them to still.

"Now, you see," smiled Thorpe. "This is exactly why I postponed revealing this information until we were within sight of our destination."

Hunt turned to glare at the man.

"Jonathan," said Dana. "You know how traumatic everything having to do with that artifact is to Hunt. I think you owe him an explanation."

Thorpe smiled. "Well, to begin with, they're paying you one hundred thousand dollars just to make an appearance today. At which point they'll explain everything. You will then be free to accept or decline their offer—which is another one hundred thousand to complete whatever assignment it is they've dreamed up. I'm not sure there's need of much more of an explanation than that."

"Yeah," said Hunt. "The reasoning of a thief. It's all about the money."

"You may not care for my chosen profession, Marc, but I've never seen you shy away from an opportunity to enhance your resources."

Hunt simply grunted. He sincerely wished they'd left Thorpe behind. But he was their contact here and he was right, there was a decent payday at the end of this road. But God. The amulet. What could anything good have to do with that crazy, frightening freak show of a thing? And was Hunt even up to dealing with whatever it was? The last time the amulet had come into play . . .

Hunt closed his eyes, tried to think of anything else. He couldn't dwell on that. How could anyone truly comprehend how he simultaneously loathed and adored the thing?

At this point, the driver, a young man in his late twenties, said, "I'm sure they told the thief very little. The nature of this adventure is quiet secret and I doubt the Keepers want someone like Mr. Thorpe knowing any more than necessary."

Hunt chuckled, Thorpe scowled, and Dana said, "Keepers?"

The driver shrugged. "Priests, monks, holy people."

"What are they keeping?" asked Hunt.

"That is not for me to say," said the driver.

***

The monastery was a small three-story building located midway up a sheer mountainside and hidden from view by towering evergreens and two neighboring peaks. The brick structure was located in a small grotto recessed into the side of a cliff. There was a narrow winding spring, several goats, chickens, and two cows visible on the eastern field adjacent the place. Dana saw only three monks as they were led through the building and into the chapel area but was certain there must be more than these, for there were four long tables in what she supposed to be the dining area, numerous overcoats hung along a wall, along with various other signs of habitation.

The young driver led the three visitors through several narrow corridors and finally into a small dimly lit room. An elderly priest, bald, tall yet hunched, arthritic hands, but with clear penetrating eyes, sat on a short stool at the far end. He smiled and nodded as the driver brought the party forward. "Please, please, sit," said the man indicating three wooden folding chairs facing him. They were the only furnishings in the space. His accent was strong, but his English clear. As they each claimed a seat, the priest said, "I am Father Abidin. Welcome to our home. The roads are steep and narrow, but I trust your journey was uneventful."

"Thank you," said Dana as she scanned the barren brick walls. Not even a crucifix adorned the room. Strange. "The trip was lovely, though I admit there is some intrigue as to why we've been brought all this way and paid such a handsome sum for a meeting that could have taken place over Zoom or even the telephone."

"Ah!" smiled Abidin. "You are very direct, Mrs. Huntington."

"I believe curious would be the accurate term."

Abidin nodded. "That would seem appropriate." He paused, surveying the party of three. "Yes. I suppose we should be about it then." He lifted his arms wide as if offering the visitors to examine the room about them. "We are a small brotherhood. Merely twelve in number, the same sum as the apostles that served our Lord. And like them, we are tasked with a great responsibility." Here, the priest paused, making eye contact with each of his guests. Dana felt his scrutinizing eyes as his gaze fell over her.

"Go on," prodded Jonathan. "We are all a bit curious here."

Abidin offered a sorrowful grin. "Our brotherhood has been tasked with preserving and protecting the sacred rod of Aaron."

"Hold on," said Hunt. "I'm not really up to speed on religious artifacts. The rod of Aaron?"

"Aaron was the brother of Moses. The rod is the sacred scepter which, along with Moses and his staff, released ten plagues upon Egypt."

Dana saw Hunt blanch. The amulet he bore about his next supposedly held a locust released during these very plagues. It had come to him through unusual channels and had once displayed supernatural properties. Its use also held terrifying memories for Hunt which still plagued him with nightmares.

"Excuse me," said Thorpe. "I'm not, well, much of a Biblical scholar either, but isn't it true that this rod was lost and never recovered back in Biblical times?"

"It was lost. This is true," said Abidin. "When the Philistines captured the Ark of the Covenant, the sacred rod was lost as well."

"So," said Hunt. "Your sect either comes from Philistine origin or you're going to claim that the rod was later recovered but never revealed to the world at large."

"Very insightful, Mr. Huntington," said the priest. "And yes, it was recovered in the second century following the earthly life of our Christ and savior. It passed through many hands over the centuries. Our sect has now been charged with its wellbeing for more than five hundred years."

"I'm guessing there's a but coming," prodded Hunt.

The priest leaned forward, narrowing his eyes, and speaking directly to Hunt. "The sacred rod has been stolen."

"Had a feeling we were heading there," said Hunt.

"And so, you've contacted us because we're rescue and recovery specialists?" asked Dana.

The priest angled his head as if unsure how to respond. "I find it very curious and likely providential that the bearer of the amulet happens to locate and recover lost and stolen articles of great value as his profession. But no. This is not the reason I have sought Mr. Huntington."

"Yeah," said Hunt. "Thorpe said something about my amulet."

"The amulet, yes. You see, the rod has been missing for over five months. We have utilized all the resources available to us: our own men, other devout individuals that we were willing to bring into our trust. But none has gained an inkling as to the sacred scepter's location."

"And this has what to do with my amulet?" Hunt's tone was markedly dubious.

"May I see it?" asked the priest.

Dana could see Hunt's unease. He always wore the pendant beneath his shirt, out of sight, and rarely mentioned it—certainly not to anyone other than Dana. As well, he never took it off. The object seemed to be both a source of comfort as well as disquiet to him. Hunt remained motionless for several seconds, apparently contemplating his next move before slowly pulling the golden chain about his neck and bringing the amulet into view. The stone was amber, not cut and formed by a jeweler but fully natural in its uneven form. Within the amber was a single locust, apparently suspended for all eternity within the golden-hued substance. Dana and Hunt had had many conversations about the locust. Amber took millions of years to form. How could it have encased a locust that lived only a few thousand years ago? But then the locust had displayed some other rather unusual properties which flew in the face of any purely scientific explanation.

The priest's eyes went wide as he leaned forward cupping the prize in his palm and examining it with a practiced eye. "In what way did you come into possession of this magnificent relic?"

"It was given to me," said Dana. "By a man who had been instructed to give it to a woman who had come from afar. At the time this seemed rather preposterous, but it later showed remarkable characteristics which quite literally saved Hunt's life. He's been in possession of it since."

Father Abidin nodded and touched the subtle gray shadow on Hunt's forehead which appeared to be the image of a scorpion. "Possession," said the priest. "The holy locust drove a demon spirit from your soul." His hand then slid down, caressing Hunt's scared left cheek, the result of a bomb blast in Iraq. "The residue of a physical battle accompanied by a remnant of a spiritual encounter. Your face tells quite the tale, Mr. Huntington."

Hunt closed his eyes, remaining silent.

"Yes, well, all of this is quite fun, really," said Jonathan. "But what exactly are you hoping to accomplish with Huntington's amulet?"

The priest offered a near sneer to Jonathan but then sighed and said, "We do not know for sure. But stories of this amber-encased locust have come to us. There are tales of it from many centuries past. In each instance, the amulet has demonstrated rather extraordinary aptitudes, but only when in the possession of its chosen bearer. It would appear Mr. Huntington currently holds that distinction. We do not know if the locust will perform as we desire. But our hope is that it will guide you to the sacred scepter. There is obviously a connection between the two. This locust, this creature, was created within this same rod and then released into the world. We can only hope that this connection will allow you to accomplish what we have been unable to do in all of these months."

"Father," said Hunt. "I've got to tell you my instinct is to pass on this rodeo right here and now. I've had more than enough of this mystical mumbo-jumbo for a lifetime. I don't honestly understand the amulet. But the thing is scary and I'm not all that sure I want it waking up again." Hunt paused, waiting for the priest to respond. When the man remained silent Hunt added, "And FYI, I'm not even a Catholic. I was raised Methodist but haven't followed any religion since I was a kid. I don't know why you'd want me for this."

Abidin offered the hint of a grin. "And yet you wear the sacred locust about your neck. Do you ever remove it?"

Hunt didn't respond.

Nodding, Abidin said, "We expect you to begin your investigation first thing tomorrow. There are some simple guidelines we wish you to follow. Your company is peculiar and dysfunctional at its core. Mrs. Huntington, you travel both with your current husband, with whom you have been estranged for several months, as well as with your former spouse who is known to be a thief by profession. Mr. Thorpe, we appreciate your acting as an intermediary, bringing Mr. Huntington to us, but your services are no longer required. You will receive a stipend for your efforts, but you are not to participate in the search with Mr. and Mrs. Huntington."

Jonathan huffed, "Well, I don't . . ."

Abidin cut him off saying, "Mr. and Mrs. Huntington, your initial funds have already been forwarded to your account. We hope the sacred locust will lead you to the scepter, but we also understand that our Lord often operates using mundane means. Therefore, we expect you to begin your investigation as you would any other, by searching for and following up on clues. Durukan will provide you with the information already gathered in our investigations. He will also accompany you on this venture."

"Durukan?" asked Hunt, stumbling over the syllables.

"Um, that's me," said the young man that had acted as their driver. Dana had nearly forgotten that he was still at the back of the room. "You can call me Duck. It's a nickname and most Americans mispronounce Durukan."

"Why do I feel like I've just been insulted?" quipped Hunt.

"You are the only American present," said Dana. "And you did mispronounce his name."

"Excuse me," said Jonathan. "I'm not satisfied with . . ."

Abidin interrupted, saying, "As well, you must be sensitive to unusual occurrences. You are entering a world of faith and mystics. What, in the past, might have seemed inconsequential might in this instance be a sign."

"Do I have a say in any of this?" shouted Jonathan.

"No!" answered Dana and Hunt. In truth, Dana felt she'd been given no leeway as well. They hadn't exactly agreed to the assignment, had they? And yet, at least implicitly, they had. The priest was already detailing their mission as if their acceptance had been a forgone conclusion. And why did it suddenly feel as if this was indeed the case. Dana glanced at Hunt. His face was pale, but his jaw set. She knew the look. He was already running through mission scenarios in his mind.

Chapter Four

"I don't understand why you're, well, letting them dismiss me as a common thief," groused Jonathan Thorpe.

"You are a common thief," said Hunt.

"No. That is entirely . . . There's nothing common about me. I'm exceptional and only deal with rare collectables. Have I told you about the Monet I acquired last month?"

"Jonathan," said Dana. "Consider who these people are. This is a monastery. They see themselves as charged with a sacred task. Not only is your profession disagreeable to their principles—and to nearly everyone else's, I might add—but Father Abidin was right. You are my ex-husband and I am with my current—estranged—husband. Show us a courtesy. Allow us to proceed on our own. Working together has been therapeutic for us, but also challenging. We need this opportunity to figure things out without the added complication that you bring."

Thorpe scoffed. "Well, yes, you're estranged and all of that, but it's not as if you'll be alone. They're sending Duck the babysitter."

"I was never married to Duck," said Dana. "He doesn't act as an impediment."

"Listen," said Hunt. "You and me, we're rivals, I get it. But you've been respectful of what we're going through. I appreciate that. And, for a lowlife criminal, you're not a bad guy."

"Well, I wouldn't go so far as to say . . ."

"But Dana's right. You've helped us in the past. And I definitely owe you one for saving my butt in Botma, but we need to fly solo here."

Thorpe stammered, "You are the most infuriating man I've ever met. I do need you to know this."

Hunt smiled. "Back at you, Thorpe."

Dana, who had been seated at a table with her laptop computer, rose and walked to Thorpe. Hugging him, she said, "You're a dear friend, Jonathan. Be safe. I hope our paths cross again soon."

"If ever," said Thorpe as she gave him a chaste kiss on the cheek. "You never know in this world how many days we might have left." He gave her a squeeze. "You be safe as well—friend. This scenario, it seems a bit dodgy. I don't want to hear that you've been injured—or worse."

Dana smiled and squeezed his hand as he stepped away from her.

Duck followed the uncharacteristically quiet Thorpe from the room offering to drive him down the mountain and into the nearest town where he could secure transportation to the airport. Hunt knew this had to be hard on Dana. She and Thorpe had once been married. But that was over and had been for quite some time. He knew that Thorpe still desired to be reunited with Dana and certainly Hunt and Dana's recent marital troubles had given him some glimmer of hope. But Hunt and Dana were working together regularly again. They'd both needed this time apart. Each had suffered traumatic experiences and had needed time to cope. But there was also a point where a decision needed to be made, one direction or the other, together or separate, and Hunt felt the point was drawing near. And in his deepest core, he feared what that final decision might bring. Yes, they worked together, but the relationship now seemed more to be that of good friends than of husband and wife. Was it even possible to recover what they'd once had?

Dana reseated herself before her computer. "I've been doing some research, both historical and concerning the recent theft of the rod."

Moving to beside her, Hunt said, "Uh-Huh. What you got?" Hunt had been surprised to learn that a monastery had internet access—it was through a landline and very slow, but it existed. He hadn't even been sure they'd have phone service. But it appeared that at least this particular brotherhood had a foot in the modern world.

"I've done basic background work on the rod of Aaron to gain some perspective. Solomon built the temple in Jerusalem in 960 B.C. The Ark of the Covenant was stored in this temple. From what I can gather, the stone tablets that contained the Ten Commandments, the rod of Aaron, and a jar of manna were contained in the ark. Aaron's rod was presumably lost when the Philistines seized the Ark of the Covenant. I've found no references to its being found in any time since."

"Which could align with Father Abidin's claim that it was recovered almost two thousand years ago, kept hidden, and that his sect has guarded the rod for over five hundred years."

"I'm sure this wouldn't be the first time something presumably lost to history has been secreted away for some special purpose."

Hunt shrugged. "Yeah. Well, whether it's really Aaron's rod or just something they believe to be Aaron's rod, our job's still the same. What have you found concerning the theft?"

"Not much, I'm afraid. One of the monks, a man referred to as Brother Bruno—his surname is Qudsi—disappeared the same night as the rod. They've found no record of him."

"This thing's been gone for five months and they haven't found this guy or any other clues?"

"There are detailed reports noting their efforts so far, but this Bruno Qudsi seems to be the only obvious lead. Qudsi had only been with the sect for two months prior to the theft. It seems likely he manipulated his way into this sect specifically with the intent of stealing the rod."

"I guess that's it then. We'll start by tracking Qudsi and see where that takes us from there. Though, I think it'd be a good idea to question the rest of the priests and monks here before we leave the site. And I definitely want to look at the place they kept the rod." Hunt paused and then added, "You okay? I mean, Thorpe leaving?"

"Jonathan is a friend, Marc. Despite his feelings for me, he's a friend only. And though I admit to relying on him from time to time, I think it best that we move forward without his distraction."

Hunt squeezed Dana's shoulder. "Yeah. And thanks."

***

The Atesi stared directly into the glorious sun as he put the phone to his ear. He loved the sun. Adored it as one might an everlasting lover. The endless fire. The brilliant eternal flames. How he wished to absorb those flames into his being to then allow it to burst from him in spectacular destruction. Such a glorious day that would be.

The Atesi cracked his neck, adjusted his arms in a series of pops and clicks. The flesh upon his frame always seemed to crawl and writhe. It was not a comfortable house for his divine being, but it was necessary. "What have you learned?" he asked his newly devout follower.

The response came quickly, the tone reverential. "I have the information you desire."

"Proceed."

"The man, Huntington, he is an American. Former special-forces commander, a unit known as Delta Force. A mission went wrong in Iraq, some of his team members were killed; he was severely injured. It was believed that he was to blame, but he escaped any charges. He then left the military. It is also believed that he struggled with OxyContin addiction until recently."

"Go on." The Atesi was already aware of most of this information, but it was helpful to allow his followers to feel useful. Humans were much like the lower creatures of the earth. They needed to be petted now and again.

"The woman is a former British spy. She had some controversy as well. Married one of her targets while undercover. Later divorced him and eventually married Huntington. Both appear to be highly skilled but volatile."

The Atesi twisted his head nearly eighty degrees relishing the stuttering pops and subtle pain it produced in his spine. "All of this, I know. Is there anything pertinent to me?"

"Yes, yes, Atesi. Several months ago, the man was possessed by the scorpion god, Anascoreth. The locust drove the spirit from him."

The Atesi smiled and nodded. The locust. That was why Huntington was interesting. And the demon god Anascoreth. That was an ancient name. He had been unaware of the Huntington man's encounter with it, but this was valuable information. "What of the thief?" he asked.

"Jonathan Thorpe is exactly as reported. The man steals high end art for paying clients."

"Very well. He has been dismissed from their company and will likely be of no consequence. I will keep an eye on the Huntington pair." The Atesi then disconnected the call without further comment and stood smiling as he gazed into the sun.

The rod had evaded him for several months. Perhaps, as surmised, the locust would be drawn to its source of creation. For the time being, though, he would simply observe. If the Huntingtons uncovered the scepter, he would then dispatch with them and take possession of both locust and rod, for he had need of each—as well as another, yet to be located item.

***

The following morning Dana and Hunt left the monastery with their escort, Duck. They had interviewed each monk and the one other priest with little success and no solid leads. No one had seen anything. The Holy scepter was guarded round the clock in a secure basement chamber but had still disappeared somewhere during the night. Brother Bruno was found to be missing later the following day, though he had not been on guard duty the night of the theft. That had been Brother Thaddaeus, who admitted to feeling groggy throughout his shift but denied falling asleep. Dana had interrogated enough people to easily read through the lie. But though he sought to hide his weakness in falling asleep, neither Dana nor Hunt got the impression he was in any way involved in the theft. Possibly—even likely—he'd been drugged into the stupor. They weren't opposed to revisiting Thaddaeus if evidence pointed in his direction, but they were satisfied with his statement for the time being. Qudsi was the obvious suspect.

A vehicle had been taken the night of the theft and found the following afternoon in the nearby village of Karawan. Likely the thief used it to flee the monastery and then either took a train, stole another vehicle, or had a ride waiting for him in Karawan.

Dana, Hunt, and Duck arrived at Karawan in the early afternoon. It was a small rural village bordered by majestic snowcapped peaks. The women wore colorful dresses and sweaters, though almost every one of them was faded with wear. The men also wore well-worn clothing, but usually of subdued browns and greens. Blazers and felt hats were common. The area was mountainous and many of the residents used mules for transporting crops and supplies up and down the mountainside. While there were several businesses; none were from any established chains, but were all individual shops run by family members. The few automobiles visible were mostly a decade or better in age. The people were friendly, but curious of strangers in their community. Most outsiders, apparently, came in on the train and only deboarded for a quick meal or supplies before continuing their journey.

The Huntingtons spent the day interviewing townspeople, showing a picture of Brother Bruno to anyone who would look, and generally getting the lay of the land. Turkey was ninety-nine percent Muslim, a Catholic monk in full garb would likely stand out and be remembered. Still, it had been five months since the theft. Unless Qudsi did something to draw attention to himself, it was unlikely he'd be remembered. As well, a man on the run wouldn't wear something as recognizable as a monk's robe but would have changed into something to help him blend. These initial interviews weren't likely to offer much by way of leads, but were necessary, nonetheless. One never knew what might turn up in an off-the-cuff comment or sudden memory.

They checked with the local sheriff—the only law enforcement officer in the village—presenting themselves as investigators hired by the monastery. Their hope was to discover that a car had been stolen that night and to then learn if and where it had been found. This could, at least, give them some direction. But it was a dead end. No cars had been stolen. There was a train station in town. They would check the travel records for the days surrounding the theft. Perhaps the thief fled via the railway.

Hunt sent Duck ahead to secure three rooms at the local inn, mostly so the couple could discuss the case out of his earshot. "What do you think of Duck?" asked Hunt as they sat across from one another at a small outdoor café. It was chilly, above freezing, but they could see their breath. Still, the air was fresh and it felt good to be out of doors.

Dana took a bite of her Manti, a Turkish dish featuring lamb dumplings with yogurt and butter, before responding. "He's rather cute, I suppose. A bit like a stray dog. Awkward. Boyish."

"I wasn't asking if he was cute," said Hunt. "I was more concerned that he was sent to keep an eye on us."

"I'm sure he was," said Dana. "And I can't blame Father Abidin for the caution. He's paid us a substantial sum and this scepter is obviously of great religious value."

"I don't like it. Last thing we need is some kid poking around, getting in the way."

"Well, he's not exactly a child, Hunt. I'd put him at nearly thirty."

"And what's his connection to the monastery? He's obviously not a monk or a priest."

"Well, I suppose you'll need to ask him. Now, how about we discuss the case while we have a moment alone?"

Hunt placed his simit, a kind of round almost doughnut-shaped bread on his plate and offered a grunt. "The Keepers have no video security system in their monastery."

Dana sipped at her coffee and said, "They're monks, not security guards."

"Nah. Not buying it. These guys are supposed to be the guardians of a sacred relic. Their gig is to keep that thing safe."

Dana couldn't exactly argue with that. "You make a good point. But even the best security details can get lulled into a sense of complacency if they go long stretches with no activity. No one outside of their small circle is supposed to know the location of the rod—or even that it still exists. It's possible they've gone decades or even centuries without an attempt on their prize. Add to that that these men are pious, likely having been schooled not in security but in theology. Under those circumstances, this could all make sense."

"Yeah, maybe. But that place still seems too lax for their mission."

Dana leaned forward. "Did you notice anything peculiar about the monastery?"

Hunt shrugged. "No ESPN? I don't know."

"No crucifixes."

"Okay. Yeah. You got me on that one. And no idols. No Virgin Mary." Hunt took a bite from his simit and then added, "Maybe they're not Catholic. I mean, Christian, yeah. They talked about Christ, but maybe they're another flavor. We normally think of priests and monks as Catholic, but hey, I'm a Midwestern boy, what do I know about religious factions in Turkey? I just assumed Catholicism. Shame on me for not digging deeper."

"I suppose we could ask about their affiliation. But I think I'll do some additional research first. I'd like to know a little more about our employer."

Hunt set his simit on his plate and then glanced right. "You notice that guy, three tables to your left? I'd swear he's been watching us."

Dana angled her head just slightly, attempting to glance at the man without obviously doing so. "Which?"

"The one that sticks out as much as we do?"

Dana smiled, with her Asian features and Hunt's scarred Caucasian face they weren't exactly inconspicuous in this part of the world.

"You got eyes on him? I'm going with Irish. Red hair and a complexion so fair he'd get sunburn under a full moon."

"I see him."

"Yeah, well he seems pretty curious about us. Trying hard to hide his interest, pretends to be checking his phone every thirty seconds, but his eyes are always on us and I'm sure he's snapped a couple shots."

"Well, that's interesting," said Dana. "We're supposed to be following the rod's trail and it appears someone is already following ours. Do you think he was sent by Father Abidin?"

"Nah. He sent Duck to keep an eye on us. Why would he need a spy?"

"True. Then who is he and why is he interested in us?"

Hunt patted his lips with a napkin, set it on the table, and rose. "Guess I'll just have to ask him."

Dana had been schooled in covert affairs. Her instincts generally relied on stealth and guile. Hunt used more of a let's-put-all-the-cards-on-the-table approach. It often unnerved Dana, but she couldn't deny his success rate. Shifting in her seat to better watch the encounter, Dana followed Hunt with her eyes. At the first sign of trouble, she'd intercede. Despite his successes, Hunt's approach frequently required Dana to rescue the lovable goof.

The red-haired man showed subtle surprise when he realized Hunt was headed to his table. Surely, this was the last thing he'd expected. "Hey," said Hunt. "Come here often?"

The man said nothing, eyes narrow, jaw clenched. His right hand slipped to beneath table level. Was he going for a gun?

"Ah. Silent type," said Hunt, either not noticing the move or pretending to ignore it. "Don't be shy. I don't bite. Well, there was that time with a Rottweiler. But he had it coming. Turnabout's fair play."

"I do not know you, sir," said the man, his Irish brogue thick and his hand coming to rest on his thigh. No, not pulling a gun—yet. But he was probably at the ready. Dana followed suit, slipping a hand into her purse where she kept a small colt.

Hunt maintained his grin. "Okay, so that's how you're going to play it. Fair enough. Here's the deal. You've been watching us. Nah, nah, don't deny it. Now, I know Dana's stunning and I make Karloff look like Cruise in comparison, but I have a feeling it goes deeper than that. Care to comment?"

The man's fingers twitched. Dana nearly pulled her weapon. But then his eyes widened, his tongue fluttered, both palms smacked hard against the tabletop, toppling his drink and causing a spoon to stutter off the table and onto the ground. He gasped, "Murder! The devil's murder!" He attempted to rise but his knees gave out. It was as if his entire body went limp. He collapsed, his chin connecting with the tabletop as he tumbled to the ground.

Hunt was immediately on his knees beside the man, his fingers against the jugular feeling for a pulse. Immediately, he jerked his hand away. "My God, the guy feels like he's on fire." Shaking his hand as if cooling a burn, Hunt shouted, "Call an ambulance! This man's not breathing."

***

The Atesi turned from the scene, grinning. He had not been seen by the Huntingtons and he'd eliminated a potential complication.

Or at least a facet of the complication. Slipping between buildings and along a narrow cobblestone lane, he located one of his recent recruits. A young woman of perhaps twenty-five years in age, short, well-muscled, with a scar on her left cheek and a pit-bull personality. He would charge her with pursuing the details of the intruder's faction. Smiling as he approached the young woman, he said, "Esel, a word please."

The woman nodded. He'd found her to be rather boisterous with her companions, but silent and sullen with him. He supposed that was natural. Mortals should fear one such as him.

Angling his head to the sun, he said. "Esel, you are a feisty thing but much too self-obsessed. You must set aside how your father disgraced you." At her apparent shock at his knowledge of her closely held secret, he leaned in closer saying, "A new and glorious destiny awaits you."

The girl said nothing but offered a hidden grin.

"Ha! Oh! That is simply delicious. You have divorced yourself of your stale religion, why? To spite your father? Come now. Answer the question." His right arm jerked and flopped, his face twitched.

Esel said, "You are unpredictable, Lord Ates Iyesi. Yet I serve at your pleasure."

"Oh! Ha! Charming. The girl is charming. Yes. It is true. I might lack predictability. But I also offer release from the shackles of mediocrity. I'm sure this pleases you like nothing else you've ever heard in your boring little existence." He wiped green and red dribble from his chin and flung it to the dirt where it sizzled and bubbled.

"Yes, Lord Ates Iyesi. I desire to please you."

"Good, good. Yes, very good." Here, the Atesi scanned the area, the meager buildings, the narrow lanes. Four birds perched on the awning above. Grinning, the Atesi said, "Observe, dear girl. And fear your god." Rubbing his hands together, he twitched and moaned. Mucus dribbled from his nose and one of the birds burst into flames. Squawking, it attempted to take flight, but fluttered to the ground in a spiraling dive. The other three birds took flight, but at the Atesi's will, each ruptured into flaming debris that rained down upon the alleyway.

"Ah! Oh-ho! Do you see? Do you see, dear girl? And this, I tell you, is but the most insignificant of my miracles. For soon will come the day when I hold the sacred scepter on the mountaintop. And in that day, none will dare oppose me. None!"

But the girl was not suitably impressed. In truth, she was weeping. Trembling. She feared him, as well she should. Ah, but this girl who wished to appear so strong, so defiant, was weak. She was not a suitable spy as he had hoped. Perhaps, she would provide a better service in her weakness.

Wetting his fingertips with spittle, he stepped forward and swiped his fingers across the trembling girl's forehead. The flesh sizzled, the girl screamed and pulled away. The Atesi laughed. "Ha! Yes, yes. Run! And when you are asked how it is you came to be marked, tell the world that you have been marked by the great and powerful Ates Iyesi. Run, girl, run. Oh, yes! Delightful."

Chapter Five

It was nearly two hours before Hunt and Dana were allowed to leave the scene. The man had died even as Hunt applied chest compressions. The medical personnel were calling it a heart attack, but Hunt was having none of it. The man's skin was hot, feverish, painful to the touch. Poison maybe? But if so, why and by whom? The sheriff questioned them both at length. Why had Hunt approached the table? Did they know this man? What made Hunt think he'd been watching them? They were forthright with their answers, restating what they had told the man earlier, that they'd been hired by the monastery to investigate a theft. They held back details about the actual item stolen, simply stating that it was a religious article, but otherwise complied. There was no reason to make an enemy of the man. They'd done nothing wrong and had nothing to hide.

Once alone in Hunt's room at the inn, they discussed the situation. "Was that an assassination?" asked Dana as she stood at the window staring at the nearby mountain range.

"My guess? Yeah. Sure, it could have been a heart attack but my gut screams murder. A heart attack doesn't cause that kind of crazy fever and did you hear what he said at the end?"

Dana nodded. "Something about the devil."

"Yeah. He said, 'The devil's murder.'"

Dana turned to face Hunt. "Cheery term. What does it mean?"

"I don't know. Maybe nothing. Maybe just an unusual expression."

Dana narrowed her eyes. Hunt could tell she was thinking about something.

"What?" asked Hunt.

"Think about this case. We've been hired by a monastery to track down a stolen Biblical relic."

"Yeah. And?"

"And then a man dies right in front of you with the words, 'The devil's murder' on his lips. The devil is a religious figure. Everything has to do with religion, or, I suppose you could say, the supernatural. And do you remember what Father Abidin said before we left? He said something to the effect of, 'Be sensitive to unusual occurrences. You're entering a world of faith and mystics. What, in the past, might have seemed inconsequential might be a sign.'"

Hunt paced the small room, rubbing the amulet through his shirt like some form of charm. "Nah. I mean, listen, I get it. We've seen enough to know there are legitimate supernatural elements in this world. But I also know that most of the experiences in my life can be explained by perfectly mundane means. We can't just assume that anything weird is some crazy spell or spirit or whatever. I say we treat this like any other situation until or unless it proves to be something different."

"And if it does?"

"Then I curse Thorpe to hell for ever dragging us into this mess. I've had enough weirdness in my life. I'd like something strictly solid, no crazy hoodoo or mystical mumbo jumbo." Hunt paused and when Dana didn't respond he said, "So far we have nothing. No one's come forward with anything on Qudsi. There's no record of a car theft on that day. We still need to check the train records for that week to see if we can track him that way. In addition, I think we should start looking for the rod itself. Sure, stay on Qudsi, they spoon fed him to us and he's still the likely candidate. But let's put out some feelers to see if anyone's tried to sell the thing. It's got to be worth a fortune."

Dana scrunched her lips in that I'm-not-quite-sure-you're-right way of hers. "Perhaps. Certainly, that makes sense if the motive is profit. But the theft of a religious artifact, especially one credited with a miraculous history within the Bible itself, might have a spiritual motivation."

"So, what do we do? Investigate every church, synagogue, and mosque?"

"No. But it seems prudent to look into any more radical sects operating nearby."

Hunt waved his hand in disagreement. "Nah. Nearby means nothing. If this thing really is Aaron's scepter and some radical sect learned its location, they could be from anywhere in the world. Radicals don't let geography get in the way of their 'sacred mission.' If that's what we're looking at, they could have come from anywhere."

"Fair enough. So, what do you propose?"

Hunt thought for a moment. "Stay on point with Qudsi but keep our options open. Cast a broad net and see if we snatch anything."

Dana nodded. "I'll call Father Abidin right now and ask him about other sects or interested parties."

Dana removed her phone from a pocket and made the call. Hunt could tell almost immediately that something was wrong. Dana's expression became taut, she asked a series of short direct questions. "When?" "How?" "Was there a note?" "Did anyone hear anything?" When finally she disconnected, she looked at Hunt and said, "Father Abidin's dead. Burned to death in his room. They're calling it a suicide."

"That's ridiculous. No one commits suicide by burning."

Dana nodded. "I spoke with the other priest, Father Tilev. He said Abidin was alone in his room. One of the monks found him when he investigated why the father hadn't come to his meal. His body was severely burned. There was a partially written note saying, 'The fires of the Atesi are upon me, I cannot…' Apparently, that's as far as he got."

Hunt frowned. "Atesi means 'fire' in Turkish. 'The fires of the fire are upon me?' That doesn't even make sense."

Dana shrugged. "The note is peculiar; I'll grant you that. Father Tilev said he'd shown no signs of depression. The only concern was that he'd complained of a fever. He said the note was partially scorched. Personally, it sounds more like Father Abidin was trying to warn the other Keepers of something rather than writing a suicide note."

Hunt grunted. "That's the second death connected to us in one day."

"Well, we can't exactly claim they were connected to us."

"I'd like to hear an argument that they're not. The guy at the café had a ridiculous fever and Abidin burns. I'm not a fan of coincidence."

"Nor am I, but occasionally they do occur. And Father Abidin didn't die by apparent natural causes like our chum at the café. The father actually burned to death."

Hunt slammed a palm against the wall and then clutched his amulet through his shirt. "Okay, we need to focus on the task. I'll take the train station and you put out some feelers, try to see if the scepter's popped up on the black market? Then I guess we can look into any radical religious movements making noise about a sacred relic."

Hunt saw Dana nod and open her mouth to speak, but there was a knock at the door. Eyeing Dana with a who-could-that-be expression, Hunt made his way to the door, his right hand coming to rest on the butt of his holstered Browning. There was no reason to believe someone was after them, but the two deaths of the day seemed too close for coincidence. Something wasn't right here.

"Who's there?" asked Hunt through the door.

The response came in heavily accented English. "Um, Mr. Huntington. It's Durukan. There is a problem with Mrs. Huntington's room."

Hunt opened the door just slightly, hand still on the Browning. "Yeah?"

"Mrs. Huntington, her room. The doorjamb is broken. It appears someone has been in her room."

Hunt opened the door fully now revealing Duck: late twenties but already balding, about five foot six or seven, dark complexioned, a wisp of a beard, with a slightly larger than average sized nose which had probably contributed to his nickname. The kid was kind of twitchy, always shifting his weight from one foot to the other. "Did you see anyone?" asked Hunt.

"No. Not in the room. I didn't enter."

Dana was to the door now, her own weapon in hand. "Right. Stay behind us, Duck. We'll investigate."

The young man nodded and moved aside as the Huntington's moved past, closing and locking the door behind them and saying, "Please be careful. Criminals don't usually have good manners." He looked both ways as if crossing a street and then followed.

The inn was billed as a farm guest house and the doors opened not to hallways but onto an exterior courtyard bordered with olive groves and a vegetable garden. No one was visible in the courtyard and the two Huntingtons moved quietly along the tan brick exterior, weapons drawn. Dana was in the lead and signaled for Hunt to stop as she approached the damaged door. He saw her angle her head to get a view of the room and then move in. Hunt was just coming through the door when she gave him the all clear.

"Well, someone made quite a ruck," said Dana as she moved through the room, gun still held in a two-handed grip. The room had been tossed. Obviously, someone had searched the place, but it took less than thirty seconds to determine that that person was no longer there.

"Anything missing?" asked Hunt.

"At a glance no. Nothing of importance anyway. Anything critical is still in the car trunk or on my person. The disturbing thing is, who is so interested in us?"

"Uh-huh," said Hunt. "Not a full day into our investigation and your room's been tossed, a guy dies in front of me, and our employer apparently burns himself. Tell me there's not more to this thing than we were led to believe."

"What did you say?" It was Duck who had followed them into the room. "Someone burned himself. Who?"

Dana turned toward Duck. "Father Abidin. I'm sorry, we hadn't had the opportunity to tell you. He's dead."

The young man went pale. His jaw quivered as he sought to hold back tears. "But, Father Abidin is . . . everything."

***

Jonathan Thorpe sat on a bench at the Karawan train station sipping tea and pretending to read whatever nonsense social media might provide. He wore a thick wool overcoat, a scarf, and a charcoal gray flat hat. It wasn't a disguise per se, anyone who looked closely would recognize him as a light skinned Caucasian and thus not a local. But it was more a means to a casual blend with his environment. He wasn't trying to impersonate a villager, but simply to avoid drawing attention. Hence his placement at the train station where outsiders were to be expected.

The air was brisk, but the heavy coat was likely a bit much. Thorpe was perspiring profusely. He was at a crossroads now and needed to decide his next move. He'd been angered at the priest for ordering him away from the investigation and even more so at Dana for so readily dismissing him. But she obviously hadn't given up on her sagging relationship with Huntington and so, at least until the bloke did something catastrophically stupid, he'd need to remain in the background.

But that didn't necessarily mean he should disappear. Thorpe had the same information as Dana and Marc. There was no reason he couldn't seek the rod on his own, run his own private operation. Besides, Huntington had his woman, why shouldn't Thorpe take the man's reward by locating the rod first? It seemed fair enough to him.

But there was another reason as well. A more pressing matter than a petty jab at his rival. Thorpe had witnessed the incident at the café. He'd been across the street, simply keeping an eye on the Huntingtons while he contemplated his options. He'd seen the man watching them and then he'd watched as the man died within moments of Huntington making contact.

Something was not right about this. The death was too coincidental to have been natural. Right as Huntington approached? Please! So, the question became, who was following the Huntingtons and why? And then, who didn't want them followed badly enough to kill their tracker? Dana was a bright girl. She'd likely already asked these same questions. Still, he didn't feel comfortable leaving when deadly foul play appeared to be in the making.

And speaking of which. Thorpe had noticed a figure lingering toward the end of the platform. He'd avoided making any obvious signs that he was aware of the woman, but he'd been here for nearly an hour now—as had she. Two trains had come and gone during that time. Pretending to read an article on his phone, he switched it to camera mode, angled it just right, and snapped a photograph of the woman. Pulling the image up onto his screen, he enlarged the picture until the woman's face filled the screen. Early thirties, black, slender. The face was as familiar as the woman was lethal. Bloody hell, what was she doing here?

Thorpe thought about making contact but decided against it. No. There was no need to tip his hand so soon. Perhaps it would be better to allow the woman to follow for a time, to keep an eye on her, see if she met with anyone and then perhaps catch her unawares. Offering a faux yawn, Thorpe pretended to reengage with social media. Lovely. Only a day in and there were already multiple complications.

***

Duck looked like he'd just swallowed a rock. He gasped, almost staggering into Dana's ransacked hotel room. Obviously, the news of Father Abidin's death came as quite a shock to him.

"Here, sit down," said Dana as she righted an upturned chair and scooted it toward the kid.

"What do you mean 'Father Abidin is everything?'" asked Hunt referring to Duck's comment upon hearing of the priest's death.

Seating himself, Duck said. "To me. Everything to me. He took me in when I was orphaned. He treated me as one might treat a son."

Okay, thought Hunt, so nothing to do with the case. "I'm sorry, kid. Not a good way for you to learn of the death of a loved one."

Dana asked, "Had Father Abidin been depressed? Did he give any indication that he was giving up?"

Duck wiped an eye with his shirtsleeve. "No. Never. You're saying he killed himself?"

"That's what Father Tilev says," offered Hunt.

"No. No. Never. Father Abidin was a man of faith."

"Even people of great faith can waver in times of stress," said Dana. Her voice was soft, comforting, she placed a hand upon Duck's shoulder. Hunt had always admired her ability to connect with people.

"No. Trust me. I understand what you are saying and perhaps, earlier, when the sacred scepter was first stolen, I might have believed it. But now? No. He was hopeful. Very hopeful."

Dana said, "Duck, do you know of anyone that would want Father Abidin dead?"

"No! Why would someone want that? He was a gentle man. A good man. What could be the reason?"

Hunt said, "Aaron's rod comes to mind. He just hired us to find it." Hunt paused, glanced at Dana and then back to Duck. "Listen, kid, I know this is hard to hear, but it's the deal and there's no avoiding it. Father Abidin was found burned to death in his room. So, if it wasn't suicide—which is unlikely based on the means of death—it was murder. Those are the only two options."

Duck looked up at Hunt, his eyes moist with tears. "I cannot believe it was suicide."

"Agreed," said Dana. "Suicide by fire makes little sense. Duck, did the Father have any enemies? Had he recently had any conflicts?"

"No. No, nothing. No one. He was liked by everyone."

Hunt asked, "He wrote something about the fires of the Atesi. That mean anything to you?"

"No."

"Had anyone come to him about Aaron's rod, maybe trying to see it or maybe to get him to sell it?"

"Again, no. Very few people know of the rod, fewer still know where it was kept. No one ever questioned him about the rod. At least not to my knowledge." Duck paused and then added, "I did hear Brother Thaddeus ask him about your amulet, though."

Thaddeus, the man on guard duty the night of the theft. "Go on. What did he say?"

"He was upset, always upset. He felt guilty that the sacred scepter had been stolen while he was on duty. When Father Abidin told him of your amulet and that it might be the key to finding the rod, he became very excited and questioned Father Abidin several times about the amulet and what made it so special."

Interesting, thought Hunt. Thaddeus could have been excited about the amulet because it brought hope for the possibility of recovering the rod, or he could have been nervous about it because he didn't want the amulet to lead to him, if he was, in fact, the thief.

"May I see it?" asked Duck.

"See what?"

"Your amulet. The locust. Father Abidin held such hope for it. I would like to see it."

Hunt paused for a moment before saying, "For the record, I don't see this thing as some sort of mystical homing beacon. I know the father hoped so, but it may just be a lump of amber with a bug inside."

"But Father Abidin said it had worked a miracle for you and that it had done so for others throughout the ages."

Hunt offered a taut grin. "I can't speak for what it's done through the ages, but yeah, it did me a solid. But since then, nothing. Just a hunk of amber."

"Still. I would very much like to see it. For Father Abidin. He had much hope for this talisman."

Meeting Duck's gaze, Hunt felt his hand quiver as he withdrew the amulet from within his shirt and into view. He prayed the kid wouldn't want to hold it. He didn't think he could allow that; he just couldn't think of . . . Hunt closed his eyes, attempted to center himself, and then opened them, gazing at the young man before him. This was not the enemy, just a brokenhearted kid. Relax. The amulet wasn't going anywhere.

Duck's eyes narrowed and then the hint of a grin creased his lips. "Ugly," was all he said.

"Yeah, kid. Ugly. And yet somehow I just can't seem to find a reason to trash the thing." *Much less let it leave my sight,* he added silently.

"Duck," said Dana. "I understand this may not seem an appropriate time and I don't mean to minimize your grief. But we need your help. It has to do with finding the rod. And please believe me, the missing artifact and the murder of your mentor are almost certainly connected. And so, helping us to uncover Aaron's rod may very well lead us to Father Abidin's murderer."

Dana was right, Hunt knew this. He'd been thinking the same thing. He wasn't sure if the kid would be up to discussing anything of significance right now, but he was a source of intelligence concerning the inner workings of the monastery and the personalities involved.

Duck met Dana's gaze for a long moment and then nodded. "Ask your questions. I will do my best to assist."

Dana offered a welcoming grin. "Tell me about Brother Bruno. Was there anything odd about him? Did he display any unusual interest in Aaron's rod?"

Duck shrugged. "Everyone had interest in the holy scepter. It was the reason for the sect's existence."

"Understood. But did Bruno show more interest than others or ask any unusual questions about the rod or its security?"

Duck contemplated this for several moments before answering. "Brother Bruno was very excited about the holy scepter. But I would not call this unusual. He was still new to the sect. We do not get new personnel frequently, but when we do, they are usually in awe of the scepter."

"And his interest in its security?" prodded Hunt.

"The scepter's security is the primary function of the sect. So how does one gauge an inappropriate amount?"

"Okay. Fair enough. You said Qudsi was new. How long had he been at the monastery before the theft?"

"Not terribly long. Perhaps two or three months."

Long enough to learn the layout of the place, the protocols, and to gain a little trust, thought Hunt.

"What was Qudsi like as a person?" asked Dana. "Did he mingle with his fellow monks or did he keep to himself? Did you have much contact with him?"

Duck fiddled with his hands in his lap, rarely making eye contact. Hunt noted a tear creeping down his cheek. "He was quiet," said Duck. "But that is not unusual. I'm sorry. I really don't think I have anything to offer. This is not a good time. May I leave? I'm sorry." With that, he rose abruptly and exited the room.

***

Dana had already said her goodnights to Hunt for the day and was sitting on her bed in her replacement room with her laptop computer. She had needed to switch rooms because of the broken doorjamb. Dana pondered the break-in. Why leave the room in such disarray? No effort had been made to hide the fact that the room had been invaded. Had the culprit been trying to make it look like a random burglary? If so, they hadn't stolen anything and so failed horribly if that was their goal. Had they been in a hurry, worried about discovery? Did they assume that since they'd broken the doorjamb there was no reason to hide the fact that someone had been there?

Was someone trying to scare them off?

There was no way of knowing, not yet at least. They'd questioned the owners of the inn, a pleasant couple in their late fifties or early sixties. They'd seen nothing and no one else was currently lodging there.

It was a small inn in a small village. Not much activity other than train passengers stopping for a night before continuing their journeys or the occasional out-of-town relatives visiting villagers.

Dana's phone rang, pulling her free of her contemplations. Picking it up and expecting to see Hunt's name on the screen, she sighed. Jonathan. What could he possibly want now? Accepting the call, she answered with, "I certainly hope you didn't call to whine about being left behind."

"Yes. Well, wonderful to hear your voice as well, darling. I'm fine, thank you. So kind of you to ask."

Dana rolled her eyes. "Hello, Jonathan. So very sorry to insult you. How may I be of service?"

"How may you be of service? Really? Am I suddenly a distant acquaintance or perhaps a business connection?"

"Jonathan, please. It's been a long, rather peculiar day. I simply would like to rest."

"If by a rather peculiar day you mean that incident at the café, I'm aware of that. Rather unsettling, I would say, and not at all coincidental. Have you learned anything concerning the man?"

Hmm. Jonathan knew of that. Had he been spying on them, thus witnessing it himself, or had he been nosing around where he didn't belong? Either would be in character and neither appreciated. "No," said Dana "He carried no identification. He spoke with an Irish brogue, but beyond that we know nothing."

"A shame, I suppose. It would have been nice to know who's following us."

"Us?"

"Yes, dear. I haven't quite begun my journey home. Stayed to do a bit of sightseeing and whatnot. Noticed I'd picked up a tail. I haven't engaged her yet. Nor have I attempted to lose her. I'm mostly curious.

Have you uncovered anything that might lend a hand in determining who might have interest in us, or in our quest?"

"Our quest? Jonathan, you've been released. They paid you handsomely and sent you on your way. I do hope you have no intention of interfering with our investigation."

"Oh, no. Of course not. Really, I'm calling you out of concern. I have a peculiar feeling about this one. I'm not certain you should continue. They've already paid you an extraordinary sum for a small monastery, perhaps you should be content with that and move on to something more mundane."

"Are you certain you're not simply trying to shuffle us aside in order to claim the prize for yourself?"

"Well, no. Dana dear, you must understand that your safety is my primary concern."

"Primary, perhaps, but not only."

"Dana. We are both being followed. One person has already died. That in and of itself should cause you pause."

"Two."

"Pardon?"

"Two people have died. Father Abidin was found burned to death in his room."

"Bloody hell, and you plan to continue with this thing?"

"Jonathan, this goes beyond recovering the rod. The reason we were hired is because of the amulet. The rod had been missing for months, but now, when the amulet is suddenly in play, people start dying. Do you actually think we can walk away—still in possession of the amulet—and not have someone come after us? I don't necessarily believe that the old piece of amber will really lead us to the scepter, but obviously there are people quite engrossed in what we're doing; and my hunch is that it's the amulet that piqued their interest." Dana had not fully formulated this thought before but knew it to be true. Whatever had been set in play, Hunt's amulet was the trigger. Other people had been sent in search of the rod and, to her knowledge, no one had died. Certainly, Father Abidin had remained unharmed until now.

"Then dispose of the bloody rock," said Jonathan. "Give it to the monastery. We both know what it did for Marc in Botma but that's done with. Hand the thing to the monks and walk away. Dana dear, if two people are dead already and you've yet to truly begin, what do you expect going forward? Do you, well, have you considered that you or your oaf of a husband might be the next target?"

Dana glanced around the small room, at the solid oak desk across from the foot of the bed, at the golden-hued couch to her left, at her suitcase lying open on the floor as she remembered the ransacked room she'd only just vacated. Jonathan had a point. They could walk away. But . . . "No," she said. "The amulet is . . . peculiar. Perhaps even problematic. Hunt is quite conflicted over the thing. But he certainly has no intention of relinquishing it, of that I'm certain."

"Even at the risk of your lives?"

"Jonathan, at this point, everything is supposition. We don't flee at the first sign of danger. We're professionals. We can handle ourselves."

"Professionals, yes, I suppose, of course, but bloody stubborn is more the thing of it. Do me a favor, would you? Speak with your simian husband. See if he agrees with me. Would you do that?"

Dana agreed to speak with Hunt on the matter, but even as she disconnected the call, she knew she was unlikely to do so. An apparent heart attack and a dead priest—regardless of the circumstances—were still very difficult to connect as an indicator of a threat on them. True, they may have been followed, and yes, her room had been tossed, but that didn't necessarily indicate danger. Curiosity, certainly. Inappropriate methods, of course. But no one had yet to approach them, much less threatened or attacked. True, this thing was turning into a bit of a mystery, but wasn't that their profession? Solving those little mysteries on the way to recovering the lost prize.

Chapter Six

The scenery was soothing. Hunt sat on a bench in the courtyard of the inn gazing over the garden to the snow-covered peeks. He wore a jacket, could see his breath, but it was a healthy chill. Invigorating, really. He'd grown up in Northwest Indiana, played hockey as a teenager, brisk temperatures, if anything, reminded him of home. And it wasn't that cold really, just a morning chill.

Hunt heard footsteps approaching from behind and, turning, saw Duck approaching. "Hey, kid," he said. Noting the young man's attire, he said, "Spider-man shirt and Batman hat. Isn't that kind of a geek fashion clash? You can't wear Marvel and D.C. together. What will people think?"

Duck grinned. "What could I ever have been thinking?"

Patting the vacant space on the bench beside him, Hunt said, "Have a seat."

Duck complied. "Good morning, Mr. Huntington."

"Nah. Trash the Mr. Huntington crap. Call me Hunt and you can call my wife Dana. We're not too formal. Well, not me. Dana has her high society moments, but she's a working-class girl at heart."

Duck smiled and nodded. "Of course . . . Hunt."

Hunt appraised the young man, attempting to determine his mood. "How are you doing this morning, any better?"

"Yes. Somewhat. Father Abidin was very dear to me, but I also know that I cannot dwell on that which cannot be changed."

"Sounds about right. Focusing on other things can be beneficial. But don't try to short circuit the grieving process. It sucks, but it's part of the deal. And it's healthy."

"I understand," nodded Duck.

"Question for you. Spider-Man and Batman, they big in monastery circles?"

Duck chuckled. "No. Not in the least. But in California, very much so."

"California? I thought you were raised here."

"Raised, yes. But not educated. I came to be with the sect because of my father. He was quite dedicated to them."

"I'm guessing he wasn't a priest."

"No. Not a priest but a lay agent they used. Our family was persecuted because of our Christian faith and were considered outcasts. When I was young, we spent much time in prayer with the monks. And then . . ." Duck paused, seemed to contemplate, and then continued. "My parents were killed in a strange mishap. I do not wish to go into the details. The sect took me in and raised me. But after completing four years of military service I went to college, UCLA, the University of Southern California Los Angeles. I have only recently returned to the monastery."

"UCLA, do they have a theology program?"

Duck gazed at Hunt as if confused and then smiled. "You think I wish to become a priest. No. I feel no such a calling. My faith is not so strong as that would require. My degree is in biology. Faith to me is . . . elusive. I catch a wisp of it and then . . ." He lifted his arms up and then separated them as if releasing something. "Whoosh. It escapes me."

Hunt nodded. "I know the feeling, kid. These last few months, some things have happened. Strange supernatural things. I can acknowledge that there are things out there, but I can't really say what form they take. I was raised in the Christian tradition and so my first inclination is to head that way, but how do I know that it's true? Just because the supernatural exists doesn't mean any particular religion really has it pegged."

"You share my mind more than you would know," said Duck. They fell into silence, each lost in their own thoughts. After several moments of contemplating the mountains, Duck finally said, "May I ask you a personal question?"

Hunt grinned. "Ask me anything you want. I'll decide whether or not to answer."

"You and Mrs. Huntington . . . Dana. You are married but are staying in separate rooms."

Hunt chuckled. "Well, you did say it was personal. Yeah. We're married. But not exactly together. Kind of complicated, really, but maybe not so much. Stuff happened to each of us—separately. And I think we've each needed time to process what those things mean to who we are now."

"And will you remain married?"

"Wow, kid, don't hold back." Hunt shook his head and gazed up at the snowy peaks. "The truth? I like to think so. But I think it might be slipping away. Neither of us have really made a move to make it happen. Maybe we're not ready. Maybe we're just kidding ourselves about any possibility."

Duck grinned. "Maybe you're chicken shit."

Hunt broke into a hearty laugh. Well, one thing about Duck, he was direct.

He was about to respond when he once again heard footsteps. "Whatever are you boys laughing about and why does it make me nervous?" It was Dana. She came to stand beside Hunt, holding a steaming cup of tea.

"Nothing you want to hear about. Duck was just putting me in my place."

"Really? Well, that sounds exactly like the kind of thing I'd like to hear about."

And exactly the kind of thing he wanted to avoid—at least for the time being. "You sleep well?" he asked.

Dana cocked her head, grinning. "Changing the subject. You really do want to avoid the topic."

Hunt tossed his up hands in surrender. "Let's leave it at this. It involves our marriage and my being chicken shit."

Dana burst into laughter spraying tea from her lips, nearly hitting Hunt with the liquid. "Oh blimey! You're right. I don't want to know."

Hunt gave Dana a moment to wipe the tea from her face and then said, "I've checked the train passenger manifests. There's no record of Qudsi hopping the rails on or around our date."

"Not surprising that. Even if he did use the locomotive it's unlikely he'd have used his real name."

"Yep. And it's been long enough that no one will remember him unless he did something to draw attention—which someone on the run would avoid doing."

Dana took a sip of tea and then said, "I've been doing some checking as well and have found no evidence of the rod appearing anywhere on the black market. I do have a few basic bits on Bruno Qudsi though."

"Alright. Hit me with it."

"Looking into his financials I've found only one credit card in his name and a minimal bank account, neither of which has been touched recently. Though, there was a substantial amount deposited and then quickly withdrawn several years ago. I haven't yet untangled that little mystery and it was long enough ago that it may or may not connect to our current situation."

"Interesting. We'll keep that in our back pockets and see what we can uncover."

"As well, he was dismissed from a previous monastery due to fanatical views."

"Anything else?"

Dana sipped at her tea and then said, "Qudsi's from Cairo originally and had placed calls there just prior to his disappearance, though I was unable to determine who those calls were placed to. Apparently, the recipient used disposable phones."

"Sounds like the kind of guy that's hiding something. Guess we're heading to Cairo."

***

Cairo Egypt

Dana and Hunt spent most of the first two days in Cairo attempting to locate known associates of Bruno Qudsi. The city was bustling, full of moving bodies and chatter. Cars and buses crowded the narrow streets and pedestrians moved along the walkways in near frenzy. Dana allowed Hunt to take the lead when dealing with locals as he'd been to Cairo before and, in addition, spoke rather fluid Arabic. Most educated people did speak at least passable English, but it was comforting to know that Hunt spoke the native tongue. He had a knack for languages, and, upon joining the military, had decided it prudent to learn Arabic, assuming that he would likely be deployed in the Middle East. He also spoke Farsi, Hindi, and Spanish, and whatever else he'd picked up along the way. Hunt liked to play the doofus, but he was in no way a fool, but rather a highly intelligent and skilled individual.

Dana had to chuckle at Hunt's knowledge of the transportation system. He completely ignored the buses and minibuses, opting instead for taxis. Duck was about to hail a black taxi, but Hunt said, "Nah. Black taxis are the old ones. Half the time they don't have air conditioning and more importantly, no meter. The driver will try to haggle an outrageous price, finally agree on something, and then haggle again once you get to your destination. We want a white taxi. They're newer. There's a meter. The driver might still play sketchy, but at least there's a base point to work from."

To Dana the whole city seemed chaotic, but as they moved around, she saw that even in the chaos there was rhythm and purpose. It just wasn't a rhythm she was accustomed to. Outdoor markets and kiosks were plentiful. The people, to Dana, seemed to be diverse in attitude. Some, entirely engaging and welcoming while others cautious of outsiders. It was at once vibrant and overwhelming.

One of their first stops was Brother Bruno's previous order, located in an area known as Coptic Cairo which was home to many Christian churches and graveyards, including the so-called Hanging church, one of the oldest churches in Egypt, and so named because of its location above the gatehouse to a Babylonian fortress. Qudsi's former station was not so celebrated and occupied a corner lot with goats on the front lawn and laundry hanging from a second story balcony. After giving a rather lengthy explanation as to their purpose—four times to three different persons—they eventually learned that the parish has had no contact with Qudsi in over a year. The priest refused to offer much more than, "Brother Bruno parted ways for personal reasons." Which essentially told them nothing. Dana did, though, get the name of another former monk, one who had, for a time, been close with Qudsi. The man now lived in a section of Cairo known as Manshiyat Naser. Upon hearing this, Hunt mumbled, "Garbage City."

Duck said, "Oh. That's not good."

Dana eyed Hunt asking, "What is it I don't know?"

Upon reaching their destination, Dana saw that the designation of Garbage City was all too accurate. Manshiyat Naser is a Christion neighborhood on the outskirts of Cairo where the city's garbage is sent. Trucks simply dump garbage on the dirt roads where the neighborhood residents then pick through it looking for items that can be sold or reused. Huge towering garbage bags of perhaps eight feet in height and four feet in diameter lined the narrow streets and the place was rank with the smells of decaying food. Goats and cows rummaged through ripped open bags looking for edible tidbits. Pickup truck beds were filled with plastic bottles or aluminum cans that could be taken to recycling facilities in exchange for money.

But strangely enough, amidst the poverty, Dana saw signs of normalcy and even joy. Two young boys played fetch with a dog. A teen-aged couple gigged and tickled each other within a narrow doorway. There were carts on the streets where residents sold fruits, grains, and random items likely foraged from the garbage. People smiled and greeted one another. The buildings were almost universally gray but many of the apartment balconies were decorated in vibrant colors, often with mosaic tiles. Being a Christian community, crosses adorned many of the buildings.

Fearing that it might be difficult to obtain transportation from the district, Hunt paid the taxi driver handsomely to wait for them with the promise of additional payment upon the completion of their journey. Few taxis frequented Garbage City.

Seth Abubaksr lived on the third floor of a well-aged apartment building. He was a rather tall man in his early forties, with the beginnings of middle-aged girth, a thick mop of curly black hair, and a cautious smile creasing his leathered features. He wore a pale green dress shirt, untucked and wrinkled, tan slacks, and Reebok running shoes. Nothing about the man screamed monk. Nor did he appear in any way disheartened by the abject poverty beyond his walls. His apartment was small, but well kept, with old but little worn furniture. Dana wondered if he lived in Garbage City out of economic necessity or out of a desire to minister to this populace.

He had been curious and maybe even a bit cautious when the trio appeared at his doorway, but soon agreed to talk with them when Dana explained their purpose.

"May I offer you a beverage, perhaps coffee. I have acquired a superb blend?" said Abubaksr after offering the Huntingtons and Duck a seat on a cream-colored sofa in his sparsely furnished living area.

"No thank you," said Dana. Hunt and Duck declined as well.

Abubaksr smiled and pulled a wooden chair over to sit before them. "So, Bruno Qudsi. I must admit, before today, I haven't thought of him in some time."

The man seemed pleasant enough and his English was quite good. Which was nice. Dana wouldn't need to rely on Hunt as a translator. She returned Abubaksr's smile and asked, "How long has it been since you've seen Qudsi?"

"Oh, two years at least. No. It must be more than that. I left the monastery before Bruno. Let's say three years."

"What's your take on the guy?" asked Hunt. "Were you two close?"

"For a time, close. Bruno can be a pleasant man, despite his rigid exterior."

"Uh-huh, and?" prodded Hunt.

"Eventually, we became less friendly. And that was my doing. Bruno would have gladly continued the friendship."

"And why did you curtail the relationship?" asked Dana.

Abubaksr offered a rather constipated expression. "Bruno was very enthusiastic about his faith."

"I would assume that's a common trait among monks," said Dana.

"This was different. Bruno had ideas."

"A little clarity would be nice," said Hunt.

"To me it was cult-like thinking. A fixation on the end times. He seemed to have deluded himself into believing he'd be instrumental in bringing about Armageddon."

"So just run-of-the-mill Sunday school stuff," said Hunt.

"Did he ever tell you how he intended to influence Armageddon?" asked Dana. "That seems a rather ambitious undertaking."

Abubaksr shrugged. "Specifically? No. He spoke in broad terms. He quoted scriptures, which usually led to debate. His interpretations were often dubious."

Dana nodded. "Did he ever mention the need of a specific object or talisman to aid in bringing this about?"

"Talisman? No. Nothing like that. As I said, it was all broad strokes, questionable theologies. He'd offer his own explanations of scripture and then cobble together different passages to support his hypothesis."

"Interesting," said Dana. "Did he seem in any way dangerous or radical? Is he someone that would commit crimes in order to bring about his desired outcome?"

Abubaksr contemplated this for some time before responding. "That is difficult to say. In the time I knew Bruno he became more and more obsessed with his interpretations. Eventually, he would hear no others. It was useless to talk with him. But he was rational. By that I mean, in every other area of his life he behaved normally. I had no sense that he was going to commit some atrocity in the name of Christ if that's what you mean. But that was the Qudsi of several years ago. How he has changed since then . . ." Abubaksr shrugged. "Who can say?"

Dana asked, "Did he ever mention a connection to anyone else? Someone of like thinking?" She was wondering if he'd become involved with someone else who might be a coconspirator in the theft.

Abubaksr nodded slowly. "A group called People of the Crimson Moon. I know little about them. But he mentioned them several times. I found this troubling. If Bruno were to become involved with likeminded individuals, I could imagine him becoming more radical in his actions." He paused and then added, "Now let me ask a question of you? What has Bruno done to cause such a stir?"

"Such a stir. What do you mean by that?" asked Dana.

Abubaksr said, "You are not the first to come to my home asking about the man."

Dana and Hunt glanced at one another and then Hunt asked, "Who else?"

"A young woman. American, by her accent."

"And what did she want?" asked Hunt.

"Much the same as you."

Dana leaned forward, meeting Abubaksr's gaze. "Who was she?"

Abubaksr sat upright in his chair, massaging his chin as if in contemplation. "No. I don't think I will tell you this. I'm sure you would appreciate confidentiality as would she. I will say, though, that she presented herself as representing a legitimate religious organization. One which I'm inclined to trust."

"That doesn't tell us anything," said Hunt.

Abubaksr shrugged. "As was my intent."

"One more thing," said Dana. "May I ask why you left the monastery?"

The man offered a tight grin. "Why don't we just say that I found I could serve the Lord better if I wasn't cloistered behind brick walls."

They got little else from the man. His information on Qudsi, while interesting, was dated and despite prodding he was unwilling to reveal more about his previous visitor. He knew nothing more of People of the Crimson Moon beyond the fact that, like Qudsi, they were fixated on the coming apocalypse. They needed to learn more about this group and Qudsi's potential involvement. In Dana's opinion, it was quite possible that Qudsi had taken the artifact for their purposes. Discussing the meeting as they left the building, both Dana and Hunt agreed that, based on Abubaksr's impression of the man, Qudsi seemed the type that would steal a religious artifact out of some misguided mission.

Duck commented that, "Seth Abubaksr was very courteous, but he was not very trusting."

Hunt allowed a mild grunt. "Goes with the territory, kid. People like us come poking around, people get nervous."

"This, I understand. But this was different. I think maybe he was nervous for a different reason."

"Alright. I'll bite. What reason?"

"I don't know. Perhaps something to do with his previous guest. What organization did he find so trustworthy?"

Curious insight thought Dana. She was about to ask Duck why he thought this, but just as they stepped onto the street Hunt clutched her by the bicep. Whispering, he said, "We've got a tail."

"Who?"

Hunt angled his head to the right. "End of the block. Female. Red-head."

"Another redhead? Do you suddenly have an issue with gingers?"

"Not at all, but they do stick out in this part of the world. I caught a glimpse of her earlier just before we entered Abubaksr's apartment. My guess is she's from the same group as the guy in the café."

Dana couldn't argue with this. The man had spoken with an Irish brogue. While far from all Irish persons had red hair, something like eighty percent of redheads were from an Irish or Scottish heritage. Dana's guess was that there was some Irish group interested in the rod. She wondered if this was the woman Abubaksr had spoken of. He hadn't given a description, other than American accent, which wouldn't fit with the Irish theory. But they'd yet to engage this woman. For all Dana knew, the stranger could be American. Red hair could be nothing more than a coincidence.

Hunt tensed beside her. "She's on the move." And then he was racing up the narrow dirt road to where the woman had just disappeared behind a building.

Turning to Duck, Dana said, "Go to the taxi. Make sure he doesn't leave without us. We'll be a few moments."

"But you may be rushing into danger. Perhaps you should wait here and let the police . . ."

Dana cut him off. "The taxi. Now!" And then she angled across the street heading toward the south side of the building while Hunt raced to where the woman had just disappeared at the north.

"I suppose I will secure the taxi," hollered Duck as Dana raced away.

Dana was forced to weave through the alleyway, avoiding people, goats, dogs, and the huge plastic garbage bags scattered throughout the area. Reaching the back corner of the tall gray building, she turned right coming along the backside of the structure. A moment later she saw Hunt round the corner at the far end of the building.

But there was no sign of the woman.

Dana pointed toward a nearby doorway and, scattering a group of rats, made her way into the building. Abubaksr's building had been cluttered with scraps of paper, broken appliances, and an assortment of random items, but this building's hallways were lined with refuse. The odor was nearly unbearable. Random people walked the narrow corridor, each giving Dana a cautious gaze. "A redheaded woman? Has anyone seen a redheaded woman?"

Blank stares. Either no one here spoke English or—more likely—no one wanted to get involved. There was no way that Dana could gain entry to individual apartments to do a room-by-room search, but the red-haired woman probably had the same limitations. Most likely she had no connection with anyone here but had simply ducked into the place to get out of sight. Likely she was making her way through one corridor or another until she had the opportunity to slip back onto the street. The only certainty was that she clearly didn't want to be confronted by Dana and Hunt.

Dana made her way to the end of the corridor and then ran up a narrow concrete stairway to the second floor. It was a similar scene to the previous level. A handful of people moving one way or another, plenty of miscellaneous trash, and no redhead.

She encountered Hunt on the third floor. It took them another five minutes to cover the remaining levels.

Nothing. No sign of her. Hunt questioned several people in Arabic, but none offered any information concerning the woman. "I don't get the sense that these people are hiding anything," said Hunt as they finally made their way back onto the street. "I think she just gave us the slip. There's no reason anyone in this neighborhood would be aligned with an outsider who was here specifically because of the rod."

"True enough," said Dana. "But was she here for Abubaksr or for us?"

"Us," said Hunt. "Let's assume the red hair is not a coincidence, that she and the guy in the café are both Irish, maybe even related. The guy was watching us, that's a certainty. Now this woman shows up in a different country, obviously spying on us and doing her best to avoid a confrontation. There's a good chance she doesn't even know who we met with here."

"Not yet. But if she's good it won't take her long to figure it out."

"And then she'll know what we know, which isn't much. Think about it, why would anyone follow us?"

"I suppose that's a rhetorical question," smiled Dana.

"The rod's been missing for what, five months? No one's found it. Now we're on the trail. Someone wants that relic and they're using us to find it."

"You do understand the risk, I assume. Apparently, some group is following us. But it would seem someone else has eliminated one of that group already as well as Father Abidin."

"Yeah," said Hunt. "Not too thrilled about those dynamics. There's way too much that we don't know here. And that's got to change."

A moment later their taxi came into view. Duck rolled the window down and said, "I hope you don't mind. I offered the driver an extra one hundred dollars, U.S. He has a pregnant wife and an ailing grandmother. He was very appreciative of your generosity."

***

Jonathan Thorpe's investigation had also led him to Cairo. He'd also learned that Bruno Qudsi had association with a group known as People of the Crimson Moon—which frequently operated out of Cairo. He'd learned very little about the group other than that they were a radical Christian group focusing their energies on end times prophecies. Qudsi's connection wasn't quite clear, but Thorpe was operating under the assumption that the monk had stolen the rod of Aaron with the intention of passing it to this group. He wondered if Dana and Marc had stumbled upon this cult connection yet and if they'd reached the same conclusion.

Thorpe hadn't seen his tail since leaving Turkey but that only meant he hadn't caught sight of her yet. Thorpe knew the woman. He'd had dealings with her before. She was a professional and wouldn't be easily evaded. Of course, she may have gone her own way by now. He had to assume she was also in pursuit of Aaron's rod and, that being the case, she'd likely be following her own leads. Truth be told, she may have been simply trying to determine what Thorpe already knew as opposed to attempting to follow him with hopes of gaining information. He wondered who she was working for now and what their interest was in this dusty old rod. There certainly was a fair amount of hubbub about it. Well, all the more reason to be about his task and find the bloody thing. He had a bad feeling about this. Simply put, there were too many interested parties in play—at least three, possibly four, that he could see—and at least one of these was apparently willing to use deadly force to achieve their objectives. The best outcome would be for Thorpe to locate the thing with haste, return it to the Keepers, collect the reward, and be done with the whole business before someone else came after it again.

Mohamed Qudsi was a short man, hunched with age, but with clear brown eyes. When Thorpe explained that he was there to talk with him about his son Bruno, the man nearly slammed the door in his face and only failed to do so because Thorpe held out his hand stopping the door.

"Sir, I mean no disrespect. I simply have a few rather quick questions."

Qudsi glared at him. "That man is no longer my son. I have nothing to do with him."

Thorpe could assume that the father had disowned the son due to his acceptance of Christianity over Islam, but he asked the question nonetheless. "Yes, well, be that as it may, might I ask what brought about such a rift?"

A hateful glare followed by, "Do you have children, Mr. Thorpe?"

"No. I've not yet had that privilege."

Qudsi scoffed. "Privilege. My son has brought shame upon this house. He goes chasing after a western god with no concern for what this might do to his family. And now he desires to hand this Jesus some scepter."

"Ah. So, you have had recent contact?"

"He was here, visiting with his mother. He left an old leather book with her for safe keeping."

"An old book? Did he tell you anything about it, perhaps its significance?"

Qudsi scoffed. "He told me nothing. It is his mother that allows him access."

"Of course, well, that's obvious, isn't it? Did he reveal anything about the book to your wife?"

"It is old. Not in a language I recognize. He claimed it was crucial to his mission. I know nothing else." Qudsi glared at Thorpe as if daring him to press further.

Thorpe considered asking to speak with the woman directly but decided against it. The man had still not allowed him to enter, it was unlikely he'd grant Thorpe an audience with his wife. "Quite interesting. Tell me, did he tell your wife anything about this scepter he mentioned, if he already has it, where it might be found?"

"No. Nothing. It is all fanciful nonsense."

Thorpe started to ask about any known associates, but the man stopped him saying, "You are not a friend to my son."

Thorpe paused for only a moment deciding on how to answer. In this instance, he believed the truth to be most advantageous. "No. Truth be told, he would likely want nothing to do with me."

"And do you follow the western god?"

Thorpe offered a taut grin and met the man's gaze. "I follow my own compass. Nothing more."

Qudsi frowned. "Then you are a dog." He paused and then added, "Tell me truly, why do you seek Bruno?"

"Well, it would appear, he has taken possession of that scepter you mentioned."

"And you desire the scepter for yourself. For what purpose."

Thorpe grinned. "The only purpose that matters. Profit."

Qudsi snorted. "As I said, a dog."

The man then closed the door. Thorpe could hear him turning the lock. The senior Qudsi would offer no more information. Not willingly at least. But that book. Thorpe had the feeling it was important.

***

Attempting to track Qudsi through financial activity, Dana had discovered that some of Qudsi's records had apparently been altered and/or deleted as if someone was systematically attempting to erase the man. It was only due to Dana's superior computer skills that she was able to recover some of what had been ditched. None of it was helpful, but the fact that he was trying to cover his movements was another indicator that Qudsi was at the heart of this.

As well, Dana could find very little concerning their employer, the Keepers. Duck shed light on this saying, "The sect is its own entity, tied to no larger organization."

"So, they're not Catholic?" said Hunt. "Priests and monks. Of the Christian faiths, that seems pretty Catholic to me."

"We have men who have come from several different Christian traditions. But the group has chosen to remain reclusive and separate in order to keep the sacred scepter safe from threats both internal and external."

"That would explain the lack of Catholic imagery within the monastery," said Dana.

"So," said Hunt. "You're afraid that some highly placed Bishop or whatever would try to take the rod and use it as some sort of power play?"

Duck shrugged. "That would be a possibility. Unfortunately, history has proven that the church is not above corruption. The scepter is too important to be used as a political bargaining chip."

Hunt couldn't argue with that. Anytime there was a power structure, there were always those willing to do almost anything to claw to the top.

On a hunch, Hunt called a contact of his, Eldon Troxel, who had once been a renowned archeologist, heading many digs in the Middle East. "Hunt!" said Troxel. "What part of the globe are you on this week?"

Hunt grinned. "Cairo, Eldon. One of your old stomping grounds."

"Eh. Yes and no. Seeing as you're outta town, I'm guessing you're not calling to invite me to a Cubbies game."

"You know hockey's my sport, El. But the Blackhawks aren't playing in Cairo tonight. So yeah, you caught me. This is one of those pick-your-brain calls that you like so much."

"Did I say I liked those? I don't remember saying that."

"Okay. So, I get the sucky friend award again this year. But how about a few tidbits?"

"Yeah, yeah. But you're paying for the next game. And for the hotdogs. You know I need those at Wrigley."

Hunt chuckled. Eldon was an accomplished academic with an amazing store of knowledge, a box overstuffed with degrees, and the heart and vocabulary of a bleacher bum. "Deal. So, here's the lowdown. I'm looking for info on Aaron's rod."

"I assume you're talking about the Biblical relic and not Aaron Rodriguez. The one used to create the plagues in Egypt, disappeared with the Ark of the Covenant."

"Yeah. You pegged it, El."

"What's your interest in it?"

"It's missing."

"Pal, it's been missing since about 586 B.C.E."

"Yes and no. Apparently, it was recovered a couple of thousand years ago and has been secreted away by religious sects ever since. The current guardians of the thing hired us to locate it. Right now, the hot theory's that it was nabbed by a rogue monk."

"Ah. I tell ya. Never trust a guy in a robe."

"Words to live by, Eldon. So, what do you know about the rod?"

"The usual. Aaron and his brother Moses both had rods supposedly endowed with supernatural power. God turned Aaron's rod into a serpent once to demonstrate power and then of course, there were the plagues. Supposedly it was a heavy pup, about ten pounds or so. Some sources say it was made of wood, others out of sapphire. There are legends about it. One being that God created the thing on the sixth day of creation and gave it to Adam. It then got passed down from generation to generation eventually ending up in Aaron's paws."

"Okay. Interesting, but a little deeper, El. It's looking like religious fanatics want it. Something about end times prophecies."

"Oh. And suddenly we're talking apocalypse. Well, rabbinical literature indicates this staff will be given to the Messiah as a of symbol of his authority over heathens. If I remember correctly, there was some sort of inscription on it. Kind of a code or initials having to do with the ten plagues. There are some writings that claim the rod, along with the Ark of the Covenant, will remain hidden until the Messianic age when the prophet Elijah unveils them."

"Anything concrete, like how it will be used or where? I'm trying to figure out where these guys might be headed."

"Concrete? Nah. I mean, listen, there's your normal cache of rumors. It was found in this century or that by this or that group, but nothing substantiated. And depending on what group snatched the thing, they could have their own interpretation. The thing shows up in Jewish,

Christian, and Islamic writings and each of those has their own catalogue of theologies and traditions. Whoever has it—if it really exists—could be headed to the valley of Megiddo where Armageddon is supposed to take place; they could go into Egypt where it was used for the plagues, to the sight of the crucifixion, to Wrigley for dogs and beer. Who knows what they're thinking? Sorry. I can't really give you a GPS on this thing."

"No problem, El. You gave me some things to think about." Hunt paused. "You know anything about a sect that calls themselves People of the Crimson Moon?"

"Nah. Doesn't ring a bell. But my deal's ancient history. If these are the people you're after they probably didn't come on the scene till recently. Most radical groups don't last for millennia."

"Fair enough. Guess I owe you a game. We'll catch one when I get back in town."

"Don't forget the hotdog."

"You'll get your dog, El. You'll get your dog."

***

Jonathan Thorpe was addicted to preparation. If anything, over preparation. When possible, he would case locations for weeks, avail himself of blueprints, familiarize himself with the ebbs and flows of the residents. True, he was sometimes forced to improvise, but it was in these incidents when things were prone to deteriorate into catastrophe.

But, in this instance, Thorpe didn't have the luxury of time. He was quite literally in a race for the rod of Aaron with an unknown number of opponents. The book left with Bruno Qudsi's mother could be instrumental in giving him an edge in locating the ultimate prize. It could also be a dead end, but he wouldn't know until he'd studied it. He required that book and he needed to obtain it tonight.

Thorpe had a keen eye, he was a student of human behavior, he knew body language, the little tells that so often revealed something momentous. When Mohamed Qudsi had mentioned the book, he'd unconsciously glanced left, into the living area. Thorpe, of course, could be wrong, but his instincts told him that the volume was somewhere in that room, likely not in plain sight. Qudsi wouldn't want a reminder of his son's betrayal visible. It would be in a drawer, a cabinet, or perhaps a closet.

Thorpe entered through the front door. The neighborhood was dark and there was sparse foot traffic at night, the lock was of a standard variety—easily picked. The only other option would have been to enter toward the rear of the house near the bedrooms where he was more likely to be heard and therefore caught.

He was inside in just over thirty seconds.

The Qudsi house was not large. There was a small living room, a kitchen/dinette, and a hallway leading to the two bedrooms and commode. It was neatly kept, the furniture relatively new, the air fresh with the scent of flora. There was a couch with several throw pillows, a wooden coffee table adorned with candles and a floral arrangement, and two cushioned chairs facing the couch. Beyond this was an arched window. Beside the window was a dresser. There was no closet in the room.

Thorpe made his way to the dresser.

Family pictures adorned the surface atop a laced doyly. None contained images of Qudsi's son Bruno. Most were of a young woman, likely Bruno's sister, the rest included the parents and other adults, who Thorpe assumed to be extended relations.

Thorpe went directly to the bottom drawer, assuming Qudsi's shame over his son's betrayal would cause him to bury the tome as far from site as possible within this tiny dwelling.

It was there. Buried beneath numerous linens. Large. Leather bound. Thick stiff-looking pages. He'd assumed the volume would be an antique, but this appeared to be ancient, likely centuries old.

Thorpe was carefully lifting it from its resting place when he heard a soft shuffle from the direction of the hallway.

He turned. The young woman from the photographs faced him. She bit her lower lip. Her eyes were wide with fear. She held a gun with both trembling hands. Bloody hell, how had she heard him? The girl was terrified and therefore prone to act irrationally. Thorpe wore all black, including a skull cap and a silk scarf to hide his face. He looked the perfect criminal which likely frightened the young woman all the more.

Still cradling the book in one hand, Thorpe held the other hand out before him in an obvious please-don't-shoot gesture.

Her first shot was wide, shattering the window beside the dresser.

Thorpe dove behind the sofa which was between him and his assailant.

The second shot passed through the couch only inches from his left shoulder.

There were now shouts and the clamor of movement from the rear of the home.

Twisting, Thorpe placed both feet on the sofa and pushed, sending the couch into the coffee table and the table toward the startled woman. A glass flower vase toppled from the table, crashing to the floor and shattering.

The young woman was firing as the table connected with her shins. The gunshot went into the ceiling.

Thorpe was on his feet now, book still cradled in the crook of his right arm. Crouching, he dodged right and then left as he made the door.

More shouts.

A bullet struck the door as Thorpe pulled it open.

He was onto the lawn and ducking between buildings as two figures, father and daughter, raced from the Qudsi home. Disappearing into the darkness, Thorpe cursed. This bloody book had better be worth this rigmarole.

Chapter Seven

Wilhelmina Calhoun was a linguistics professor at The American University in Cairo, a private English language research university. While the school was founded in 1919 by the United Presbyterian Church of North America, it soon found it difficult to maintain its Christian roots for its mostly Egyptian student populace and shifted to the more generic mission of promoting good moral and ethical behavior. But while there were no longer any official religious ties, that didn't mean all faculty and teaching was completely free of religious pursuits.

Calhoun was in her mid-forties, attractive, but seemed to do her best to hide this fact. Her hair was cut short, not in any masculine way, but businesslike, nothing that would draw attention. She wore a blue blazer over a cream blouse. There was no visible jewelry or make-up, and her tortoiseshell eyeglasses were narrow rectangles of the type librarians the world over had adopted as an unofficial uniform accessory. She had a pleasant smile and a professional demeanor. While great strides had been made in bringing women into the workforce and even into positions of influence, Thorpe still wondered about the pressures a woman of authority must endure in such a male dominated society. Even in a so-called American university, many in the Middle Eastern culture likely frowned upon women holding certain positions.

After the initial pleasantries, Calhoun offered Thorpe a seat across the desk from her and said, "So, tell me about this book you wish me to examine."

Thorpe said, "Yes, well, to be honest, I know very little about it. I acquired it from the very angry father of a rogue monk."

Calhoun offered a musing expression. "Oh, now that's curious. I'd say you've piqued my interest. You claim you want it translated."

"The whole volume, no. There's a certain page. It's been book marked and there's a folded piece of paper with rather cryptic notes. These drew my attention."

The professor smiled. "All very mysterious, Mr. Thorpe. May I see it?"

Nodding and mumbling something inane about its potential value, Thorpe reached into his leather briefcase and withdrew the volume, placing it on the desk before her.

The professor's eyes widened at the sight of it. "A codex. This is ancient." Examining the binding, she added, "Perhaps dating as early as the fourth century A.D." She glanced at Thorpe with a rather severe glare. "There's quite a problem with the black-market sale of antiquities. If I were to investigate, would I find that this manuscript was missing from a museum or university, or perhaps an archeological dig?"

Thorpe offered his best smile. "Quite honestly, I have no knowledge of its history. I received it from a private individual that was given it by his son. I know nothing more." Thorpe felt this was close enough to the truth to mollify the professor for the time being. Despite the potential value of the codex, Thorpe was more interested in the translation. If he could learn of its connection to the rod, he could worry about the old book later.

Still eyeing Thorpe with suspicion, Calhoun carefully opened to the first yellowed page scanning the text. "Aramaic?" she said. Her voice was warm, like a morning cup of tea. She tugged her right ear, an unconscious habit, perhaps. "A text written in the language of Jesus. I have a feeling you sought me out for more than just my linguistic skills."

"Yes, well, your studies of historical Christianity were obviously a factor in choosing you. This is, I assume, a religious text. I was hoping that in addition to translation you might also offer some interpretation."

Another suspicious glance at Thorpe, an ear tug, and Calhoun scanned the first few pages, um-humming and nodding as she read. She turned the pages with great care, nearly caressing the brittle sheets as she scanned text. "The content appears to be quite ancient, attributed to Zarathustra; a prophet born somewhere around six hundred B.C.E. Obviously, this is not an original. Codices were not developed until the first century A.D. The original text, if truly originating with Zarathustra, would have been written on parchment or papyrus. But someone long ago painstakingly copied this."

"That is all quite fascinating, truly. And I so wish I had the time to delve into the deeper meanings. Perhaps at a later date. But currently my interest lies specifically in the marked page."

Calhoun glanced over her glasses. "That's how it is then." There was bite to her tone. She carefully flipped through the pages to the book-mark, adding, "Apparently there's nothing of use anywhere else in this document."

Thorpe caught her displeasure but remained silent. For his purposes, there likely wasn't anything else of use within those pages for it was likely Qudsi had marked these passages for his specific purpose.

Coming to the designated page, Calhoun first read the handwritten note which had been slipped into the codex and then began studying the page. She um-hummed and nodded, but said nothing for several minutes, causing Thorpe to wait patiently. Likely, this was her rebuke to him for hurrying her along to the designated page. Twice during this time Thorpe sought to speak, but she waved a finger and shushed him like a schoolmarm disciplining a schoolboy. Thorpe hated adhering to any-one's rules but his own, but he needed the woman's cooperation and so remained silent and still. How humiliating!

Eventually the woman glanced to him with a smile and said, "Much of this text concerns the rod of Aaron. A very peculiar topic for Zarathustra. Is that of interest to you?"

"Yes. Most certainly. That is indeed of interest."

Leveling her gaze at him, she said, "There has been a lot of talk about Aaron's rod recently. Just whispers among the faculty, really. It seems another professor has been approached with questions concerning it. Why the interest?"

"Well, I cannot speak for your whispers, but the rod has, well, been stolen, actually."

"Stolen? I wasn't aware that it had ever been found."

"Yes. Well, all very hush hush and all of that. But a certain sect has held it secure for centuries. It's been taken and I'm seeking to recover it for them."

Calhoun nodded, tugged her ear, frowned. "Well, that's all very interesting. I'm not sure that I believe someone has the actual rod of Aaron. So many supposed authentic holy relics are of dubious origin, but this does explain the recent murmurs."

"Yes. Of course. Now, the text. Is there anything pertinent within?"

"You really are in such a rush," said Calhoun. And then glancing at the text, she said, "The key passage concerns an insect returning to its nest."

"An insect? Whatever does that have to do with the rod of Aaron?"

"The implication seems to be that the rod is the nest."

"Interesting. And this insect, what exactly is supposed to happen when it returns?"

"Please understand, there are hundreds—thousands—of ancient documents, many religious in nature. They claim everything from frogs inheriting the earth to humans rising to divinity. Most are valuable for their cultural context, but not for their factual accounts of the supernatural. Everything here could be fanciful."

"Of course. Certainly. But, again, the insect and its return?"

"Why, according to this, it's the catalyst that ushers in Armageddon."

"Yes. Lovely. Of course it is."

"Listen, Mr. Thorpe. I can give you a rough translation of this single page. But if you want any sort of worthwhile analysis, I'll need to examine surrounding passages and get a more faithful interpretation. Would you be willing to leave the codex with me for a day or two? I'm actually on my way out to meet my new granddaughter. I won't be able to give it much attention till morning."

Thorpe hesitated, considering the book's potential value. Certainly, he could sell it for an impressive sum. And he had a good idea of what the insect in the passage might be. But what if there was more that he was missing? Something that could potentially give him an edge on the Huntingtons. "I suppose. Yes," he said. "But I really must learn what there is to be learned at the earliest possible instant."

Calhoun nodded. "I am fully aware of your impatience, Mr. Thorpe. I promise to do my very best to give you my report promptly." She paused, tugged her ear and added, "And Mr. Thorpe, I will be putting feelers out about a missing codex. If I find that you've acquired this by illicit means I will not return it to you."

Thorpe nodded. Lovely. Just lovely.

***

The Atesi watched as Thorpe left Dr. Calhoun's office. Thorpe perplexed him. Huntington, he understood. In fact, it had been the Atesi who had made the priest Abidin aware of the man and his relic. He'd thought Huntington, with his amulet, would lead him to the sacred scepter. And he still believed this. But Thorpe had proven to be helpful as well.

The codex for instance.

The third piece to the puzzle.

Still, though Thorpe might prove tangentially useful, Huntington was the chosen bearer of the insect. Should the locust awaken, it could prove the deciding factor. Better to give Huntington every opportunity to succeed.

The Atesi gazed up into the sun, receiving vigor from its eternal flame. He stretched his arms, flexed his muscles, attempting to bring the fleshly limbs into compliance with his magnificent essence. As always, the flesh resisted. It had its own will, however nominal. The Atesi concentrated, bringing all under his dominance. A wisp of smoke danced from his forehead and then dissipated into the breeze. Satisfied, that his appearance and bearing was adequate to maintain his illusion before the woman, he entered the building, strode to his right, and approached the professor's office, entering without knocking. Calhoun was at her desk, the codex open before her. She looked up. "May I help you?"

The Atesi smiled, more of a leer really. "You? Not in particular. But I have a profound interest in that document."

Her eyes narrowed as she sat straighter in her seat. She tugged her ear, an unconscious reaction. "If you're interested in the codex, you'll need to talk with someone else. I have no authority to grant anyone access." Her expression was curious, more so than the situation warrant-ed. Perhaps the Atesi's appearance was not so faultless as he had hoped. But this was of no concern. The woman was nothing.

He angled his head, causing popping sounds to erupt from his neck. "Oh, I have interest. And I need no one's permission to take it." A small stream of smoke emerged from his right cheek, twirled about, and then danced toward the ceiling.

"Who are you? What exactly do you want?" The irritation in her voice was now replaced with creeping panic.

"Who am I? Why, I am the Atesi."

"Atesi? The Turkish deity Od Iyesi? What is that supposed to mean?"

"It means that I wish for you to kindly die so I may take possession of this volume."

She was about to respond, surely with some threat or command, but the Atesi stepped forward, locking eyes with her. "Tell me, Wilhelmina Calhoun. What exactly is the sensation when your heart suddenly ignites?"

Both mouth and eyes went wide. Her hands came up to her chest. She gasped.

"The flames, they burn hotter and hotter," smiled the Atesi.

Calhoun's eyes were now crimson. A pulsing vein grew on her forehead, throbbing faster, faster. Her face was blue, her skin taut. She attempted to stand, bracing herself with her desk. Her mouth worked as if to speak. And then she fell to her left, thudding on the carpeted floor where she twitched and gurgled before gasping her last.

Ignoring the corpse, the Atesi stepped forward, closed the codex, and then lifted it, cradling it under his right arm as he exited.

***

Dana and Hunt had spent much of the day separately searching through records, attempting to gain useful information from Qudsi's former associates about both the man and this shadowy group known as People of the Crimson Moon. It was late afternoon and they'd decided to grab some food and compare notes. They'd sent Duck on some minor errands, mostly so they could talk in private.

Dana had chosen a restaurant in the beautiful Al-Azhar Park for their meeting. It was one of the few areas in the city with much greenery and offered a nice view of the pyramids. It was probably a rather touristy choice, but Dana felt they needed to allow themselves little gifts here and there just to remain sane. And it didn't hurt that the place was at least marginally romantic. Dana truly didn't know where things were going with Hunt. If she was true to herself, she'd admit defeat. They'd been separated for nearly a year and a half now and neither had made a solid move toward reconciliation. Though they'd resumed working together, they didn't even live in the same state. Still—and perhaps this was simply wishful thinking—it seemed Hunt gazed at her with that certain curl of his lips. That grin of appreciation. And of love?

How long had it been since he'd said he loved her?

How long since she'd said it him?

Bloody hell, thought Dana. *What do you truly expect to happen? We've become good friends, nothing more.*

"This shawerma's good," said Hunt, holding up the lamb and pepper kabob and bringing her back into the moment. "You should try some."

Dana took the offered bite, though, to be honest, she was already filling up on her mahshy. The plate almost overflowed with spiced meat and vegetables.

"I talked to several more of Qudsi's former associates," said Hunt between bites. "More of the same. Borderline heretical end times theology. Not an aggressive guy, but the consensus is that if you put him with the wrong crowd . . ." Hunt shrugged to finish off the thought.

Dana said, "I've managed to accumulate some tidbits on People of the Crimson Moon, but nothing actionable. It seems they're quite mobile, never headquartering in one place for more than a few months.

They operate mostly within Egypt, but there's been activity in other Middle Eastern countries as well. I've found nothing on a current location or on the goals of the group."

"Anything on their leadership? I'm thinking names."

"Three so far. But all dead ends. They're aliases. Barely able to withstand the first level of scrutiny. I've found no connection to actual identities."

"Think you can penetrate their screen?"

"I'm working on it. If I could uncover any photographs, I could plug their images into facial recognition programs. But for now, I'm at a blockade. There was mention of a high-ranking member penetrating the Keepers."

"Qudsi?" asked Hunt through a mouthful of kabob.

Dana shrugged. "I would assume so, but the reference gave no details. I think we should operate on the assumption that it was Qudsi."

"You check social media?"

"Yes. Bruno had a Facebook page, but it hasn't been active in over two years. He had less than sixty friends, most of which appear to be online-only acquaintances he'd made through various Facebook groups, mostly religious in nature as well as a few scattered archeology pages. I've identified a handful that might be true friends or colleagues."

"Good. That's better than I'd hoped. I wasn't sure a monk would be on social media."

"I wouldn't consider Qudsi an average monk."

"Fair enough. Give those to me. I'll try to contact them. What about People of the Crimson Moon? Any social media footprint?"

"None. They don't seem to want any attention drawn their way. If they do have social media, say for recruiting or communication purposes, they're not using the Crimson Moon name."

Hunt took another bite of lamb. "We've talked to Qudsi's former associates. I'm wondering if we should contact any of the other Christian ministries in the city. Being a minority religion in a Muslim society, I'd guess they'd be a fairly close-knit group."

"Hmm. I suppose that would be a logical step."

Dana saw that Hunt was about to speak again but a short man, perhaps fifty years in age, with frenzied black eyebrows, and the loose jowly skin of a bloodhound, slipped onto the seat to Hunt's right. "Mr. Huntington. I'm so sorry to intrude."

Hunt at first appeared startled and tensed for battle, but obvious recognition then spread across his features. "Brother Lachie. What are you doing here?" And then before the man could answer, Hunt turned to Dana saying, "Lachie was stationed at the same monastery as Bruno for a while. We talked earlier."

Dana nodded. "I was hoping it was something like that and not some bizarre attack. I would hate for my food to get cold while I knocked you senseless." She offered a wicked smile. Just a little jab to let the man know he was dealing with competent people.

"My apologies," said Lachie. "I didn't feel that I could speak freely in front of the others."

"No, problem," said Hunt. "I get it. Shawarma?" Hunt indicated his plate.

"Oh. Yes. Don't mind if I do." The man picked up one of the kabobs and began greedily devouring the meat from the stick. Hunt glanced toward Dana raising his eyebrows.

"So," said Hunt. "What is it you couldn't tell me earlier?"

Lachie nodded, wiping juice from his chin with the back of his hand and saying, "Madu."

"Madu? What's Madu?"

Lachie nibbled at a pepper, pulling it from the skewer with his teeth. "A man. I don't know a first name. I only know him as Madu."

Dana leaned forward on her elbows. "And who is this Madu?"

"Ah. Yes. I don't know his connection to Bruno Qudsi, but the two would meet periodically."

"How frequently?" asked Hunt.

"No set pattern. Two weeks apart now, three months later."

"And what makes you think this Mr. Madu would be of interest to us? Is there a connection to People of the Crimson Moon?" asked Dana.

Lachie reached for another kabob, but Hunt slapped his hand. "Don't be greedy, Lach. I'm a growing boy. Need my veggies."

The man at first appeared startled and then, offering a twittering smile, answered Dana. "People of the Crimson Moon. I have only heard of them today from Mr. Huntington. The reason for my visit is because of the nature of the conversations between Brother Bruno and Mr. Madu."

"And that was what?" asked Hunt, now attacking his last kabob before Lachie could make another attempt.

"That is the thing. I don't know. They were always very secretive."

"So, you have no idea as to the nature of their conversations, but that's why you're here?" asked Dana.

"This I do know. Bruno Qudsi did not want anyone to know of these meetings. I only know of them because I tend the grounds and saw the man come and go. The two would walk the perimeter of the property, well out of earshot and away from prying eyes."

"Except yours," said Hunt.

"Yes, Mr. Huntington."

"Were you ever close enough to hear any conversations?"

"No. Though I did see Bruno pass papers to Madu on two separate occasions."

Hunt shoved a piece of meat into his right cheek. "I'm guessing you don't know what the papers were?"

"No. I wish I could be of better assistance."

Dana asked, "Do you know where we can find this Madu? Does he live in Cairo?"

"He is Egyptian. I can say this much. But I know no more about him."

Hunt asked, "Who seemed the more dominant, Bruno or Madu?"

"Dominant? I couldn't say. Again. I was tending the grounds. Not spying. I know very little."

"Right," said Hunt.

"Is there anything else you can tell us?" asked Dana.

"He was well dressed. I have the impression he was wealthy." Lachie paused, scratching his fleshy jowl. "Maadi. I once heard him mention Maadi."

"And what is Maadi?" asked Dana.

"A wealthy neighborhood south of Cairo," said Hunt. "On the east bank of the Nile. It jives with the idea that this guy has money."

"Yes," said Lachie. "Very nice. Very green. Like this park."

They questioned Lachie for another ten minutes but got nothing of further use from him. Finally, they thanked him for his time and let him go. "Thoughts?" asked Dana after the little man had scurried away.

Hunt shrugged. "He's got a healthy appetite."

Dana smiled. "I meant about this Madu, you oaf."

"Yeah. I knew that. Not sure I'm totally on board with Lachie. He gave me no indication that he knew anything at all when I saw him three hours ago. And how did he know where to find us? Did he follow me? On the other hand, he may have given us our first solid lead. It's not like we can give it a pass."

"Well, then I suppose we need to meet this Mr. Madu. Though I do share your concerns about Lachie. I'll investigate them both."

***

Lachie hurried down the steps and around the corner from the dining establishment and then, slowing, walked down one of the narrow park walkways. Retrieving a disposable phone from his pocket that was given to him only an hour earlier, he pressed speed dial for the one number entered on the device. The call was answered on the second ring. "You have news, Lachie?"

The monk hesitated, stroking his fleshy jaw.

"Lachie?"

"Yes. Yes, I did as you asked, Mr. Madu. I told them about you and hinted at where you could be found."

"And did they suspect anything?"

"They asked many questions, but no. I don't believe so. The questions, to me, seemed the type that would be routine." Lachie paused and then added, "When should I expect my payment? The need is urgent."

"You will have the money to bring your sister home by the time you return to the monastery. I am a man of my word, Lachie. You have nothing to fear from me."

"Thank you, Mr. Madu. Thank you."

The line went dead. Lachie stared at the phone for a moment, wondering if perhaps they'd been disconnected. He then did as instructed, breaking the phone in half over the back of a park bench and then depositing it in a trash receptacle.

***

Hunt received a call from his archeologist friend, Eldon Troxel, while they were in a taxi returning to their hotel. "Eldon," said Hunt. "Hope you're not calling about those Cubs tickets already."

"Nah. Nothing so apple pie and Chevrolet as that, buddy." There was an uneasy tone to the normally jovial voice.

"What's up, El? There a problem?"

"Yeah well, maybe, maybe not. I got a call. Some guy asking about you. Or more specifically, asking about our last phone conversation, what you wanted to know. He knew I'd been an archeologist and figured you'd be asking me questions along those lines."

Hunt swore under his breath. "Thanks for the head's up, El. Sorry to drag you into this. What did you tell him?"

"What's there to tell? I told him you were asking how the curse on the Cubs finally got lifted."

"You didn't."

"I did. It didn't make him happy. He probed. I evaded. He asked if it had to do with Aaron's rod. I told him A-Rod never played for the Cubs."

Hunt chuckled. "You're a piece of work, El."

"Funny. That's what he said."

"So, you didn't tell him anything?"

"Nah. There's nothing to tell. But I don't take kindly to bullies. This guy was a bully."

"Anything you can tell me about him? Did he have an accent? Did he sound old, young? Did he give you a phone number?"

"Accent, yeah. Hard to peg, though. Old, young, couldn't tell. And no phone number or any other info. He tried to sound threatening without making any real threats. But I didn't buy into it. I hung up on him."

Hunt chuckled. Eldon was a pistol. "Tell you what, I'm not going to call you again until this is over. If you're contacted, post something on your Facebook page. Something we can use as a code. Maybe, 'Go Cubbies' and I'll contact you from another number."

"Go Cubbies? I post that almost every day."

"Okay, how about, 'Chicago's my kind of town?'"

"Yeah. That'll do." Eldon paused and then added. "You okay, Hunt? You into something dangerous down there? This thing kinda creeped me out."

"Could be, El. Still figuring it out. But it looks like someone's monitoring my calls and that doesn't make me feel bright and cheery."

"If someone's tapping your line then the Facebook thing won't work. They may be listening right now. They'd know the code."

"Damn. Okay. If it happens again, just call me or Dana. We'll just keep the conversation short and not say anything important."

"Yeah, well, I don't like it. You be careful there. Get another phone. Watch your back."

"Yeah. You too. Watch your back, I mean."

"Got it. Now get back here and sit your butt down on the bleachers."

"As soon as I can, El. See ya."

"Yeah. See ya."

They disconnected.

Hunt glanced to his right and said, "You catch that?"

Dana nodded. "Someone's gotten into your bloody phone. But it's not tapped, otherwise they wouldn't have had to ask your boorish friend what you'd discussed. More likely, they've accessed your phone records to see who you've called."

"Well, now I feel much better."

"This is getting quite convoluted," said Dana. "We're supposed to be hunting for the rod. Why does it feel like we're the ones being hunted?"

"Because we are. I'd just like to know why and by whom?"

They tossed around some theories, none of which really seemed to fit, discussed their next step, and then arrived back to the hotel more perplexed than they'd been before Hunt's discussion with Eldon. They both agreed that the next logical step was to interview Madu. They'd see where to go from there. This type of investigation was often one tiny step leading to another tiny step until something finally broke open.

Parting in the corridor between their respective hotel rooms without a kiss, they each entered their rooms.

A large leatherbound book sat at the center of Hunt's bed.

Chapter Eight

It was late evening when the knock came on Jonathan Thorpe's hotel room door. He'd already retired to silk pajamas and a glass of chardonnay when he heard the sound. Placing the goblet on the coffee table, he moved to the door peeking through the peephole. A smile crept across his lips. He'd been wondering when—and if—she'd make contact.

Opening the door, he said, "Tina, dear. So nice of you to stop by. And knocking on the door this time. No breaking and entering. That's simply brilliant. Though, I do apologize. I'm not exactly dressed for company."

Tina Collins smiled up at Thorpe. He'd always enjoyed her smile. Her disposition and her motives, on the other hand, were perpetually suspect. "Your silk jammies, I can handle, darlin'. As long as you promise not to drug me and tie me to a chair this time."

"Well, promises, no. Of course not. But the fact that you're entering with permission does offer some hope of a more pleasant encounter than we'd had in Dresden." Thorpe stepped aside, allowing her to enter.

She was a petite black woman, slender but well-muscled and not to be trifled with. She spoke with a sweet and sassy drawl but could strike with the venom of a scorpion. Thorpe both admired and feared her. Their previous encounters had been fraught with conflict and duplicity.

"I was wondering when you were going to make contact," said Thorpe. "You've been following me for days."

Collins smiled. "On and off, darlin'. You're not all that interesting. But I've been keeping tabs on you. Just enough to make sure you're staying out of trouble."

"Trouble? Why, Tina, what kind of scoundrel do you suppose me to be?"

"Why, Johnny. The worst type. Just clever enough to cause a mess and too arrogant to realize when you're in over that charming little head of yours."

Closing the door, Thorpe met her at the center of the room. It was a large spacious suite with lush carpets and fine linens. Unlike the Huntingtons, who maintained a rigid budget, Thorpe spared no expense when traveling. "Oh, that pains me. Only just clever enough? You still don't know me, now do you? And it's Jonathan, not Johnny." He paused and then added, "I've just opened a bottle of chardonnay. Would you care for a glass?"

"Oh, Johnny. The last time we met, you drugged me. I think I'll pass."

Ignoring her irritating insistence on the use of the name Johnny, Thorpe shrugged. "Different circumstances and, to be clear, I did not drug you with a drink. But very well. I'm sure you're here to discuss Aaron's rod. We might as well get on with it." He indicated a couch at the western wall of the room, offering her a seat. He sat across from her on an elegant golden lounge chair. "Well, I suppose, you first," he said once they'd both settled. "It is you, after all, who sought me out."

That broad winning smile again. It seemed to encompass nearly half of her face. She was rather adorable—in an entirely terrifying fashion. "Well, darlin'. As usual, you're into something way over that self-important little head of yours."

"Yes, well, insults aside, would you care to enlighten me? To what exactly is it that you refer?"

"The rod of Aaron, Johnny. It's real and there are dangerous people prepared to do absolutely any despicable little thing to get their paws on it."

"It's real. As in, this is in fact the rod spoken of in the Bible. Not just some random staff that was found centuries ago and then given the designation as some holy relic?" Thorpe knew that many so-called authentic relics were rumored to be of dubious origin and likely not the actual items claimed. Item's such as Mary's belt, the bones of the three wise men of the gospels, the actual cross of Jesus. The Catholic Church was averse to investigating these items too closely for fear they might be found to be forgeries. They wouldn't want to damage anyone's faith over a belt or a piece of bone that may or may not date to the proper century, after all.

Collins nodded. "I believe that's what I said. Please try to keep up, darlin'."

"Yes, yes. Certainly. It is the actual rod of Aaron. Go on."

"Professor Calhoun is dead."

This hit Thorpe like a punch to the belly. "Calhoun? That is, well, I just met with her a few hours ago."

"Yes, darlin', and it seems she passed soon thereafter. I know you well enough to know you had nothing to do with it. Directly, at least. Though, I'd lay money that it was your visit that got her killed."

"So, it was murder."

Collins scoffed. "An apparent heart attack. But you don't believe that any more than I do."

"Right. Of course." Thorpe paused to think for a moment and then said, "There was a book. I'd, well, I'd left it with her. I don't suppose you know anything about that?"

"No, Johnny. In fact, I was going to ask you why you'd sought her out."

"Yes, well, an ancient book. A codex. Written in Aramaic. She was a linguistics professor. I needed a marked page translated. She'd just become a grandmother. Just today. She was going to see the baby. She seemed much too young to be a grandmother, don't you think? She couldn't have been more than forty-five. I suppose that is old enough, but only just. It seems such a . . ."

"Stay on track, darlin'. Tell me about the codex."

Thorpe shook his head and then lifted his eyes to meet her gaze. "No, Tina. Not quite yet. Tell me, what's your involvement in this?"

"I've been sent to retrieve the rod of Aaron."

"Of course, well that I've ascertained, haven't I? Who exactly sent you? I assume it wasn't the CIA. Do you still claim to work for them? Or Joshua Tull, that madman who thought he was some sort of god or whatnot. He's been your employer for some time now."

Collins grinned. "Johnny, I'm working for the Vatican."

"The Vatican? Really? Tina dear, you do understand I find that hard to believe. Your track record is rather, well, shall we say, dodgy?"

"Oh, I'm not that bad, really." She winked. Thorpe wasn't in the mood for games.

"I saw you kill your own partner in cold blood."

"Haas wasn't my partner. More of an overly aggressive complication. You should thank me. He'd been prepared to blow Dana Huntington's head to oblivion."

"Yes. That is true enough, I suppose. But you coerced me into stealing a militarized bacterium."

"Darlin', if I didn't play the part, I'd be dust and bones right now. Besides, at that point, I honestly didn't know Tull's insane scheme. I'm going to assume you've never been deep undercover. It's not something I'd recommend. I was forced to . . ." Collins paused, breaking eye contact. "There were compromises. Many compromises. Things I was forced to do that still keep me up at night. I was ordered to continue, to allow his terrorist activities to move forward, because the agency wanted to get to the heart of the organization. Not just Joshua Tull, but all the leadership. Do you realize how many people died, Johnny? I wasn't in a position to stop the attacks, but the fact that I was ordered to stand aside and do nothing . . ." She paused, bit her lower lip. "Let's just say absolution feels far and away."

Thorpe gazed at her, still unsure if he could trust her story. "And this southern bell drawl of yours, that wasn't part of your cover? It always seemed a bit contrived."

Here, she stiffened. "Why, you racist pig. What, am I not urban enough for you? I'm black and so that means I must talk like I'm from the hood?"

"No. I, well, that isn't what I meant."

"Sure it was. For your information, I was raised in rural Kentucky. My daddy owned a farm. The drawl is as much a part of me as that condescending smirk is a part of you." There was a long moment of silence. Thorpe could think of no response. She was right. He'd made unfair assumptions. Where had that come from? He'd always thought himself better than that.

Finally, Collins shuffled forward on the couch, leaning elbows on thighs. "So, are we going to continue with this little dance, or are we going to get to the nitty-gritty?"

"Right. The nitty-gritty. And you're going to, well, hold to the Vatican claim?"

"Johnny, you're going to have to trust that I just might not be the villain you think me to be." She paused, appraised him, and then continued. "The Vatican is concerned about the rod falling into the wrong hands. Especially now that the insect is involved."

"The insect?"

"Again, Darlin', keep up. I've been briefed on Marc Huntington's amulet and its apparently miraculous properties. Though I'm not so frisky about jumpin' onto the supernatural bandwagon as some, my employers are quite adamant about keeping your rival's little bug away from the old rod."

"Yes, well, supernatural elements aside, my understanding was that the Vatican wasn't even aware of the rod's existence. The sect that's guarded it for centuries is tied to no specific denomination and, to my knowledge, didn't want the Vatican to know of it as they felt it might be misused by some power-hungry cardinal or another."

"The Vatican's been aware of the rod and where it's been housed for centuries. Not much gets passed them, Johnny. But they thought it best to allow the Keepers to maintain control. Probably for the same reasons as the sect themselves. The Vatican didn't trust others within the Vatican to act responsibly with such a significant relic."

Thorpe set his chardonnay on the coffee table and said, "Listen, Tina. I think you know me well enough to understand that I don't, well, go racing off after fairytales. I've never been one to give credence to the supernatural or God or any of that rot."

"And here comes the but." Collins offered her luscious smile.

"Yes, Tina. There is a but. Huntington's amulet. When we were in Botma several months ago. That locust came alive. Wings flapping, an annoying little buzz. It drove demonic spirts from Huntington."

Collins laughed. She actually laughed. "Johnny! Oh, Johnny. I never thought I'd hear such a thing from you."

"Be that as it may, I was there. I witnessed it. Something very unusual did occur."

"Darlin', I'm not denying that. I work for the Vatican, remember? Their whole deal is the supernatural. Now the rod may or may not have miraculous properties. I'm not willing to commit to either side on that. But there are people who believe it to be very powerful and who will do anything to acquire it. And that's why I'm telling you that you're in way over your head. You're just this self-important little thief. You've been somewhat useful in the past, but, if not as a friend, at least as someone who doesn't want to see that cute little head of yours ripped from your neck, please pack up and go home. This isn't for you."

"Tina, dear. You never fail to stroke my ego. And I appreciate whatever level of concern it is you are trying to convey. All very touching, that. But I have no intention of stepping away from this."

"Johnny, I'm serious. People are dying. It's not worth whatever profit you think you're going to make from this."

"Tina. I can't walk away."

Collins appraised him for several moments, sighed, and then nodded. "You won't walk away because there might be danger for Dana Huntington."

Thorpe offered a taut grin. "Am I truly that transparent?"

"Well, the word I was thinking is pathetic. But yes, Johnny darlin', you are. And for what it's worth, it's kind of cute."

"Yes, well, that's not exactly what I was going for."

"Well, then I guess that settles it. You won't go away and I can't just leave you stumbling around making a mess of everything. I'm sure my employers won't be thrilled about it, but you and I are going to have to work together."

"Now wait just a minute. I never agreed to . . ."

"Just shut up, Johnny. I'm doing you a favor." She leaned forward, slapping him playfully on the thigh. "Now cheer up. I've got a lead on a group in Luxor. Pack your fancy jammies, we're taking a road trip."

Chapter Nine

Hunt and Dana had pondered the peculiar book found on Hunt's bed for nearly an hour before giving up for the night. The book was obviously quite ancient, though neither Hunt nor Dana were experienced enough to make an educated guess as to the age. The language was one that Hunt didn't know, though he recognized it as a Semitic language with some similarities to both Arabic and Hebrew. If he were to guess, he'd say Aramaic, the language spoken in the Middle East during Christ's time. Somehow that made a crazy kind of sense. They were, after all, pursuing a Biblical relic. They'd need to find someone with the proper expertise to help them uncover just how this book figured into things—and who left it for them. Hunt would have liked to contact Eldon Troxel, maybe text him some photos of some of the pages, but Eldon was on someone's radar. He didn't want to inadvertently endanger the man.

The book being a dead end for the time being, they decided to go with their initial plan to follow up on Brother Lachie's lead of the man named Madu. It didn't take Dana long to locate Madu's address based on the information they'd been given, and they decided to meet with him the following morning.

Rashidi Madu was a bear of a man. Easily six foot four, three-hundred and fifty pounds. Hunt couldn't tell how much was muscle and how much fat, but Hunt was five foot nine, a solid one-forty-five, and the man towered over him. The face was round, clean shaven, the hair black with wisps of gray toward the top front. The eyes, small and dark, the glint of intelligence in his gaze. His dark skin only hinted at the beginnings of age lines, though Hunt placed him in his late forties. Madu stared down upon Hunt, Dana, and Duck, smiled, and said, "I'm sure you must have the wrong residence, because I don't know you." His tone was not harsh or angry. If anything, he seemed amused.

Hunt shrugged. "Yeah. Sorry to knock unannounced. I figured I stood a better chance of getting to talk with you if we just showed up rather than calling ahead."

Madu smiled. "Well, that was rather brash. But I'm not easily offended. Still, I am curious. Who are you and what do you want?"

Dana stepped forward, offering her most charming grin. "My name is Dana Huntington. This is my husband Marc and our companion, Duck."

"Duck?" chuckled Madu.

"Durukan," said Duck, not meeting the man's gaze. "Duck is a nickname." To Hunt, the kid always seemed just short of twitchy. Nothing outright irritating, but a bit odd. At first, Hunt thought maybe the young man was on some sort of drug. But over the past few days he'd come to think that maybe it was just excess energy. Now, he just seemed nervous, as if Madu intimidated him. Hunt couldn't blame him. The man was an elephant dressed in silk.

"So," said Hunt. "Here's the deal. Dana and I were having a nice meal yesterday when we were approached by a man who said you might be able to point us in the direction of a guy named Bruno Qudsi." Hunt sensed Dana tense as he said this. She was never quite comfortable with his direct approach. But Hunt felt it gave him an edge. He had a knack for reading reactions, even the tiniest of movements or changes in baring. People were never so transparent as when they were surprised.

And this man was not surprised. Oh, he feigned a mild shock. After the slightest pause, he offered an exaggerated rise of the eyebrows. But this didn't ring true. Madu knew they were coming. This meant Hunt's gut feeling about Lachie had been accurate. They'd been set up.

With a subtle shake of his head, Madu said, "Bruno Qudsi? I've not heard that name in quite some time."

"You sure about that?" asked Hunt. Dana glanced at him. He was giving her a cue that he'd picked up on a deception.

Madu appraised Hunt. "No. I don't believe I have. But does it matter? You've obviously come to ask me questions and I have no reason to hide that I once had dealings with Qudsi. Come in. Come in. We might as well be civilized." He stepped aside, ushering them into a massive foyer.

A trap of some sort? Maybe. But they weren't going to learn anything if they played it safe. Hunt stepped past Madu and into the home.

The place was only just shy of a mansion. Hunt gazed up at the ceiling three stories above and at the marble half pillars evenly spaced about the walls. The furnishings were exquisite, all white and gold. The floor was a superb tile mosaic of white, brown, and blue. Madu was obviously not only wealthy, but the kind of person that sought to impress with his wealth. Dana often told Hunt he was too hard on the rich. That there was nothing wrong with acquiring fine things if one had the means. At the core he agreed with her. He and Dana made a very good living and Hunt felt no guilt about this. But there was a difference between owning quality items for one's own use and enjoyment and being ostentatious for the purpose of causing others to be impressed, or worse, to feel inferior. This man struck Hunt as being of that ilk.

Hunt decided he didn't like Rashidi Madu.

"May I offer any of you a beverage?" asked the large man as he led them into the adjoining room where he signaled for them to select seats all facing a long glass-topped coffee table. "I have an excellent selection of wines."

"We're fine," said Hunt, answering for everyone. "And we won't take much of your time."

Again, Dana eyed Hunt. She'd picked up on his tone and was likely trying to interpret just what he'd sensed.

"Nice of you to allow three strangers into your home without us giving you much of an explanation," said Hunt as he selected a chair. "It almost seems risky."

Madu shrugged, seating himself across from Hunt as Dana and Duck found their seats. "Perhaps I'm foolish, but I sense no danger from you."

"I'd say you're right on that count," smiled Hunt. "We come in peace." He decided to back off on some of the edge. He didn't trust Madu, but he still needed information from him. There was no point in making an enemy of the man this early into the conversation. Clearly, Madu wanted them here for a reason, one which would certainly become clear in the coming minutes. But until that point, Hunt meant to glean as much information as he could from the man.

Dana leaned forward signaling to Hunt that she wanted to take the first shot at questioning Madu. "I'm curious," she said. "You said you had dealings with Bruno Qudsi. May I ask the nature of this business?"

"Some years ago, yes. Real estate transactions, nothing pertaining to his station within his brotherhood."

"Brotherhood?"

"The monks. The monastery."

"Of course," said Dana. "May I ask how a monk, whom I believe is sworn to poverty, was involved in real estate transactions?"

Madu grinned. "This is why we met in private, away from prying eyes and ears. Qudsi was involved in a land purchase and did not want his order to know."

"Why?" asked Hunt. "What I mean is, why purchase land at all if he was sworn to a monk's life?"

"His exact motivations, I couldn't say. Qudsi was one to play the enlightened mystic. Everything was mysterious. I believe he enjoyed the drama."

"Brilliant," said Dana. "What type of real estate? Was it a home, commercial property, undeveloped land?"

"You see, that's the most curious thing. Qudsi purchased desert land. Miles away from civilization. It was government land and took quite a bit of finessing to acquire."

"And you don't know why?" asked Hunt.

"Oh, I have my suspicions. As I said, Bruno Qudsi relished in the dramatic. And so, while he covered his purchase in secrecy, he couldn't help but allow little hints to slip out here and there. He liked to prickle my curiosity, you see."

"Interesting," said Dana. "And what, may I ask, are your suspicions?"

"That there's something beneath the sand. Some ruin that he's learned of. Something fresh for academics to study or for fanatics to plunder."

Dana nodded. "That's quite interesting. Did he indicate this to be the case? That there were ruins beneath the sand?"

"In so many words, no. With a passing phrase or wink of the eye, I believe so."

"Why do you think Qudsi was interested in these ruins—if they actually exist?" asked Hunt.

Madu pondered for a moment. Hunt wasn't sure if the man was truly searching for an answer or determining just how much to reveal. Thus far, the man had been surprisingly forthcoming. Hunt was waiting for Madu to hit them with whatever scheme he'd set. "I don't believe the land purchase was for him personally," said Madu. "And I'm sure it wasn't for the monastery."

"Alright. I'll bite," said Hunt. "Why purchase the land? And for whom?"

"A group. Very secretive."

"This group have a name?"

Madu smiled. When he spoke, his tone held the first hint of menace. "I believe you already know the answer to that, don't you, Mr. Huntington?"

And there it was. Madu was finally showing his hand. "I've got my hunches. But let me ask you something. Are you a member of this group?"

"People of the Crimson Moon? No. never."

"Yeah? Then why did you have Lachie nudge us in your direction?"

Madu chuckled, deep and rumbling. "Really, Mr. Huntington? You're an intelligent man. You must have determined that there is more than one party interested in the sacred scepter."

"Yes," said Dana. "We have concluded that, and we'd simply love to learn just who those parties might be."

A smile and a nod. "Of course you would. And I truly wish I were at liberty to give you more information. But, for now, no. I have been forthcoming concerning Qudsi, giving you what I believe to be valuable information in your quest, but I am constrained concerning my affiliations. But let me say this. There are many who think you, Mr. Huntington, are key to the destiny of the scepter. I am not of this mind. I believe it is only that which you possess that is of value."

"Oh?" said Hunt as he resisted the urge to clutch the amulet through his chest. "And what is it that I possess?" The words were soft, nearly a whisper, as he attempted to obscure any sign of panic from his voice.

"Mr. Huntington, please, no games. May I see it? I know you keep it on your person."

Duck spoke for the first time since entering the room. "He wants the amulet, Hunt. Don't let him have it."

"I know what he wants. And it's not going anywhere." The words were nearly a shout. Hunt clutched the arm of the chair, resisting the urge to flee the room. His pulse raced; there was a throbbing at his temple, sweat on his brow. Hunt struggled to maintain composure. This damn amulet had become an obsession from which he found no relief.

"Mr. Madu," said Dana in her most disarming tone. "Why is there such interest in Hunt's amulet?"

"Once again," said Madu. "Let's set aside the games. I'm sure you're aware of the prophesies concerning the insect and the rod. Certainly, you know what it is you hold."

"What I hold is the ugliest damn piece of jewelry on the planet," said Hunt. "And we'd love to learn about whatever lore has everyone in such an uproar." He was sweating profusely now. Why did this damn thing have such a hold on him?

"If you've not yet discovered the truth of the insect, then this is of your own doing. Now please, Mr. Huntington, the amulet."

The gun was in Madu's hand before Hunt could react. Wherever he'd hidden the weapon, he'd done a good job of it. Hunt hadn't noticed telltale bulges in any of the usual places a man might carry a gun on his person. Maybe he'd hidden it beneath the cushion of his chair. Maybe Hunt was off his game because of that damn locust. But none of that mattered. Madu wanted the amulet and there was no way in hell Hunt would part with it. Of course, by all logic, Hunt should just give Madu the amulet. It certainly wasn't worth dying for. But logic had nothing to do with it. The thing never left his person. Even when he slept or showered. Never.

"The amulet, Mr. Huntington," pressed Madu.

Hunt shook his head. Sweat dripped into his right eye, causing him to blink.

"Is it really worth your life?"

Hunt managed a shrug. "Is it really worth taking someone's life?"

Madu cocked his head. "I was hoping we could avoid violence. But I will do what I must do."

Hunt had to get his head back in the game. The man's focus was on Hunt. He should keep it that way. Reaching into the front of his shirt with a quivering hand he withdrew the locust amulet. "This ugly piece of crap really worth all of this nonsense?" he said, dangling the thing. Then, looking to his right, he added, "What do you think, Duck? Twenty bucks at a flea market?"

Madu looked to his left. Toward Duck.

And away from Dana who sat to Hunt's left.

She was quick, lunging forward, striking Madu's gun arm with a sharp chop.

The gun didn't fall free, but the arm did drop, pointing the pistol toward the floor as the gun discharged. Splintered ceramic shards struck Hunt's arm and Madu's cheek as Hunt launched himself at the man, connecting with him mid-chest and sending Madu and his chair tumbling backward.

Hunt felt like he'd just been doused with a bucket of ice water. Whatever mind fog had gripped him evaporated as he focused on the scene. Dana was still clutching Madu's right arm, attempting to dislodge the weapon. Hunt lurched forward, punching the larger man's jaw.

Sliding free of the toppled chair, Madu swung his free arm left to right, slamming Dana against the floor, while simultaneously kicking Hunt free, causing him to stagger backward.

The gun hand was free and coming up, aiming at Hunt.

Duck kicked Madu in the left ear. The man had still been on the floor beside the chair.

Duck kicked again, this time in the nose.

And then again.

And again.

The chest.

The belly.

The chin.

The ear.

The kid was in a fury.

Duck wore heavy army-issue boots, likely from his time in the military. The damage to Madu's face was already significant.

Dana pulled his gun arm, up, back, and down, freeing the gun as Madu allowed a pained wail.

Duck was still kicking. Screaming. Crying. The kid had completely lost it.

"Duck!" screamed Hunt as he pulled him away from the howling man. "Duck! Get a grip. What are you doing?"

Duck tried to pull free.

"Soldier! Stand down!"

Duck stopped what he was doing, huffed, wiped his nose, and then lifted his head to look at Hunt. It had been a crazy idea, but Hunt knew Duck had served in the military. He'd hoped that maybe some of the military discipline would kick in if he addressed him as a soldier. Apparently, it worked.

Dana was now holding the gun on Madu, instructing him to remain where he was. Hunt pulled Duck away.

"You okay, kid?"

Duck stared dumbly at him, wiping tears from his face with his sleeve.

"You could have killed him," said Hunt. And secretly, somewhere within, he felt the man deserved to die. Madu had meant to steal the amulet. The amulet! But that danger was past. Hunt had regained control of himself. It was just an ugly hunk of amber. Nothing to be concerned with. Nothing . . . Hunt shook his head, fighting with the grip of that thing. This wasn't the time to go down that rabbit hole.

"He could have killed you!" screamed Duck. "Or Mrs. Huntington! Or me!"

Focusing on Duck, Hunt held him at both shoulders ensuring that the kid was looking at him. "Yeah, he could have. Maybe. But Dana and I are pros, we know what we're doing. I appreciate the help. Really. But, he was down. The first couple of kicks were enough to take him out of the game. Dana had secured the weapon. There's no need to go lethal unless there's absolutely no other choice, you get that?"

The young man glanced to Madu who was leaning on one arm, his bloodied face dripping onto the once-pristine floor. Duck wiped another tear from his face but said nothing.

"I understand," said Hunt. "Tough situation. Adrenaline kicks in, you go a little nuts. Now it's time to bring it down. Madu's under control."

Duck nodded. "I'm sorry. I don't know what that was. I usually don't . . ." He trailed off, at a loss for words.

Hunt gave him a pat. "No harm, no foul, kid. Everyone here's still breathing." He paused, grinned. "And thanks for the save. Nice to know you're on our team. Why don't you go outside? Get some fresh air. After that little display, I think we'll get more out of Madu if you're not hovering over our shoulders."

Duck nodded and walked away silently, looking back once with a peculiar intensity as he opened the door and exited. Hunt knew that he'd been only moments from going as berserk as Duck had. He'd just managed to repress it a little longer.

Madu was in a half-reclined position, leaning on one arm as Dana held the gun on him. Hunt scanned the area, noted a restroom at the hallway entrance, and marched to it. A minute later he returned with a damp towel. Checking the chair for additional hidden weapons and then righting it, he handed Madu the towel and said, "For your face. It's not ice, but it's cold. Maybe it'll help keep the swelling down till you can take care of it properly." Indicating the chair, Hunt added, "Have a seat. You've got some explaining to do."

Madu glanced at Hunt, nodded, and then rose with a grunt, before plopping into the chair. He then brought the towel to his face, tapping it gingerly and wincing. The nose was clearly broken and Hunt suspected the left cheek was likely fractured. God, Duck had done a number on the guy.

"Brilliant," said Dana. "You look like bleeding Sylvester Stallone at the end of a Rocky film."

"You know Rocky?" smiled Hunt.

"You bloody well know you made me watch those wretched things. Stop gloating."

Hunt chuckled. She was right. He had made her watch them and he was gloating.

Keeping the pistol trained on Madu, Dana said, "Would you mind telling us what that was all about?"

Still holding the damp cloth to his face, Madu said, "I would think that obvious. I desire the amulet." His voice was nasal, a result of the broken nose.

"Right. Brilliant. Can we, perhaps, go a level deeper? Why do you want the amulet? What's your role in all of this?"

"You don't understand what you've stumbled into."

"Enlighten us," said Hunt.

Madu pulled the towel away from his face revealing his swollen and distorted features. "I do not know how you came to be in possession of the locust. But it's clear you do not understand its significance."

"Still not telling us anything," said Hunt.

Dana glanced at Hunt and then said, "Father Abidin seemed to believe that Hunt's amulet could somehow lead us to Aaron's rod. That seems a bit of a fantasy to me, but we do acknowledge the amulet has displayed some unusual properties."

Madu chuckled, though obviously it pained him. "Unusual properties. What a very sterile way of describing it. Yes. The amulet may guide. That is entirely possible. But do you not understand what will happen once amulet and staff are brought together?"

Hunt said, "We're still kind of new to this spiritual mumbo-jumbo stuff—no disrespect intended. How about you pretend we're idiots and explain it in simple terms?"

Madu gazed at Hunt as if contemplating him. The dark eyes were narrow and cold, his posture tense. Eventually he nodded and sighed. "There are prophesies. They are obscure. Little known even amongst scholars. But they pertain to the scepter and the insect. They are largely discounted, but some believe them to offer key insights into things to come."

"Right," said Dana. "So, if these prophecies are mostly discounted as false, why do you believe they are authentic?"

"It is precisely because early church leaders found the prophecies to be credible that they discounted them and sought to have all copies of them destroyed."

Dana cocked her head. "I'm not quite sure I follow."

"The prophesy of the locust was too dangerous. If, knowing what was to come, the wrong people with the wrong motives were to gain access to both insect and staff, the entire world could be endangered. It was better that only a few learned men from each generation knew the full truth. Therefore, when we learned that you now possessed the amulet, we sought to intervene."

"Bingo!" said Hunt. "There's the magic word. 'We.' Who's the 'we', Madu. Who are you working with?"

Madu tapped his face with the towel again, wincing at the contact. At first, Hunt thought he was simply buying time, thinking about whether to reveal who he was working with. But then Madu looked up at them, his face wet with perspiration. He said, "Hot. Do you feel it? So very hot."

Dana glanced at Hunt. "Look at him. It seems he's suddenly feverish."

He did look feverish. Just like the guy at the café. But before Hunt could respond, Madu screamed the high warbling screech of a thousand agonies. He fell from his chair and began beating at himself as if attempting to extinguish flames. "Ahhh! Sons of Light protect me! It is The Atesi! The Atesi!"

He rolled about the floor, flopping this way and that almost as if being tossed about by unseen hands. He convulsed, shuddering and hacking. Dana still held the gun, but seemed uncertain, likely wanting to help Madu, but fearing it might be a ruse to get her to lower the weapon.

Hunt stepped forward, kneeling beside the man, clutching him, attempting to steady him. Touching Madu's skin, he said, "He's burning up."

Grabbing Hunt by the biceps, Madu screamed, "You must not let The Atesi acquire both pieces! Do you understand? Protect your amulet!"

He convulsed. Bile dribbled across his right cheek. Unintelligible words spilled from his lips. And then he was dead.

"Dana. He's not breathing." Hunt dropped to Madu's side, opening his shirt. He couldn't believe how hot the man's skin was. It nearly burned Hunt's hands at the touch. "Madu! Wake up, damn it! Wake up!" But it was painfully clear that Madu was gone. There was nothing left to be done.

Hunt slid to the side. His hands were pink—slightly burned—from the brief contact with Madu's skin. What was that? What had just happened? Hunt gazed at Madu. It didn't make sense. What could do that? He didn't know of any poison capable of what he'd just witnessed.

"What did he mean by The Atesi?" asked Dana, who was standing over Hunt's left shoulder. "Father Abidin's note mentioned the Atesi as well."

Rising, Hunt shook his head. "Yeah. I remember. Atesi is Turkish for flame or fire. Which makes sense, the way Madu became so feverish. But he was talking like it was a person. Keep the amulet away from the Atesi. I don't get it."

Dana said, "He mentioned Light as well."

"Yeah. I caught that. Something about Sons of Light. I don't know." Hunt stared down at the dead man. "We can't stay here. I don't know if he had a wife or maybe house staff, but if someone comes in and he's dead—and obviously beaten—we'll be blamed for the death." Hunt was thankful that they'd finally stopped relying on the somewhat unreliable taxi cabs and rented a car when they arrived in Luxor. A taxi driver would be a witness that they'd been here at the time of the death.

Dana nodded and then, bending, reached into Madu's right pocket, withdrawing his phone. "We'll call the authorities from his phone once we're a distance away."

"That'll work. We'll need to ditch the phone after that, though."

"I'll offload his call history before making the call. Perhaps we can determine who he's working with."

Hunt moved across the room. "We can probably spare a couple of minutes. I'm going to see if I can find anything helpful."

He saw Dana scanning the room before saying, "There are security cameras. I'd best hack into his system and delete any data accumulated in the past hour." She crossed to the foyer and said, "I'll locate the system hub and work my little magic. Let's plan on being free of the residence in under five minutes."

Hunt nodded. "I'm on it."

Hunt didn't like hiding their actions from the authorities. And if Duck hadn't pounded the guy bloody, they'd have simply contacted the police and done things properly. But they were in a foreign country, there'd been obvious violence, and a man was dead. There was no telling how long they'd be held while things were sorted out—if they were ever sorted out. No. They'd need to play cloak and dagger on this one. Wipe away any fingerprints, delete security recordings, and get some distance away.

Pulling rubber gloves from a pocket and slipping them onto his hands, Hunt made his way down the hallway opening doors until he found Madu's office. If there was anything pertinent to find, it would likely be in here. He only had time for a quick search, so needed to target the most obvious place.

There were several occult-oriented books and objects on Madu's shelves. The guy was obviously enthralled by the supernatural. Hunt scanned some written notes on the desk, finding no reference to the rod. But there was a slip of paper with the words, "Did The Atesi kill the professor?" scrawled across it. Who was this Atesi and what did he or she have to do with any of this?

More questions. No answers.

Hunt spent another five minutes in the room, going through drawers and scanning shelves, but found nothing. He was about to remove the hard drive from Madu's computer when Dana entered. "I think it best we leave that be," she said. "On the off chance we're found out, we don't want to be guilty of anything. A stolen hard drive could be considered motive for murder. I've altered the security recordings and wiped down everything we might have touched to eliminate prints. I'd love to stay and have a looksee in his computer, but I've got a bad feeling about this."

Hunt nodded. If Dana felt it was time to vacate, then he wouldn't argue.

They were off property in less than two minutes.

Chapter Ten

It had now been more than twenty-four hours since Madu's death and they'd found nothing further on Bruno Qudsi. Yes, Dana had been able to determine that through a series of rather convoluted transactions he had purchased some seemingly worthless desert land, but there was no evidence that he'd even visited the place, much less developed it or gone digging for lost treasures.

Dana had also dug into Madu's background and found nothing unusual. He seemed to be exactly as he'd appeared, a wealthy real estate broker. True, he was heavily involved with various flavors of spirituality, but as far as she could ascertain, he was not connected to any radical faction that might be on the hunt for mystical relics. Of course, it was entirely possible that the man had simply been successful in covering his movements and connections.

Hunt had gone back to the monastery to question Brother Lachie about his contact with Madu and learned that Lachie had never actually witnessed any contact between Qudsi and Madu but had been coerced by Madu into delivering his message to the Huntingtons. Madu had desired the meeting but hadn't wanted to make the contact himself. Curious, that. Why the deception? Madu had alluded to working with someone else but had died before revealing this connection. Had he been attempting to hide this person or persons? Was that the reason for the ruse? Or was it something deeper?

Dana had just decided to take a break, maybe a short walk outside to clear the brain fog, when her phone buzzed. She expected it to be Hunt. He'd taken Duck with him to see if they could dig anything else up about Qudsi's land acquisition from the Deeds Registry, but this was a blocked number. Dana hesitated, but then decided to answer.

The voice was soft, only a whisper. It was female, slightly accented. "Mrs. Dana Huntington?"

"Who is this, please?"

The woman paused before answering. "My name is Khepri Qudsi. You tried to contact me earlier this week."

Bruno's sister. This was an interesting development. "Yes, Miss Qudsi. Thank you for returning my call."

There was another pause. When the woman again spoke, it was so soft that Dana had to increase the volume on her phone to hear her. "I am sorry I did not respond sooner. My father, he has forbidden any contact with my brother or those involved with him."

This didn't surprise Dana. They'd contacted the father as well. The man had berated them as westerners with their western god who had corrupted his son. He'd then disconnected the call. "I understand," said Dana. "I don't want to cause you any trouble."

There was a pause, and then, "Before we talk further, I must tell you something. If I feel that in any way you deceive, I will disconnect the call and never contact you again."

"I will be forthright, I assure you."

There was another pause. Dana could almost picture the young woman contemplating her next sentence. "Have you or anyone associated with you been to my residence?"

Quite curious, this. "No, we have not. I attempted to contact both you and your father. We reached your father, but he . . ." Here, Dana hesitated. "He was less than helpful."

"And you know nothing of any break-in at our residence?"

"Absolutely not. May I ask for details concerning the break in? Was anyone hurt? Was anything taken?" Perhaps the rod of Aaron?

"You may not. We will discuss it no more."

There was a long pause, surpassing thirty seconds. Finally, Dana asked, "Khepri, are you still there?"

"I am worried about my brother," said Khepri, her voice strained. "I believe he may be in danger."

"Be assured, he is in no danger from us," said Dana.

"That is yet to be determined. You've not yet told me why you seek my brother."

Dana hesitated for only a moment. She felt it important to be forthright about their part in this. If the woman already knew their purpose and Dana tried to present their interest as something else, the woman would likely become uncooperative. Better to lay things out directly and hope for the best. It almost seemed like something Hunt would do. "We're looking for him because it appears he may have stolen something of great value. But we wish only to reclaim the item and intend him no harm. We are not police and have no intention of detaining him. Our sole interest is in recovering this item. Could you please tell me what you know, Khepri?"

The woman did not respond.

"It's alright, Khepri. You can talk with me."

There was a shuffle and Dana feared Khepri was about to disconnect, but then she said, "My brother is frightened."

"So, you've had contact with him?"

"Yes."

"Was this before or after he fled the monastery?"

"After."

Brilliant. This was the first person they'd spoken with who'd had contact with Bruno since the theft. "What was the nature of your contact?"

"He said there were people after him and that he might be in danger."

119

"Did he say why they were after him or who they were?"

"No. He was very vague."

"Khepri, can you tell me anything about his plans? Where he was going? Who else was involved?"

"I don't know. Not most of what you have asked, at least."

"Anything, Khepri. We can never know for certain just what might become helpful."

Khepri offered a soft hum as she apparently thought through the conversation. Finally, she said, "Bruno said a man came to him. He asked him many questions and threatened him."

"Did he say who this man was, what he wanted?"

"My brother would not say what the man wanted. He said it was something quite important, but that he didn't want me involved."

"This is important, Khepri. Did he mention the man's name?"

"He did. But that was months ago."

"Try to remember. It could be important. It might help us find your brother before something horrible happens."

"It was a short name." She paused, nearly growling in frustration. "Maa something."

"Maa?"

"Yes."

"Think, Khepri."

The woman allowed another growl and then offered, "Madu. The man's name was Madu."

Madu. Very interesting, but quite literally a dead end. "Did he give you any information about this Madu person?"

"Only that he was very angry that my brother would not give him what he desired."

Perhaps this was why Madu had been so forthcoming with information about Qudsi. He might have hoped that the Huntingtons would succeed where he failed, after which he would attempt to steal the rod from them. "Did he mention any other names? Or maybe a group or organization?"

"Not that I remember. I was not thinking about those things. I was thinking about my brother's safety."

"I understand, Khepri. That's only natural."

"There was . . ." The young woman paused. "I'm still not sure that I should tell you this."

Dana decided to remain silent, to allow the young woman to move forward without undue pressure.

After a few moments, Khepri said, "A man broke into our home two nights ago. I shot at him, but he escaped with a book that belonged to my brother."

Dana's stomach tightened. "A book? What type of book?"

"Old. Very old. I know nothing more of it."

Very curious. Dana couldn't help but to believe this was the book found in Hunt's hotel room. "Are you sure you don't know anything else about the book?"

"Only that he felt it was important."

Dana paused, pondering her next question. Finally, she asked, "Did your brother mention a group calling themselves People of the Crimson Moon?"

"I don't believe so. Does this Madu belong to this organization?"

"He may have, but I don't believe so." Dana paused, thought for a moment, and then said, "I'm going to ask you the most important question. Please be truthful in your response."

"I will do my best."

"Do you know where your brother is now?"

There was a very long pause. And silence. No rustling. No little growls. Just quiet. And just when it seemed the woman was not going to respond, she said, "Luxor. My brother was going to Luxor."

"Brilliant. And did he by chance tell you what he intended to do in Luxor?"

"He said there were people there who shared his mission."

"Magnificent. Khepri, let me ask you another question. You spoke with your brother. Do you have his phone number?"

The woman groaned. "I don't think I should give you that."

"Then you do have it?"

Silence.

"Khepri, we mean your brother no harm. Our only concern is the return of something important to the monastery. I can't say the same for anyone else that's after him. This might be as simple as a short conversation with him."

Again, the hesitation, and then, "I'm very concerned for him."

"And you're right to feel that way. Khepri, please. Give me the number."

***

Hunt paced the hotel room, his yo-yo twirling up, down, up, down. "So, Bruno's sister just hung up on you?"

Dana set her teacup on the dinette table and said, "Someone had obviously just entered the room. She didn't want to be found talking with me."

Hunt flipped his yo-yo into an around-the-world. "Yeah. I get that. So, she said Bruno had contact with Madu?"

"Yes. He apparently interrogated Bruno. But it doesn't appear he acquired the rod. The only certainty is that Madu was after both the rod and your amulet."

"Doesn't matter. Madu's dead." Hunt pivoted, and then paced in the opposite direction. "But I am curious about this Atesi guy Madu mentioned. He must be important for Madu to scream his name as he died. Last words are usually important."

Dana said, "I've done some research, but I don't know if any of it plays into the real world."

"I'm listening."

"The Atesi is a mythical Turkish entity made from an eternal flame."

"Okay. Here's something I'm not getting. Aaron's rod is a Christian artifact. Well, Jewish originally, I guess. Old Testament, right? So, why would a Turkish entity be interested? Both Turkey and Egypt are predominately Muslim countries."

"I might be able to help you with that," said Duck who had been sitting quietly on the couch throughout the conversation. "Aaron is a figure in all three religions: Judaism, Christianity, and Islam. Islamic tradition accords Aaron the role of a patriarch."

"So, Aaron's rod could be a prize for someone from any of the three religions?" said Hunt.

"Yes. I would think so," said Duck.

"Interesting," said Dana. "And now we have this Atesi bloke who, according to my research, is some sort of Turkish entity predating Islam. Why would The Atesi want the bleeding stick?"

"Well, I'm not willing to assume he's really a spiritual entity," said Hunt. "He could just be some guy with a flair for the dramatic."

"I would love to believe that," said Dana. "But Madu's death was unusual to say the least. And he was screaming The Atesi's name as his temperature rose to lethal levels."

Hunt nodded. "So, where does that leave us? If this Atesi really is a spirit, we can't exactly track him. If he's human, we know nothing about him. Madu's dead and connected to some other person or group—but obviously not to the Atesi—and Qudsi's still AWOL, most likely in Luxor. And to top it off we have some ancient book written in a dead language that was apparently stolen from Qudsi and deposited on my bed for reasons I can't even begin to guess."

Dana said, "I've put out feelers to locate a translator. I'd be truly amazed if the bleeding thing didn't have something to do with the rod, though I'd absolutely love to learn who left it for you." Dana finished her tea and added, "According to my research, People of the Crimson Moon have had some recent activity in the Luxor area, so I'm inclined to follow that thread."

Hunt thought for a minute and then nodded. "I'm onboard. But maybe see if you can get anything more out of Qudsi's sister. I'd love to have a starting point when we get to Luxor."

"Oh, but we do," smiled Dana. "She gave me Bruno's phone number."

Hunt turned and scowled, allowing his yo-yo to drop lifelessly. "And you're just telling me this now?"

Dana grinned a mischievous grin. "I doubt he would answer a call from us, but I might be able to use a dash of computer magic to trace his phone usage through meta-data."

"Yeah. Meta-data, bring me up to speed."

"Meta-data is essentially the data within the data. I won't be able to listen to his conversations, but I should be able to access a list of all of his calls, from which number and to which number, duration of calls, and even—due to the GPS on his phone—his location at the time of each call."

"And his most frequent location is probably his current residence."

"One could assume."

"And the numbers he calls most . . ."

"Could be his contacts within People of the Crimson Moon."

Chapter Eleven

Luxor Egypt

Jonathan Thorpe and Tina Collins arrived in Luxor nearly a full day prior to the Huntingtons. Collins had gained some intelligence on a fringe group that had recently been active in the area. Thorpe was still disturbed by the death of Professor Calhoun. The woman had been an innocent and would be alive today and enjoying a new grandchild if not for Thorpe's intervention in her life. And his trust in Collins went about as far as he could launch an elephant with a slingshot. Truth be told, Thorpe was not having an enjoyable experience.

But Collins could be very persuasive and, for the time being, he felt it better to keep her close than to have her wandering about, potentially reaping havoc on this entire operation.

Thorpe smiled to himself. Curious. That was just about the same reason she'd given for bringing him along. What would that be called, mutually assured non-destruction?

"What are you grinning about?" asked Collins as she turned, offering a bit of a grin of her own.

"Only that we're a curious pair."

"Why, Johnny darlin', we're no kind of pair at all. We're just a couple of reluctant adversaries who can't seem to stay clear of each other's paths."

"Yes, well, of course, that was more or less my thought on the matter as well."

Thorpe drew in a long breath and gazed about his surroundings. The air was so hot and dry as to have passed through a hair dryer. But the city astounded him. Home to roughly a million people, Luxor still felt like it existed only for the past. From his hotel room this morning, he had seen ancient pillars, and statues, and great structures dating back millennia, glowing golden in the rising sun. He'd heard Luxor referred to as the world's largest outdoor museum and now he understood why. The spectacular Luxor Temple loomed large as a backdrop to the city with its stone sentinels and hieroglyphic-laden walls. The Medinet Habu, which served as the mortuary temple of Ramesses III was no less spectacular. Thorpe had spent much of his life around fine art and relics but felt sheltered for never having seen the likes of this—even from the distant vantage of the hotel balcony—until now.

That said, the modern-day city was booming with life. Thorpe and Collins were currently moving along a crowded sidewalk as motorcycles weaved between buses and automobiles, street vendors hawked produce and trinkets, businesspeople rushed to appointments. The place was a perpetual contradiction between new and old. Jaded as Thorpe might be, the city ignited something in him.

"Daydreaming, Johnny?"

Thorpe glanced at the smiling Tina Collins. "Ah. Enraptured by the city, I suppose. Rather stunning and all of that. Now, about this man we're after."

"Anubis Maalouf. At one time he was connected with a group calling themselves Sons of Light."

"Anubis? If I remember correctly, that's some sort of Egyptian god."

"Well, I don't think the man claims any connection to deity, but yes, Anubis was the god of embalming and of the dead." Collins chuckled. "What possibly could his parents have been thinking when they slapped that name on his birth certificate?"

"Yes. Certainly. Perhaps they were undertakers. Now, do tell me about this Sons of Light group and their connection to the rod of Aaron."

"Sons of Light is a fringe Christian group known to actively acquire ancient religious relics for their own purposes. It seems they've shown interest in the rod and I'm hoping our Mr. Maalouf might be able to point us in the right direction."

Collins held out a hand, signaling Thorpe to stop. At her signal, they moved close to the wall of the nearest shop, allowing the bustling foot traffic to pass them by. Removing her phone from a pocket, Collins angled it toward Thorpe showing him a picture of Maalouf. "This is Maalouf. If my intelligence is reliable, he should be exiting one of the next three westbound buses and entering that clothing shop across the street."

Thorpe studied the image. He hated playing second to Collins—to anyone really. He was accustomed to running his own operations and being subject to no one else's whims or potentially faulty information. But Collins apparently had resources that weren't at his disposal and so he'd found himself falling into her shadow. The entire scenario was quite humiliating for one with his talents.

"And this Maalouf is connected to the mysterious Sons of Light?" asked Thorpe.

"Even better, Johnny. He's formerly connected. No longer in the fold and more likely to dish out some of their secrets."

"Ah. Of course. Silly me. I should have thought of that. Why ever would we want someone with up-to-date information?"

Collins glanced back at him with a knowing grin. "Why, Johnny, you look perfectly constipated. Is your ego really that delicate that you can't take advantage of a lead offered by an ally?"

"I'll tend to my own ego, thank you. I was simply pointing out that, though this bloke might be eager to spill his vast abundance of knowledge, it's unlikely that it will be pertinent to our current situation."

"You see, Johnny, that's why you've never been more than a thief. You can scope out a place and learn the habits of someone's house staff and crack their security codes. You can take a million-dollar painting right through their front door with that Cheshire grin of yours. But you don't understand the varying dynamics of human behavior. You live in an itsy-bitsy little world dominated by you and only you. You allow yourself to learn only enough about a person to tease your curiosity and benefit your goals. It must be a terribly lonely existence."

Thorpe smiled, ignored the multiple insults, and silently gazed across the crowded street. There were reasons Thorpe preferred to work alone and nonsense like this was one of them. Tina Collins was obviously a talented operative, but that didn't mean she knew the first thing about him or his motivations and foibles.

They remained for nearly thirty minutes, each standing quietly, each scrutinizing every man to exit a bus, until finally Thorpe nodded toward the street, saying, "I believe that would be your man." He pointed toward a short middle-aged man just exiting the bus. He was wearing western-style attire, carrying a briefcase and a smartphone. The man looked once in each direction and then marched to the clothing shop.

Collins nodded. "You have very good eyes, Johnny. One more thing for you to be proud of. Make sure to keep that ego good and stoked." And then she walked into the street making her way toward the tiny storefront. With an exasperated sigh, Thorpe followed, weaving between the cars that were inching by at a crawl due to traffic congestion. Had Collins always been this condescending or was she still smarting from their previous encounter when he'd drugged her? He certainly hoped she wasn't that petty. It had been nothing personal.

Upon entering the tiny shop, Thorpe perceived several things about Anubis Maalouf. He was indeed short, likely only five foot three or four. He stood with a hunch. One eye seemed to be perpetually closed. He dressed quite shabbily for someone working in a clothing boutique and wore a large golden cross about his neck.

But, most importantly, he had a gun trained on them.

"Well, isn't this simply brilliant," muttered Thorpe as he came to stand beside Collins. "Did your intelligence sources tell you he was likely armed?"

Collins kept her eyes trained on the weapon as she whispered, "Not now, Johnny."

"Please raise your hands to where I can see them," said Maalouf. His left eye twitched. "Do nothing quickly."

"Of course," said Thorpe. "Why would I ever do something to startle a man with a gun? Tell me, is this how you greet all of your customers?"

"Mr. Maalouf," said Collins. "I'm with the Vatican, here at your request. There's really no need for the weapon."

Maalouf's squinted eye twitched, almost a flutter. He massaged the cross with his free hand. "I don't believe you." Reaching into his pocket and then holding up his phone for them to see, he added. "I view the video on this each morning before entering the shop. The two of you were across the street, spying, waiting for quite some time. You cannot deny it."

Collins offered her most charming grin. "Oh, sugar, you got us. Yes. Of course, we were waiting. But that doesn't mean we mean you any harm. You contacted the Vatican with concerns. They sent me to follow up. We remained secluded prior to your arrival as a precaution. You did indicate to my superiors that you might be in danger."

"You have a gun," said Maalouf, angling his head toward the slight bulge at Collins' ankle. The eye twitched again.

"That I do," said Collins. "And, as of now, I have no intention of using it. Now, may I show you my Vatican identification so we can get past this pesky little standoff?"

Maalouf scrunched his lips as if contemplating and then nodded. The gun remained trained on Collins as she used two fingers to withdraw her I.D. from a pocket and hold it out for Maalouf to see.

"Now," said Collins. "Will you please put the weapon away?"

Maalouf directed the gun at Collins and then at Thorpe and then back to Collins. "My apologies, but I can trust no one."

"That is entirely unfortunate," said Thorpe as he offered Collins a quick nod. "I for one have had much the same difficulty as humanity is, well, problematic. But to trust no one at all, tell me, did you have abusive parents?"

Collins made her move just as the man, now focused on Thorpe, was about to respond. She crossed the distance to Maalouf in thee bounding steps, slamming an elbow to his chin while one hand grabbed the forearm and the other twisted the pistol from his grasp. Collins had Maalouf unarmed and on the ground before Thorpe could process what had just occurred.

"Bloody hell," said Thorpe as he stepped forward, taking the offered gun from Collins' outstretched hand. "Once again I'm reminded of why I should avoid crossing you."

Pulling Maalouf to his feet, she said, "Johnny darlin', there's a chair behind the counter. Bring it to me."

Thorpe complied.

The diminutive Collins essentially slammed the mewling Maalouf into the chair as Thorpe stood astonished at the woman's ferocity.

Holding her own weapon on Maalouf, she said, "Now, sugar, we came at your request because you indicated you had valuable information for the Vatican. Now, I just want to have a nice little chitchat. Can we do that or do I need to get aggressive?"

Maalouf whimpered. "I'm in danger, Miss . . .?"

"Collins. Tell me about the danger."

The diminutive man looked from Collins to Thorpe.

"Please," said Thorpe. "Do tell us everything and we'll be happily on our way."

Collins said, "You can begin with who you're so afraid of. I'll take a stab and say Sons of Light?"

Maalouf looked first at Collins then at Thorpe. "Then you know," he said. "You already know."

"Yes, we know about Sons of Light," said Collins. "If that's what you're talking about. Though I'm just aching for some details." Collins moved the gun just a little closer to the terrified man's brow. "Care to share?"

Thorpe said, "Tina, dear, don't you think you're being a bit too, well, shall we say aggressive? The man's obviously frightened."

"Not now, Johnny." Keeping the weapon trained on Maalouf's temple, she said, "You contacted us, said you'd been with Sons of Light, claimed to have valuable information concerning the group and the rod of Aaron. I'm anxious to hear this information."

Maalouf was perspiring, his eyes wide. He worked his mouth, but no words came forth. "Tina," said Thorpe. "Allow me." Not waiting for a response, Thorpe knelt before the man. "Tina. The gun. Please."

With a sigh, Collins withdrew the weapon. "That better, darlin'?"

Nodding, Thorpe addressed the trembling man. "You must, well, forgive Tina. She is a dear, really, but there is that rather nasty aggressive streak. Now, about this Sons of Light group."

Gazing past Thorpe to where Collins stood, hands on hips, gun still in hand, Maalouf seemed to steel himself. "I became involved with Sons of Light perhaps a year ago. They have an ancient pedigree. They are supposed to be defenders of righteousness, to fight away the darkness."

None of this told Thorpe anything, so he simply nodded and said, "Go on."

"They knew of the scepter's existence and the prophecies surrounding it. But it wasn't until it was stolen that they learned of its centuries-long hiding place."

"So, Sons of Light don't have Aaron's rod?" said Collins.

"No, no. But they seek it."

"You see," said Thorpe. "This is the thing I don't understand. You were with this supposedly righteous sect. But you left and are now, well, let's be honest, terrified of them. Care to enlighten me?"

"Their methods. Their violence. They claim a sacred destiny, but I could not disregard their methods."

"Sugar, that's all well and good," said Collins. "But we're interested in the rod. If Sons of Light don't have it, do you have any idea who does? Were Sons of Light following any leads that might be viable?"

"There was an imam. A Muslim cleric. He tends to have knowledge."

"Knowledge?" asked Thorpe. "What type of knowledge?"

Maalouf worked his lips into a twist. "Everything of consequence. You might say he has his finger on the spiritual pulse of the city."

"Well, yes, I suppose he might be helpful," said Thorpe. "But you apparently contacted Tina's people with claims that you had knowledge. I assume there is something, beyond the idea that someone else might know something, that you'd like to share."

Maalouf's eyes went wide. Again, he worked his lips. "There is a book, a codex. The other factions, People of the Crimson Moon, they do not know its significance. Sons of Light will do anything to acquire it."

They bloody well may have already done so, thought Thorpe. "This is important," said Thorpe. "Where does Sons of Light meet? How do we locate them?"

Thorpe thought Maalouf was about to leap out of his skin, the way he trembled.

Collins said, "Darlin', there's nothing to be afraid of. The Vatican can protect you."

It was then that Thorpe heard the door to the shop open. He turned just in time to see a woman, white, with bright red hair, lob a baseball-sized object into the shop.

Collins screamed, "Grenade!"

Leaping to his feet, Thorpe was diving behind the counter as the explosion tore through the tiny storefront.

Chapter Twelve

Luxor Egypt

Dana, Hunt, and Duck pulled into the residential neighborhood in the late morning, about ten AM. It had taken some real finesse, but Dana had managed to pull the needed meta-data from Qudsi's cell carrier, pinpointing the address from which most of his calls had originated. It troubled her that there had been no calls to or from the phone in over two weeks. Dana sincerely hoped the man had simply ditched the phone, but not changed addresses as well.

The home was on the first story of a three-story flat and belonged to a man named Sabra Tavakkoli in a neighborhood that Dana considered to be just two steps up from dodgy.

Dana had learned that Tavakkoli had been Qudsi's roommate in his first year at university. The phone had also been in Tavakkoli's name. It appeared that the phone had never belonged to Qudsi, that he'd simply borrowed it to call his sister. But even this being the case, Tavakkoli was a contact of Qudsi's and thus a potential lead.

Tavakkoli's wife—a small woman, broken English, and in traditional Middle Eastern attire—answered the door and after a bit of persuasion, agreed to begrudgingly answer their questions. Yes, she knew Qudsi. He had stayed with them for a short time, but he and her husband had run off on some sort of nonsense. She knew little more than this and seemed ready to condemn her husband to eternal flames for bringing Qudsi into their home. The woman made little eye contact, her answers were curt and absent elaboration.

Dana felt oddly ill-at-ease as they left the apartment. It seemed to be another dead end, but something didn't sit quite right. She'd held out hope they'd finally acquired a lead on Qudsi and couldn't help but feel that she didn't get the full truth from the woman. Strolling past a street vendor selling peaches from a cart, she turned to Hunt saying, "What are your opinions?"

"Besides the fact that Tavakkoli's in for the tongue lashing of a life-time when he gets home? I think this was a bust. How are you doing on finding a translator for that ancient book?" asked Hunt as, angling left to avoid three young children chasing a cat, they neared their rental car.

"I've put some feelers out at nearby universities but not had success in finding anyone. We might need to enlist your boorish friend, Eldon."

"Why do you insist on calling him boorish?"

"Because he's boorish, obviously."

"I'll call him if I need to, but he's been compromised. I don't want to endanger him."

They were at the car now. Hunt depressed the button on the key fob, unlocking the doors. Duck slipped into the back seat, Dana into the front passenger side, and Hunt walked around to the front of the vehicle and was approaching the driver side door when a black van skidded to a stop beside him.

Before Dana could think to respond, the sliding door of the van opened and two men leaped out, each grabbing Hunt, and pulling him forcefully into the van. Dana was out of the car and racing toward the van in an instant, but the door was already sliding shut and the van pulling away by the time she reached the front of the car. Even as she sprinted after the fleeing vehicle on foot—a useless exercise to be sure—she pulled her phone from her pocket and snapped a photo of the license plate. The van disappeared around a corner only a moment later.

Cursing, Dana ran back to the car, hollering at Duck, who was running toward her, "Get back in the car. Hurry!" She had a key for the ignition as well. They might still be able to catch the blokes.

***

Hunt was just about to open the rental car door when he was grabbed from behind. Two men yanked him, one on either side, dragging him up and into a van. They immediately pushed him into a bench seat situated along the driver side interior wall. One of the men was still pulling the door shut as the van pulled away with a jerk and a squeal.

The first man—Caucasian, burly, and balding—pressed down on Hunt, holding him at both shoulders while the second—a bodybuilder type—hurriedly frisked him. "Stay put and you won't be hurt," barked burly as he released his grip and seated himself beside Hunt. Bodybuilder, now finished frisking Hunt and finding no weapons, moved to a short bench at the back of the van. He settled beside a redheaded woman. Hunt recognized her as the woman he and Dana had chased through an apartment building in Garbage City. She was well-dressed in business attire, maybe forty-five years old, stocky, but solid. Her green eyes seemed to have a perpetual squint and her painted red lips were a stark contrast to her milky complexion.

Glaring at the woman, Hunt said, "You ran from us last time I saw you. What's with the change of heart?"

The woman offered a tepid smile. "It seemed it was time we spoke. You and I seem to be racing down the same rabbit holes, as it were." She spoke with a thick Irish brogue, as had the red-haired man at the Turkish café. This bore out his conclusion that they were probably connected in some way, maybe even related.

"You could have just asked. Why abduct me?"

"I don't know you and therefore don't trust you. I desired a controlled environment." Her tone was condescending yet simultaneously conversational.

"You know my wife's probably already chasing us. This could get dicey."

Another grin, this one haughty. "No. Right now she's likely cursing us for disabling your vehicle. We have plenty of time for a leisurely conversation."

Hunt didn't like it. The men were still beside him. No one had pulled a weapon. But there was no mistaking that he was a captive. "Alright. So, talk. How about starting with who you are?"

A shrug. "Aye. Well, I suppose it would be fair to begin with your questions. My name is Alice O'Broin."

"Yeah. That doesn't tell me anything. What's this all about?"

"Ah. Don't play the eejit, Mister Huntington. You are after the rod of Aaron, as are we."

"And who is we?"

"An ancient order known as Sons of Light. We seek to acquire sacred artifacts in order to utilize them for their divine purpose."

"Alright. I'll bite. What purpose is that?"

"To bring a final universal peace to the world." She actually said this with a straight face.

"Okay. Right. How's that working for you?"

"Naw too well, I'm afraid. My fear is that the rod of Aaron might have fallen into unsavory hands. At first, I thought you might be in the employ of one of these factions. But after researching you, I've concluded that you're naught but a pawn. You were brought in because you possess the insect. If you believe anything different, you're a fool." She angled her head, again offering that tepid grin.

"Well, thanks for the kind words, but so what? All I'm trying to do is to recover the rod for its rightful owners."

Here, O'Broin chuckled. "Aye! Rightful owners? Could there even be such a thing for a relic that belongs to the ages? Tell me, Mister Huntington, what have you learned thus far? What is the next step in your investigation?"

Hunt had no desire to tell her anything and so responded with a question of his own. "Sons of Light. I met with a man who said something about Sons of Light when he was dying. Care to comment?"

O'Broin hesitated before responding. "Oh? What was this man's name?"

"Madu. And by the way, he tried to steal my amulet. Hope you don't have similar plans. Obviously, you know about it. You mentioned 'the insect.'"

O'Broin seemed momentarily stunned. When she spoke again, she was less confident. "Madu. I was not aware that he had passed. Did you . . .? I mean, were you the one . . .?"

"Nah. I had nothing to do with his death. His temperature shot up out of nowhere. It was pretty creepy. Didn't seem natural." Hunt paused and then added, "He was one of yours, wasn't he?"

She nodded, her haughty façade crumbling ever so slightly. "Madu was . . . He had become a problem for us, a bit of a rogue, too fanatical. I suppose we should have kept a tighter leash on the man." She paused and then added, "He is not the first of our number to die this week."

"In Turkey. The man at the café," said Hunt.

"Aye. Patrick. My cousin. I fear he and Madu may have fallen prey to the same evil."

"Yeah? And what evil is that?"

O'Broin seemed to gather her thoughts. After several moments she straightened, reestablishing her posture of superiority, and said, "You pursue a man by the name of Bruno Qudsi. We believe he might also go by another name, the Atesi. If this is indeed the case, he is a very dangerous man, with abilities that are beyond those of the natural world. This is why we meet, Mister Huntington. I must convince you to give up your search and leave it to those of us who recognize all that is involved."

Hunt chuckled. "And now you're going to tell me to give you my amulet, right? Because you have some great enlightened understanding."

"Enlightened? Hardly. I have feet of clay, the same as you. But aye, Mister Huntington, we are educated in these things and it would be wise for you to relinquish the amulet to us. For we have studied such matters for years. We have knowledge that may protect us, where you . . ." She shrugged. "Honestly, I'm surprised you've made it this far without catastrophe. So, I ask you, with respect and courtesy, will you release the insect to our care?"

"Not going to happen. And as to respect and courtesy, that went out the window the moment your two brutes hauled me into your rolling Gitmo."

O'Broin offered a subtle nod and said, "You do realize that the long-awaited week of the holy convergence is nearly upon us and as long as you are in possession of the insect, you will be in danger. Your wife and your companion as well."

"Guess we'll take our chances. No offence, O'Broin, but I don't know you, I don't know your organization, and you haven't exactly given me any reason to trust you."

Her lips descended into a bit of a pout. "I had hoped to persuade you to a logical choice. We are in a much better position to both protect and utilize the insect than are you."

Hunt was already growing tired of this and allowed irritation to creep into his voice. "I'm still saying no. Are you going to try to take it from me?" His thoughts were hostile, nearly irrational. He had to protect the amulet. He could not relinquish it, even if it meant a fight to the death. Hunt clenched his fists in frustration. It was almost as though these emotions came from beyond himself.

O'Broin offered that too-sweet grin again. "Naw, Mister Huntington. Sons of Light may use drastic methods when necessary, but we don't routinely work that way. As I said, our Mister Madu was a rogue. He believed in taking things by force. But that is not our method. I encourage you, please reconsider. Give us the insect, or, at the very least, work beside us. I don't believe it is worth losing your life over an amulet you don't particularly like and barely understand."

"Guess I'll just have to take my chances on that."

O'Broin offered an exaggerated pout, nodded, and said, "That truly is a shame. I suppose, to some, life is of little value."

***

The van carrying Hunt was just rounding the corner and out of sight as Dana launched herself into the rental car and practically slammed the keys into the ignition.

The car wouldn't start.

The engine wouldn't even hint at turning over.

Dana slammed her palm on the dashboard. The bloody car wouldn't start! Popping the hood with a knob beneath the dashboard, she nearly leapt from the driver's seat and raced to the front of the vehicle to inspect the engine.

"What is wrong?" asked Duck as he exited the car and came beside her.

"Whoever took Hunt disabled the car." She immediately saw the problem. A cluster of wires had been ripped free. Suppressing a curse, she turned to Duck. "Go back to the flat. Tell Mrs. Tavakkoli we need to borrow her car."

"But Mrs. Tavakkoli barely said a word to us. I don't think she liked us."

"Duck! It's a bleeding emergency. Convince her!"

Dana returned to the mess of wires, not bothering to listen to Duck's mumbled response as he turned and rushed toward the building. Cursing, she separated the wires, inspecting them, attempting to determine just what went where.

"Damn it!" she screamed. What was she thinking? There was no time for this. Hunt could be nearly a mile or better away already. It would take a miracle to acquire his trail. Straightening, she scanned the narrow street. She could try to hotwire one of the nearby cars, but, again, the van was already gone. "Idiot!" she screamed, pulling her phone from her pocket. She had the bleeding license number. Why hadn't she called the police? Pulling her phone free of her pocket, she was about to access the emergency number when she heard a racket coming from the direction of the flat. Duck had been knocking on the door—pounding really—and there had been panicked shouts from inside.

And then there was the slamming of a door.

Not from the front where Duck stood, but from the rear.

Still holding the phone, Dana moved around the back of the car and then alongside the building.

And there he was, racing from the apartment down a narrow alleyway. It was Bruno Qudsi, or at least she supposed it to be. He was short, box-like, and carried a long narrow case. She assumed this to contain the rod of Aaron. Bloody hell, he'd been there all along and panicked when Duck came back to the door, likely assuming he'd been discovered.

Dana broke into a run as Qudsi cut left between two aging apartment buildings.

Dana was quick and made the intersection in only a few seconds. He was within sight again. Qudsi raced across a street and between another set of decades-old buildings. Dana followed, bolting out in front of a bicyclist who skimmed her right leg before toppling with what she assumed to be a curse. Dana stutter-stepped through the encounter without slowing.

Rounding a corner and emerging on a commercial lane, Dana saw Qudsi go through the doorway of a small corner shop. Her instinct told her he wouldn't remain in there and risk becoming trapped and so she angled left toward the rear of the building assuming he'd exit near her.

He didn't

Dana heard a shout and the clang of a door from the front and raced around the building and toward the front. Qudsi was on the opposite side of the street. Racing between oncoming cars, Dana nearly danced across the boulevard barely averting honking automobiles.

Qudsi was now racing along a downward sloping walkway leading to a small park area. Dana raced forward and catapulted over the metal guard rail separating her from the sloping grade, landing only perhaps twenty feet behind the fleeing Qudsi. She felt a slight twinge in her left knee upon impact but shrugged it off. With a howling roar, she lunged at Qudsi, catching the tail of his jacket and causing him to stumble almost to the point of falling.

Grabbing him by the elbow, she twirled him around. He jabbed a knee into her belly. Startled, Dana released her grip allowing Qudsi to push her forcefully at the shoulders. Dana stepped back and, connecting with a large egg-shaped rock with her heel, fell onto her buttocks.

Qudsi was racing away as Dana leapt to her feet and reinitiated pursuit. She was skilled in several martial arts disciplines. The only reason Qudsi had been able to subdue her was due to her own arrogance. She hadn't expected any real resistance from the monk. She wouldn't let that happen again. Charging after Qudsi, she connected with his back. He stumbled forward but regained his balance. When he turned to face her, Dana greeted him with a roundhouse kick connecting on the lower back just above the left hip.

Qudsi let out a howl but managed to slam three quick punches into Dana's gut. She countered with a chop to his right shoulder which sent him to the ground and the case flying from his grip, landing several feet from the battling duo. She moved in the direction of the case, but Qudsi grabbed her ankle preventing her from moving forward. She twisted, kicking the man in the left cheek with her free foot. He fell backward, but managed to curl his legs, catching Dana in her shins, and causing her to hop and scoot in order to free herself.

Eyes on the case and still disengaging from the fallen monk, Dana didn't notice the approach of two more men until they were upon her. One slammed her in the side with his fist, the other grabbed her left arm.

A quick downward jerk, pull across, and then up and Dana had freed her arm. Spinning, she leapt forward and up in a powerful vertical jump. Jutting her legs forward at the last moment, she thrust her knees against the other man's upper chest causing him to tumble backward.

Landing, she turned to face Qudsi and the other assailant. Lunging forward, she crowded the second man, preventing him from getting off effective blows as she peppered him with a series of quick punches.

Ducking, she avoided a swipe by Qudsi and then brought her elbow down on the top of his head, causing him to crumble to his knees.

Turning toward where the case had fallen, she saw the third man running across the park, case in hand. Dana had just begun pursuit when a 1980s era sedan pulled to a stop in front of the fleeing man.

A man exited the car: tall, hooded. He stepped in front of Qudsi's accomplice, and, producing a long metal bar from within the folds of his coat, struck the man across the face, sending him to his knees. Snatching the case, the newcomer shoved it into the back seat of the car and then slid into the driver's seat and pulled away. The entire encounter took only a matter of seconds.

Dana raced after the hooded man as he pulled away. One of Qudsi's companions shouted in anger, waving his hands while Qudsi cursed and bellowed.

Obviously, the hooded man was not with them. The only logical conclusion was that a third party had just acquired the rod. Were these the same people that had abducted Hunt? Dana shot to her right, angling across the open space, attempting to intercept the car before it could get beyond this tight area and accelerate. Her left knee throbbed, whether from the fight or from the leap she'd taken earlier, she wasn't sure, but her gate was uneven, her pace slower than it should have been. Though Dana had a shorter distance to traverse, the car made the intersection ahead of her, turned the corner and sped from view.

Cursing, Dana turned back toward Qudsi, but he and his companions had already disappeared between buildings and were lost from sight. Damn! Who had that been? Who now had the rod?

Chapter Thirteen

Jonathan Thorpe regained conscious with a prolonged moan. The world was fuzzy, just a kaleidoscope of moving colors. There was a low tone in his ears, almost like an electrical hum but with a bell-like quality. His eyes fluttered as he attempted to focus. There were voices. None he recognized. Speaking . . . Arabic, maybe?

A shadow moved into his still cloudy vision. Human in shape, leaning over him from the right. And then another, this from his left.

They conversed. The person on the right flashed a light in Thorpe's eyes, first one and then the other.

The bell-like tone continued, but eventually his vision came into focus. He was in a room, brightly lit. He could now see four people grouped about him, three in medical garb and one in a police uniform.

He blinked again, attempted to rise, and then thought better of it, collapsing back into a pillow.

He ached. A general all-purpose ache. But he didn't notice severe pain in any specific points on his body. That was likely a good sign. If there was real damage to something, the pain would be much greater at that point. Likely he'd taken a good pounding, but nothing more.

Either that, or he was on quite effective pain killers.

The man with the penlight was leaning over him again, saying something, still in Arabic.

"English, please," moaned Thorpe. The man was obviously a physician and most educated people in Egypt spoke English and French as well as their native tongue.

"Very well. English," said the doctor. "How are you feeling, Mr. Thorpe?"

"Truth be told, a bit battered. Would you mind dimming the lights a notch or two? They're quite irritating."

The doctor turned to a young man, also in medical attire, and nodded. The young man complied with Thorpe's wish.

"There. Is that better?" asked the doctor.

"Much."

"Very good. Do you know where you are?"

"Well, at first guess, I'd say a hospital."

The doctor nodded and then lifted Thorpe's arm, striking his elbow with a small mallet. "Yes. And where do you believe the hospital to be?"

"Egypt. Most likely Luxor."

The doctor shuffled right, tapped both of Thorpe's knees with the mallet, and then moved to the other side, repeating the process on the left elbow. "Mmm, good. Do you remember your date of birth?"

Thorpe gave the date.

The doctor put an arm behind Thorpe, pushing him gradually into a sitting position. "How well can you hear me?"

"There's a hum in my ears, but I can make out what you're saying."

"Lift your left arm."

Thorpe complied.

"Your right."

Thorpe did this, though the arm was stiff, the movement painful.

The doctor released Thorpe, allowing him to sit without assistance. "Good, good. You may lay back. Do you know what happened to you?"

Thorpe closed his eyes and thought for a moment. Everything was a jumble, but the pieces were reassembling. "Explosion," he said at last.

"Good, good," said the doctor.

At this point, the uniformed man stepped forward, barking something in Arabic. The doctor seemed to put up some sort of feeble resistance but was overruled by the officer. Nodding, the doctor turned to

Thorpe saying, "Do not let him upset you. You've got a concussion. You must rest."

As soon as the doctor moved away, the police officer was hovering over Thorpe. "Jonathan Thorpe, am I correct?"

"Well, as you've likely already seen my passport it would do little good to deny it."

"Agreed. Tell me, Mr. Thorpe, what are you doing in Luxor?"

Thorpe was generally not a fan of law enforcement. He considered them low level keepers of inane laws enacted by even more inane bureaucrats. But in this instance, there was no advantage in being evasive. Thorpe readjusted with a grimace and said, "Looking for a very old stick."

The officer frowned. "I will tolerate no nonsense, Mr. Thorpe. A man is dead."

Thorpe nodded. He assumed the officer was referring to Anubis Maalouf. There was little possibility he had survived the blast. The best news was that the officer had said nothing about other casualties. I.e., Collins likely survived. "Allow me to rephrase," said Thorpe. "I am pursuing an ancient artifact stolen from a monastery."

"And what is your interest in this artifact?"

"The artifact itself, very little, but the monastery is offering a sub-stantial sum for its return, and that is of great interest."

The officer grunted, showing obvious displeasure, and then said, "What was your connection to Anubis Maalouf?"

"None whatsoever. He was simply a lead. We were questioning him concerning the artifact."

The officer seemed to consider this for a moment. "Why would someone kill him, or were they attempting to kill you and your compan-ion?"

"Yes, well, all good questions. But as I don't know who threw the grenade, I'm at a loss for any meaningful response. But speaking of my companion, did she survive? Is she well?" Thorpe couldn't exactly call Tina Collins a friend, but he had a grudging respect for the woman. And, if he was to be honest with himself, she wasn't entirely awful.

"Aw, sweetie. So nice of you to ask. I was beginning to wonder if you'd ever get around to it." It was Collins, she'd been standing in the doorway and now entered the room followed by another police officer. Her face was swollen and bruised. There was a gauze bandage on her forehead. She walked with a slight limp. The first officer turned, watching her as she said, "No need to answer any more questions, darlin'. We're getting out of here."

The officer began to protest, but the man who had entered with Collins cut him off and ordered him from the room. He then gave Collins a glare and exited.

"Very impressive," said Thorpe. "Dare I ask how you managed that?"

"Oh, darlin'. The Vatican has pull like you'd never imagine." Turning to the remaining medical staff, she added, "A little privacy, please." The doctor nodded and then exited, followed by his staff.

Thorpe stared at her. "This Vatican claim is real, then? You actually work for them."

Collins simply smiled and went to the small closet at the corner of the room and began retrieving Thorpe's clothing.

Thorpe pressed further. "I've heard conflicting reports concerning the Vatican, some say they have their own intelligence bureau and maybe even some military units, others that this is simply myth."

Collins tossed Thorpe's clothing on the foot of the bed. "I'm sure some people do say those things," said Collins, offering a perfectly infuriating non-answer. "Now climb out of bed and get dressed. We need to leave. The doctors say your capable of moving. Just be careful of your head. Sounds like you took a good knock to the cranium."

Thorpe moved gradually to a sitting position. "It seems you've survived satisfactorily. No major injuries, I presume."

"Bumps and bruises. I've had worse. I ducked behind the half wall beside the counter. I got lucky."

Thorpe nodded and swung his legs around, preparing to stand. "Why did they kill Maalouf? Or was it, well, us that they meant to eliminate?"

"Maalouf was obviously a security risk to Sons of Light. He'd contacted the Vatican concerning them and was passing information. I suspect that was motive enough."

Thorpe moved gingerly to the foot of the bed, grabbing his pants and slipping them on while still wearing the hospital gown. His head swam and his vision wavered, but he managed to perform the task. "Yes, well, Sons of Light. I'm curious as to their connection to the rod."

"I contacted my people at the Vatican while you were out and learned a tidbit or two about them. It seems they've kept a pretty low profile, but word is they have a militant undercurrent. They claim to be the Sons of Light mentioned in the War Scroll which is a document of the Dead Sea Scrolls dating to the first century B.C.E. Apparently the Sons of Light are supposed to battle the Sons of Darkness during the end times."

"Well, that sounds entirely nonsensical. If the scroll is from the first century, B.C.E., that's before the birth of Jesus. Maalouf wore a cross. I was under the impression this was a Christian group."

"It is. The Vatican believes that though they claim a direct connection to the group mentioned in the War Scroll, they've really just adopted the name and mission. This group, though, does date back at least two centuries. The Vatican found nothing of them prior to that time."

"If this sect goes back that far, the current members might quite like-ly believe they are part of the true Sons of Light spoken of in the scroll."

Collins nodded. "Exactly my thoughts, darlin'. In any event, they're after the rod. Maalouf gave us a lead before he died, an imam that's well connected. I have a pretty strong idea who that might be. I say we pay him a visit."

Thorpe slipped out of his hospital gown and grasped his shirt. "Love-ly," said Thorpe. "Though you might need to support me a bit. I believe my discharge might be a tad premature."

Collins smiled. "Anything you need, darlin'."

They were free of the hospital five minutes later.

Chapter Fourteen

El Kab, Egypt

The email came from a woman named Brigid Daniels. She claimed to be an archeologist and was responding to Dana's request for a translator. Dana had agreed to meet with her, had then done a quick background check on the woman, found nothing to concern her, and so, along with Hunt and Duck, had come to the meeting place at the designated time.

The meeting place was not at all convenient.

About a two-hour drive from Luxor, El Kab was on the east bank of the Nile and was rife with ruins of an ancient settlement, rock cut tombs, the remains of ancient temples, and pretty much anything else to make an archeologist drool. Dana had tried to convince the woman to meet them in Luxor, but she'd insisted that if they were to meet, it would be in El Kab. Though there was nothing troublesome in her brief background check, Dana got a sense that there was something more to the woman than what she presented. She'd seemed a bit agitated, overtly controlling of the situation, but this was not necessarily a bad thing. Even if the archeologist was keeping something back, it likely meant she knew that Dana and Hunt were on the trail of the rod of Aaron, and if she had interest, or even a connection with that, all the better. She might prove to have more uses than simple translation.

The downside was that it would mean she had an agenda of her own. And depending on what that agenda might be, it could be a complication—or even a danger. Dana and Hunt hadn't ruled out the possibility that this was a trap. But they'd decided to come regardless. At this point, they weren't willing to miss any opportunity that might bring them closer to their goal. Hunt had been taken and then released by a group seeking the rod and Dana had come within sight of the prize only to have it spirited away by a yet-to-be-identified party. In many ways, they were starting over with no leads on who now held scepter. Qudsi and his ilk had disappeared again, so any information they might have on the hooded man was out of reach. The old book might well be their only lead.

While the area closest to the Nile was green and fertile, the rest of El Kab appeared to be sand. Seemingly endless sand, spotted with ruins of structures made from sandstone. Tan on tan everywhere they looked. Dana had only marginal interest in archeology as a science, but she was awed by the sites they passed as they drove through the area. These structures dated back centuries—millennia—and still stood as silent testaments to the past. Most of the buildings were low functional struc-tures. And yet they were impressive in their rugged simplicity, in their ancient design, in the mysterious hieroglyphs carved into their stone.

As instructed, they parked their rented jeep about a quarter of a mile away from the ancient Coptic monastery where Brigid Daniels did her work. Hunt positioned the jeep adjacent three aging buses likely used to shuttle staff and volunteers to their overnight accommodations.

Hunt wiped sweat and sand from his brow with a bandana. "Did your archeologist say why she wanted us to wait all the way out here?"

"No," said Dana. "But my impression is that the woman is overly cautious. I'm curious to learn why."

"Oh!" said Duck, excitement in his tone. "She's coming. Look. She's coming."

Dana and Hunt both looked toward the monastery. A lone female figure was making her way in their direction. As she drew closer, Dana could see that she wore a brightly colored tie-dyed shirt and a floppy wide brimmed hat with a florescent peace symbol stitched to the front. She was black, slightly tall for a woman, and seemed relatively fit. Likely no older than thirty, her hair was long and braided in dreadlocks.

"She is very pretty," said Duck with a cautious grin.

"Keep your mind on the task at hand," said Hunt. "But, yeah. She's cute."

Choosing to ignore the two men, Dana climbed from the jeep and walked toward the approaching woman. She noticed Daniels glance in either direction as if expecting someone to appear out of the desert. "Hello," said Dana as they drew near to one another. "I'm Dana Huntington."

"Brigid Daniels," said the woman through a curious smile. She pulled earbuds free, allowing them to dangle below her shoulders. Dana could make out faint music coming from these. Was that The Grateful Dead? "Pleased to meet you," said the archeologist. Her accent was South African. This matched with Dana's background check on the woman.

Dana explained that her husband and companion were with her and, with Brigid's consent, waved them over. Hunt hefted the satchel carrying the mysterious book and leapt from the jeep.

After introductions, they began their march to the ancient monastery. Brigid warmed some as she explained, "This site has been in one stage of excavation or another since the late eighteen hundreds. Throughout most of the twentieth and twenty-first century it's been led by the Belgians, but other groups are allowed some access from time to time. We can sit over here in the shade." She indicated a long white tent about five hundred feet to the right."

They sat at a six-foot-long folding table in a tent that appeared to serve as something of a combination mess hall, office, and storage facility. Rows of tables were lined with various artifacts each accompanied by cards indicating what the item was, where it was found, by whom, approximate dating, and any other useful information. The tent could probably accommodate nearly two hundred persons, yet, while there were other team members coming in and out, Dana's sense was that it was a moderate-sized crew, likely about sixty to one hundred persons. The volunteers were an eclectic mix. Several were college age, likely students of archeology on their first digs. The others were a real mixed bag, various ages and ethnicities. She'd heard that people often volunteered to work at dig sites as some sort of adventure holiday. Bloody good for them, she supposed, but the Caribbean seemed a much more appealing vacation locale. A couple of people nodded at the Huntingtons, a couple more stared, likely wondering who they were, but mostly they were ignored. Brigid offered lemonade and all eagerly accepted.

"Tell me," said Brigid with an eager grin. "What is this book you spoke of and how did it come into your possession?"

"Good question on both counts," said Hunt. "We don't know anything about the book. I'm guessing the text is Aramaic, but that's a lay person's speculation. As to how we got it, I walked into my hotel room and it was sitting on my bed."

Brigid cocked her head, staring at Hunt, a curious grin tickling the corner of her lips. "Really? How very James Bond."

"God's honest."

"Okay. That's cool. But, if that's true, why are you so hot for a translation? Isn't it possible that someone left it there by mistake, maybe thinking the room belonged to another? I mean, mysterious artifacts don't appear out of nowhere except in movies, right?"

Dana eyed Hunt and then said, "Dr. Daniels, allow me to pose a question before we answer that."

Brigid shrugged. She seemed to be swaying slightly to the music still slipping from her exposed earbuds. Interesting woman. Not what Dana would have expected of an academic.

Dana continued. "I have a peculiar feeling that you know something of us. Or, at least, of what we are doing here. Is that an accurate assumption?

Brigid's grin expanded involuntarily. "I . . . have been made aware of your quest."

Dana said, "And so your offer to help us with the translation is motivated by what?"

A pause. A grin. A chuckle.

Hunt interjected. "Hey, we're not here to cause any problems. But we do put everything on the table. That way we all know the score. Simple as that."

Brigid threw her arms up in mock exasperation. "Oh, what the hell. I have a friend. A mentor, really. He learned of your search for Aaron's rod. He's a university professor. When he saw your request for a translator come through his department, he suggested I contact you."

"And why was that?" asked Hunt.

"He has a passion for such things. For Biblical artifacts. For their place in eschatology. He thought that perhaps the translation would prove interesting and might even help to unveil some as yet unknown knowledge. You must understand, this is what we do. We uncover artifacts and writings. Every significant piece adds to our knowledge of the culture. If your book is genuine, it might prove quite valuable from an academic or historical perspective."

"I see," said Dana. The story made sense and might well be true, but she wasn't entirely convinced that this was all there was to it.

After a moment's pause, Brigid grinned and said, "Sooo, are you going to allow me to see it?"

Dana made eye contact with Hunt, who shrugged and then hefted his satchel onto the table. "Hope you brought your reading glasses, some of the text is kinda faded." He slid the large leather volume free and handed it to Brigid. "As you can see, one of the pages is marked. I'm guessing that's the page that pertains to our search. But like I said, this thing showed up out of nowhere. For all I know it's restaurant reviews for the best first century pizza joints."

Brigid carefully opened the tome to the first page. Dana noticed that Duck was watching the woman quite closely. She wasn't sure if it was simple attraction or something more, but his expression was one of deep concentration. She couldn't blame him, she supposed, Brigid was quite pretty with her soft oval face, smooth skin, and large brown eyes. Surely, she would catch the eye of many young men.

Dana noticed Brigid's expression change as she scrutinized the book. At first, mild curiosity, but then something more, something nearing urgency. No. Not urgency, more of giddiness. Her mouth curled into a barely suppressed grin, her eyes nearly lit the room with excitement, she twirled her hair, she swayed left and then right to her music, all the while entirely engrossed with her task. Dana and Hunt allowed her several minutes of silence, but eventually it seemed Hunt was simply too curious to remain quiet. "So, I'm guessing that's not an ancient edition of 'Fifty Shades of Grey.'"

Brigid seemed almost startled at the words, she'd been so engrossed. "Oh, God, no." She nearly snorted a laugh. "No, this is . . . So cool. I mean, I'm sorry. That was unprofessional." She paused, cleared her throat, and said, "I believe this to be the Achaemenid Codex. My God, you have no idea what you have here." Suddenly she was a schoolgirl who'd just been asked to the prom by the school's star athlete.

"Sorry," said Hunt. "Not up to speed on the ancient bestseller list."

"Right. Of course. I'm sorry. The Achaemenid Codex is a compilation of lessons and prophecies dating from about 500 B.C.E. and attributed to Zarathustra, a Persian sage who still has followers into the present day. Until now, the oldest known surviving text of Zarathustra was only 800 years old, so it's assumed that most of his teachings were passed on through oral tradition, which is where that text apparently originated. But there have been rumors that many of his more secretive teachings and writings were assembled into a lost document, the Achaemenid Codex, which was reportedly assembled somewhere around 450 AD. I believe this to be that manuscript."

Dana simply stared at the book. She'd known it was ancient. The leather was old and worn, unevenly colored. The pages stiff and yellowed, virtually no flexibility whatsoever. But she had no idea that the tome might date back to within a few hundred years of Christ.

"Okay. So, what are we looking at here?" This from Hunt.

"That is yet to be seen. I've only just glanced at the text. But, Zarathustra was one of the first to promote a sort of monotheism, the god Ahura Mazda, which means Wise god. His culture was not ready to denounce all other deities, so Zarathustra promoted Ahura Mazda as the greatest god among lesser immortals. His teachings are thought to have had a major impact on the emerging religion of Judaism. And, if you were to read his writings, you'd see several similarities to Judaism. This codex supposedly spoke of events that had yet to happen during his life, in particular 'the last turn of creation' in which the physical world is destroyed and then renewed. It's rumored there were many secret teachings, some of which were prophetic."

Dana nodded, asking, "If the author was Persian, why was this written in Aramaic?"

"Any writings of Zarathustra were likely originally written in cunei-form. This would be a translation, but it is likely the only volume where these writings and thoughts were collected. It's quite significant."

Hunt asked, "Same line of thinking, if this prophet guy was Persian, what would he have to do with Aaron's rod?"

"The rod was thought to have been taken when the southern kingdom of Judah was conquered by the Babylonians. Babylonia was part of the Persian Empire. Zarathustra may well have been aware of its existence."

Hunt nodded. "So, what about that marked page? What do we have there?"

Brigid carefully turned the stiff and yellowed pages. The Hunting-tons allowed her several minutes to study the text. They knew that translation was rarely a quick process. She scribbled notes on a spiral pad, passed her fingers over the passage, frequently moving back over what she'd just read. Her eyes were narrow, the tip of her tongue slipped out of the corner of her slightly curled lips as she bobbed to her music. Finally, Brigid said, "This page deals with the insect and the rod."

Dana and Hunt glanced at one another in unspoken communication. This was becoming a theme.

Brigid smiled, winked, and added, "And yes, I am aware that you possess the insect."

Well, that was a bloody interesting bit of intel. Dana wondered just how she'd come about that knowledge but didn't want to challenge her until the woman had delved into the book. The last thing she wanted was for Brigid to put her tail between her legs and scurry off like a frightened animal. "And what, may I ask, does it say about the insect and the rod?" asked Dana.

"Well not to be the harbinger of doom, because, well, who wants that? But the key passage explains that the two will be brought together to bring about the 'last turn of creation', or what you would likely call Armageddon."

"Well, that's bleeding wonderful," sniped Dana.

"It also offers a warning to beware the flame, which will consume and deceive. The flames offer nothing but death. The flame is the Atesi."

"Atesi," said Hunt. "We've heard that name before."

Brigid seemed taken aback by this, glancing from Hunt to Dana. "How do you know of this? What do you know?"

"Next to nada," said Hunt. "The name was spoken in fear by a dying man. We did a little research, learned that the Atesi is some kind of Turkish deity or something."

Dana leaned forward. "What do you know of the Atesi?"

Taking a deep breath, Brigid carefully closed the ancient volume and said, "The Atesi is more commonly known as Od Iyesi. He is the Turkish and Mongolian god of fire. Some know him as the Od Khan, king of fire or blazing spirit. Od Khan is a fire spirit in the shamanistic legends of Mongolia. These all refer to the same deity, though the name Atesi is the least known and is a corruption of Ates Iyesi. Some manuscripts describe him as the color of blood. Some say he rides a goat. His mate is said to be Yalun Eke the fire mother. He's in no way connected to the Muslim faith practiced in Turkey today for he predates Islam."

"Alright," said Hunt. "That's all interesting, but what does this Ates Iyesi have to do with my amulet and Aaron's rod?"

Brigid shook her head. "The Ates Iyesi of mythology has no connection to the rod of Aaron or to end times prophesy."

"That's right peculiar," said Dana. "Considering all that's happened so far. It seems someone calling himself the Atesi killed at least one man, possibly more, and my instinct is that it had quite a bit to do with Aaron's rod."

Hunt said, "A woman who is also pursuing the rod told us that she believed the original thief of the rod might actually be the Atesi."

"No," said Brigid. "Ates Iyesi is a spirit being. He cannot be the one you pursue."

Hunt said, "Yeah. I get that. Maybe this guy believes himself to be this deity. Maybe he simply assumed the title for some sort of dramatic effect. I'm not ready to say he's actually some mythical god. He's probably just some thief with an over inflated ego looking to get rich off a sacred relic. But I'll tell you what. The whole flame thing, the Atesi being some sort of fire spirit, that kind of fits with what we saw. Madu was burning up when he died and he was screaming the Atesi's name through it all. And it sounds like the Atesi's been responsible for at least two other bizarre deaths that we know of."

"What else does it say?" asked Dana. "About this Atesi and the insect and rod?"

Brigid glanced at the leather-bound codex and then to Dana. "This will take time. I can begin with this section, moving to the pages just before and after the marked page. It would make sense that if there's more on this topic it would be in proximity." She paused, tapped a rhythm with her fingernails, and then said, "Listen. This is a very strange time. I don't really think it's my place to tell you all I know and so I'd like for you to meet with the man I spoke of earlier. My mentor Dr. Ghilardi."

"And how is this Ghilardi supposed to help us?" asked Hunt.

Noting Hunt's dubious expression, Brigid rolled her eyes and chuckled. "Oh, he's no danger to you, I can assure you of that. He has great knowledge of Aaron's rod and of the coming apocalypse. But unlike so many others, he has no desire to bring the end about. His goal is to protect the truth." She shrugged and grinned. "It's kind of cool when you think about it."

"That's all great," said Hunt. "But I don't see how that helps us find the rod."

Brigid smiled. "Trust me. I can't promise that he'll point you directly to your goal. I mean, how could anyone do that, right? But I have faith that his insights will benefit you."

Dana glanced toward Hunt. "Bloody hell, why not? We've got nothing to lose."

"I'll tell you why not," said Duck. This was the first time he'd spoken since sitting down.

"Oh?" said Dana. This was curious.

"I've seen her before. I can't remember the context, but I'm sure it was at the monastery."

"In Turkey?" clarified Dana.

"Yes. Absolutely. I'm sure of it." Duck was studying her. Dana could tell he was trying to remember just when he'd seen her.

Dana saw Brigid tense at this. The young woman clenched her fists, her grin reverted to a scowl, she avoided eye contact.

Hunt grinned and said, "Well, now I'm curious. Care to comment?"

Brigid adjusted in her seat, suddenly uncomfortable. "I assume he's speaking of the monastery run by the Keepers. I've done research there in the past."

"In Turkey? You're dig is here in Egypt," said Hunt.

"And your home is in the United States and yet you've obviously traveled here and I'm assuming to the house of the Keepers as well. I'm an archeologist. When word reached me that this little monastery might hold an important Biblical relic, I decided to investigate. It was nothing more sinister than professional curiosity."

"Interesting," said Dana. "And when was this?"

Brigid hesitated. It seemed she was contemplating her answer. "It's been several months. Maybe seven or eight months ago."

If this was true, it would have put her there approximately two to three months before the disappearance of the rod. "And did they permit you to see Aaron's rod?" asked Dana.

Brigid offered a scoff. "They wouldn't even acknowledge that it existed."

"So, you wasted a trip to Turkey?" asked Hunt.

"Essentially, yes. The monks were pleasant enough. They made me feel welcome, offered to let me use their library for research, but no, I didn't achieve my goal."

Dana and Hunt made quick eye contact and Dana said, "Then I suppose we should be about seeing your Dr. Ghilardi, shouldn't we?"

Duck was about to protest but Hunt silenced him. Hunt was obviously on the same page as Dana. She didn't believe Brigid was telling the whole story, but that was all the more reason to accompany her. Perhaps they were closer to the rod than they'd believed.

Chapter Fifteen

Somewhere outside of Luxor, Egypt

Brigid Daniels insisted on blindfolding the trio as they neared Professor Ghilardi's secluded home. After reaching Luxor, they'd driven through tightly packed residential areas with narrow streets and high-rise apartment buildings, but Hunt had the feeling Brigid was simply weaving about the city attempting to confuse her passengers as to her true destination. Eventually, Hunt could tell the difference in traffic patterns. He no longer heard numerous vehicles about them, the car was turning less frequently, most likely traveling on a single road for a prolonged period. Soon the street became bumpy, with dips and potholes. When finally they arrived at their destination and were permitted to remove their blindfolds, Hunt found that they were situated before a small modest home surrounded by trees and on an unlit road. Whoever this Ghilardi was, he liked his privacy.

"Guy doesn't get out much, does he?" said Hunt as he stood beside their rented jeep stretching the kinks from his body. The ride had not been a comfortable one.

Brigid simply giggled and said, "Only as much as is needed." Hunt was still trying to get a bead on the young archeologist. She had that free-spirited counter-cultural thing going on, but she was obviously guarded where this Ghilardi was concerned. He had a sense she was normally an open and honest person, but that she was potentially involved in something that required her discretion.

"Wait here," said Brigid as she moved toward the small home. "I'll let him know we've arrived."

"I don't trust her," said Duck as Brigid disappeared through the front doorway. "She is very pretty but I don't trust her."

"Nah," said Hunt. "I think the problem is she's been instructed to be cautious. Think about when she blindfolded us. She kept apologizing, and she was fumbling all over the place. She didn't like what she was doing. I won't go so far as to say this isn't a trap, but if it is, I doubt she's at the heart of it. Just keep on your toes and don't overreact. We wouldn't be here if this Ghilardi guy didn't want a sit down."

"She is very pretty," added Duck, repeating what seemed to have become his mantra. "But I still don't trust her. Would it be wrong to show interest in a woman you don't trust?"

"Let's save that for another time, Romeo," said Hunt.

"This Ghilardi is using some sort of scrambler," said Dana as she gazed at her phone. "I can't get a signal and my GPS is entirely offline."

"Makes sense," said Hunt. "Wouldn't do any good to blindfold us and cart us out to nowhere if all we needed to do is access an app to learn our location." Hunt paused, gazing at the doorway. "Brigid's waving us in."

"Yes. And she doesn't look happy about it."

"Yeah. Let the fun begin."

As they approached, Brigid looked at the trio and said, "I'm very sorry. I promise, I didn't know."

They learned what she meant as they entered the small living area.

There was a gun pointed at them.

Dana blurted, "Oh bloody hell."

The man was tallish, perhaps six foot one, black, head shaved bald, trim. There was a small blue tattoo beneath his left eye. Some sort of symbol. It appeared to be a rolled scroll bearing three crosses. The man angled his head toward Brigid. "Check them for weapons, dear. And collect any you find."

Brigid shook her head. "They're cool, Hugo. You don't need to do this." She seemed entirely embarrassed by the situation, shifting from one foot to the other and fiddling with her earbud wires.

Ghilardi narrowed his gaze. "You may very well be correct, but in this present climate, we cannot be too careful. Now please, relieve them of their weapons."

Brigid nodded and apologized repeatedly as she frisked each of them, finding one gun each on Hunt and Dana and a knife at Hunt's ankle.

"Is that it?" asked the man when Brigid straightened. She nodded and he instructed her to put the weapons in a wall safe which had already been open when they'd arrived.

Once the weapons were secured, the man lowered his pistol. The firm no-nonsense face melted into a warm—even charming—smile. The transformation was nearly disarming. "I apologize for the inhospitality, but these are peculiar times. Your weapons will be returned when you depart. Please, sit. May I offer anyone a beverage?"

All declined, the man nodded and, as he almost casually placed the pistol on a small end table, said, "My name is Hugo Ghilardi. I'm very pleased that you've seen fit to visit my home. Again, I apologize for the precautions. But, peculiar times, eh?"

Hunt and Dana seated themselves on a loveseat and Duck on a wooden chair. Brigid remained standing, earbuds dangling, jangly guitar riffs, soft but noticeable, emerging from the white plastic. Ghilardi sat beside the end table containing the pistol. The man's accent was French, his tone cordial. Hunt was rather surprised at his age, which he took to be mid-forties. When Brigid had referred to him as her mentor, he'd immediately pictured a much older man. Hunt should have known better than to make assumptions based on incomplete knowledge. He wondered at their relationship, merely mentor and student, or something more?

The room was small but brimming with the stuff of archeology and religion. Ancient terracotta vases, oil lamps, and idols lined the shelves. Crosses adorned the walls. Over-stuffed bookcases bent at the weight of the numerous volumes piled upon the shelves. Rarely an inch throughout the room was left unencumbered by some object or another. And there was a peculiar odor. The smell of old books to be sure, but something else as well. Incense, perhaps.

Ghilardi smiled. "Marc and Dana Huntington. I had never known of you until this week and now it seems your names come up daily." He turned his gaze toward Duck. "I'm sorry, young man. You, I do not know."

"Durukan," said Duck.

"Durukan," smiled Ghilardi. "Welcome."

"I'll bite," said Hunt. "Our names come up daily? Sounds a little creepy to me. Want to explain?"

Ghilardi chuckled. "Brigid and I are part of a small group of academics determined to keep sacred artifacts out of the hands of fanatics. While we are scientists, we are not so narrow minded as to believe that there are no extraordinary aspects to the universe." He offered a shrug. "You pursue the rod and therefore have come to my attention." He leaned forward, elbows on knees. "We currently seek to prevent the revered rod of Aaron from misuse. As I've become a hindrance to some, attempts have been made on my life. And now you are vulnerable as well, for you would return the sacred scepter to the Keepers."

"Sounds like you're just one more group clamoring for the rod," said Hunt.

Ghilardi shrugged. "Our purposes are more academic in nature. We have no desire to initiate miraculous events. But we've found ourselves in the unenviable position of attempting to prevent certain parties from short circuiting preordained events to their own ends."

"All well and good, Hugo, but what I'm really wondering is if you know where Aaron's rod is."

A chuckle and a smile. The man's reaction revealed nothing. "I would venture to say that only the person in possession of the rod has that information."

Dana said, "You've mentioned that there are several parties seeking the rod. Can you tell us anything about them and perhaps venture a guess as to which might have the rod?" Good girl. She was hitting the same question from a different angle.

Ghilardi's expression became stern. "You must stay away from groups such as People of the Crimson Moon. They can be dangerous, for only one thing matters to them and that is the end of existence as we know it. And please, do not assume that this is a fanciful goal. The fate of the world is truly held in balance should the wrong people control this relic."

Interesting. He went straight to People of the Crimson Moon. "Alright," said Hunt. "That's nice and scary, but the rod was just taken from Crimson Moon. We're looking for a lead on who has it now."

Ghilardi opened his mouth to speak but then paused, seemingly mid thought. His eyes narrowed. He gazed at Hunt, rose from his seat, crossing to him and staring at his forehead. "Fascinating. May I touch it?"

Hunt knew exactly what the man had noticed, the faint image of the scorpion god Anascoreth on his forehead, the remnant of a demonic possession some months before. He wasn't too crazy about someone touching him, but he nodded his head in agreement.

Ghilardi's fingers slid over the shadowy skin like feathers on a breeze. "How long," he asked. "Since the possession, I mean?"

"Less than a year."

"Fascinating. And the spirit was driven out by what means?"

Here, Hunt hesitated. He wasn't sure if this man knew about the amulet and what his response would be if he learned that it was in Hunt's possession even now.

Ghilardi smiled. "Ah. I see. You hesitate because you don't want me to know of the locust. Word has already come to me. It was the insect, is that true? It drove the spirit from your form."

Hunt nodded as his stomach tightened. Already, Hunt was eyeing the pistol situated on the tiny end table. Could he reach it in time if Ghilardi made a play for the amulet?

Apparently not noticing Hunt's sudden anxiety, Ghilardi returned to his seat. "I've seen this before. The faded remnants of past possessions. Very little is written about such things and only a very powerful spirit could leave such a mark. I assume you carry the locust with you. A spiritual bond would have been formed as the insect entered your consciousness to drive the offending spirit away. I can't imagine you'd willingly part with it."

Hunt offered a grunt. That simple statement clarified so much of what he'd experienced these past months. "I never had it explained to me before, but yeah. If anyone tries to take it, I get this insane urge to protect it. Almost like it's my child. I've never understood that until now."

Ghilardi nodded. "I had hoped to convince you to leave it with me for safe keeping—in fact, that is why I encouraged Brigid to bring you here—but seeing this, I know this would not be an option for you. My only advice is that you guard it with your life. The insect is a very powerful entity."

"No," said Hunt. "It's not. If anything, it's dead. It's shown no sign of life since it drove the demon from me." Though, Hunt noticed, only now as he spoke these words, that the amulet had acquired a peculiar warmth since entering this home. Something he'd never noticed before. He wouldn't mention it to Ghilardi—maybe to no one—but it was noticeable. Was it possible that the thing was waking up? Could it have been Ghilardi's touch, or had the process already begun before that moment? Hunt couldn't remember.

Ghilardi said, "The locust, dead? I would surely doubt it. Do not be deceived, there is a significant difference between dead and dormant. The locust originated in the rod. It will seek to return home."

"This is all fascinating," said Dana. "But Brigid brought us here to discuss an ancient volume."

"You refer to the Achaemenid Codex. Brigid has told me that you possess it." Here, he paused, offering an intense expression. "You might be interested in knowing that one of my colleagues, a University professor named Dr. Wilhelmina Calhoun, was slain earlier this week. She contacted me only minutes before her death to tell me that an ancient tome—perhaps the Achaemenid Codex—had just come into her possession. No such volume was found after her death."

"Bloody hell," said Dana.

"Any suspects in the killing?" asked Hunt.

"The obvious suspects would be those that now possess the codex."

Hunt chuckled. "Yeah. Of course, they would. But you let us in here. Before that, you suggested Brigid contact and then meet with us. I'm guessing you already vetted us and determined murder isn't our M.O."

Ghilardi's gaze bore into Hunt. "Yes. I did my research. And no. I do not believe you to have been involved. But, for the record, they're not calling it a killing. Dr. Calhoun died of an unnaturally high fever." He paused, sighed, and said, "I assume by this time you've heard rumors of the Atesi."

"The name's come up," said Hunt. "Brigid gave us a brief lowdown. A Turkish fire god. Or, at least, someone pretending to be him."

Nodding, Ghilardi said, "As miraculous as it sounds, it appears the authentic Atesi is actively involved in these events. Likely, he caused Calhoun's death."

"And then left the codex for us?" asked Dana. "What sense does that make?"

Ghilardi shrugged. "Who could possibly understand the motives of an ancient spirit being?" He paused, seemed to contemplate, and then said, "But that is not the matter at hand. You wish to know about the Achaemenid Codex. I must caution you; its role is likely more ominous than you believe."

Hunt narrowed his gaze. "Cut with the dramatics, Hugo. Get to the point and tell me how any of this helps us."

Ghilardi chuckled. "Help you? I was hoping that by now you would realize that locating the rod might be the most disastrous thing you could possibly do."

"And why's that?"

"You hold both the codex and the insect. Certain passages within the codex may well contain verbiage meant to usher in the last days."

"Wait, wait, wait. The codex is part of this too? As in, the rod, the bug, and the book together are needed to initiate Armageddon?"

"Quite possibly." He paused, adjusted in his seat, folded his hands together. "Look, you won't find this in the Christian Bible, nor the Quran, the Bhagavad Gita, or any other mainstream religious writing. But there are numerous lesser-known ancient texts, many dealing with the latter days. And yes, there is cause to believe that the Achaemenid Codex holds the key to unlocking the power of the rod and the insect." Ghilardi clasped his hands together and leaned forward, elbows on knees. "As you hold two of the three inciting elements of Armageddon and seek the third. I propose that you allow me to guard the codex. It would be quite disastrous should all three requisites be brought together by the wrong parties."

Dana said, "I'm sorry, no. I understand your concern, but this has become a bit of a jigsaw puzzle and we're not exactly sure where your piece fits. We'll keep the codex and the amulet even if it means muddling along on our own."

"No," said Brigid, perhaps more forcefully than she intended, for she followed it with a giggle and a roll of the eyes. "I mean, yes, of course you're free to do as you please, but allow me to go with you."

Ghilardi was now the one to protest. "Brigid, you don't know these people and believe me, as long as they hold those two relics, they are targets."

Hunt said, "I have to say, I'm with Hugo on this one. He's worried that you don't know us, but we don't know you either. I'm not sure I feel comfortable with you tagging along."

Brigid offered a careless shrug. "Before meeting with Hugo, you were prepared to leave the codex with me for translation."

"That was before we knew it was part of some crazy Armageddon box set."

Brigid twirled her earbud wire. "Yeah, maybe. But I bet it wouldn't hurt to have an expert along. Someone who understands the historical and religious significance of each element and the potential motivations of those who seek them."

Dana said, "As much as I dislike your proposal, I see some logic in what you say."

Ghilardi said, "Brigid, I must insist you reconsider."

Smiling, she strolled over to her mentor, bent, kissed him on the forehead, and said, "You always seek to protect me, Hugo. And I appreciate that. But this is significant. One of us should be involved.

And we both know it won't be you." With that, she turned toward the Huntingtons and said, "You guys ready to get down and dirty on some ancient prophesies?"

Chapter Sixteen

Luxor Egypt

It wasn't that Hunt felt Ghilardi was working against them. He didn't get any sense of malice from the man. In fact, the professor had become rather helpful once it was determined that Brigid would accompany them. But he did have the feeling that Ghilardi was withholding something. It was just something in his tone, in subtle hesitations or unconscious eye movements. The question became, was he holding back something of substance, or was it simply something he didn't wish to share with strangers? Hunt was hoping that by keeping Brigid close they might learn more about Ghilardi and any potential problems.

Besides, Ghilardi seemed quite certain much of what had happened was the work of the Atesi.

This brought a whole new dynamic to their search and the sudden arrival of the book. If this Atesi character was truly the murderer and had stolen the codex, the question of how the volume had come to be in Hunt's hotel room became more relevant. Had the Atesi put it there, and if so, why? What could he possibly gain by placing this in their hands? And if not the Atesi, then who? Had someone stolen the tome from the Atesi, or were they mistaken in believing the spirit being was involved at all?

Professor Calhoun's unusual death seemed a near match to Madu's, the Irishman at the café, and even Father Abidin's. And it fit what Ghilardi believed to be the Atesi's abilities. As such, both Hunt and Dana felt it was important to talk to the university personnel that had found the body, maybe even see if there was any video footage of who had entered the office and exited with the ancient volume. But they determined they needed to question someone from People of the Crimson Moon as well. Yes, the sect had lost the rod, but it was possible that they knew who had taken it. Ghilardi had learned that Crimson Moon members sometimes used the Luxor Market as a safe public meeting place. Hundreds of people, plenty of commotion, it was a place they could meet with contacts in plain sight and disappear into the crowd at the first sign of trouble.

They decided that Hunt would take Brigid and visit the market, flash Qudsi's picture around, see if they could learn anything. Dana and Duck would go to the university and question campus security about Calhoun's death and try to gain access to security footage.

The Luxor Market was busy with merchants and customers moving about the narrow unpaved walkways. There was a general buzz of energy. The entire market was open air, most shops simply occupying an open space with three walls and no roof. Donkey drawn carts moved along the way. Bicyclists weaved between meandering pedestrians. Attire was mostly traditional Middle Eastern, but there was a smattering of western dress as well. As such, Hunt in no way felt out of place. It seemed nearly anything could be found from groceries, to clothing, to electronics. Every merchant had a specialty, whether it be spices, or shoes, or fresh fish. In many ways it was not unlike an American flea market—only much richer and more colorful in atmosphere. Though chaotic, the climate was friendly and Hunt had no difficulty getting people to talk with him.

They were about a half hour into their investigation, having just shown Qudsi's picture to two merchants passing the time with a game of dominos, when Brigid pulled her earbuds free and asked, "So, you and Mrs. Huntington. You're not sharing a hotel room."

Wow. Between Brigid and Duck, nothing was off limits. Offering what he hoped was a nonchalant grin, Hunt said, "Um, no. We're not."

Cocking her head and twirling her earbud wire, Brigid said, "I don't mean to be nosey, but it doesn't make sense. I mean, not that it's any of my business, but . . ." She shrugged and grinned.

Hunt sighed. He really didn't want to go into this. "It's a difficult time."

Brigid offered a nervous giggle. She was embarrassed by her social misstep. "Listen, I'll shut up. I do that. I mean, stick my nose where it doesn't belong. All I was trying to say is that you don't act like a couple who should be separated. You obviously have, like, this connection." She walked a few more steps and then added, "I'll shut up now."

Hunt said nothing. There really wasn't anything he wanted to say. There was a lot of history and both he and Dana had been emotionally damaged by factors beyond their control. But there was an additional reason for his silence.

He'd seen something.

Actually, he'd seen someone.

Hunt had first noticed him as they'd strolled from the tourist section of the market into the area frequented primarily by locals. The man had been perhaps fifty feet behind them as they'd made their way amidst the teeming walkway. Hunt wasn't suspicious then, but he'd been trained to remain alert, to always assess his environment. When he saw the man three more times in the next ten minutes, always about fifty feet back, always glancing in Hunt's direction while pretending to study some product or another, it became clear he had a tail.

Hunt turned to Brigid and said, "We may have a problem. I want you to stay in the crowd. Talk to merchants. Buy something if you need to, just stay engaged with people. Try to blend. I'll be back."

Hunt was already moving away before Brigid could protest. He kept a casual pace, not wanting his tail to realize that he'd been seen. He wove between carts and pedestrians and slipped into a narrow alcove with rugs hanging throughout the space. Positioning himself amidst the forest of hanging rugs, he waited for his tail to pass by. The man was obviously searching for him, his head turning right and then left as he moved quickly past.

Stepping back into the main thoroughfare, Hunt was about to approach the man when someone grabbed him from behind. He jabbed backward with an elbow, but only skirted his attacker, who hissed, "Calm down, Huntington. These people are dangerous. I'm trying to save your life."

The voice was female, the accent Irish. "O'Broin?"

"Aye. Now stop your struggling before he sees us."

But it was too late. The man had turned back, likely assuming he'd missed Hunt in one of the many shops and was preparing to retrace his steps.

The man's eyes went wide, his jaw tightened. And then there was a gun in his hand.

O'Broin was the quicker shot. Hunt hadn't even realized she was armed, but the shot echoed in his right ear as the offending man crumpled to the ground no more than thirty feet in front of him. Cursing, Hunt broke away from O'Broin and raced to the man who lay dying in the dirt. There were shouts and screams from all about, people fleeing for fear of being shot, but this was all in Hunt's peripheral. He wanted to know if this man was Crimson Moon, why he'd been following him, and if he'd pulled the gun to fire at Hunt or at O'Broin.

The man was gasping for air as Hunt dropped to his knees beside him. The wound was to the chest. There was a lot of blood, the man likely didn't have long to live. Hunt grabbed a silk scarf from a nearby table, bunched it up, and applied pressure to stay the bleeding. "Hold on, buddy. We'll try to get you through this." Hunt leaned in, applying his entire weight, but there was too much blood, he needed proper medical equipment and personnel if this man was going to live. "Someone call an ambulance! Fast. This man's dying!"

The man's right arm came up clasping Hunt by the bicep. "Huntington," he gasped. "You're working for the fire . . ." he trailed off, his eyes fluttering.

"What are you saying?" And then "Will someone please call an ambulance!"

Another gasp. "The fire demon . . ." He drifted away, not finishing the thought. "You work for a devil."

"The Atesi? No. I was hired by the Keepers."

His eyes narrowed, perhaps assessing Hunt's comment for truth. "Keepers deceived by Atesi. Crimson Moon can help . . . You must relinquish the insect. Too dangerous to . . ." He gasped, his chest heaving.

"Come on, buddy. Stay with me."

The man's eyes fluttered again and then focused on Hunt. "You are wrong about us. You must help us to retrieve the sacred scepter from . . ."

"From who? Who has the scepter?"

The man coughed. Blood was dibbling from his lips. "Bring us the scepter before the fiery one can . . ." The man's eyes fluttered again. This time they remained closed.

It was then that he heard Brigid scream. Hunt whirled, catching a glimpse of Brigid being forcefully pulled around a corner.

Hunt had to aid Brigid, but he couldn't leave a man to die. Continuing to apply pressure, he glanced around, looking through the crowd, up and down the narrow way. Yes. Good. Two police officers were making their way through the crowd from the north. They'd have emergency medical training.

Hunt looked frantically around, selecting a young man of maybe twenty from the circle of onlookers: short, with glasses, baseball cap and iPhone. "You! Yeah, you. Quickly. Come here. Press on his chest. As hard as you can. Keep the pressure until those cops come." Hunt nearly pulled the kid to beside the dying man and, grabbing his wrist, pushed his hand down on the blood-soaked fabric. Hunt felt bad leaving the man like this, but Brigid was in trouble.

Rising, Hunt raced south toward the spot where Brigid had disappeared, leaping over obstacles and fighting through the crowd. He had to be a sight. Both his hands and shirt sleeves were bloodied.

He rounded a corner, collided with a cluster of frightened marketgoers, bounded off them and raced forward. At some point he realized O'Broin was close behind him. Where had she been since shooting the man? Hunt still didn't know what to think of the Sons of Light woman, but hoped she'd stay out of the way. He wasn't convinced that she was innocent in all of this and had no idea why she was even there. Had she been following Hunt, or following his tail?

Rounding another corner, Hunt collided with a table full of woven baskets containing colored beads. The baskets and beads spilled across the way and Hunt raced on leaving the startled shop owner shouting curses at his back.

A slight jog left around a cluster of people and then a right turn and Hunt found Brigid. She was just ahead, maybe a hundred feet forward of him, and was facing a man whose face he had memorized. Bruno Qudsi held her at both biceps. The man was shouting something at her. Hunt hollered her name. Both Brigid and her assailant turned. Qudsi raised a weapon and fired.

Hunt dove to the left, rolled, and then scampered to a crouch. But even as he did so he realized that he had not been the target. O'Broin, gun in hand, had collapsed to the ground.

Glancing to where Qudsi and Brigid had stood, he saw no trace of Qudsi. Brigid stood with tears on her cheeks, but she appeared unharmed. Damn it! Again! O'Broin might be dying. He couldn't ignore her. Twice in a handful of minutes, he'd been delayed in pursuing a Crimson Moon man because of an injured person.

Moving quickly to O'Broin and dropping to his knees, Hunt snatched her gun, flicked the safety, and jammed it into his pants at the tailbone. He saw that the gunshot wound was above and to the right of the heart. It probably hadn't hit a major organ. Unless a main artery had been damaged, she'd likely live. "Listen to me," said O'Broin. Her voice was just above a whisper. "Oh, mate, trouble follows you, don't it?" She coughed, nodded, and resumed. "You're a pawn, you do realize that. I once thought maybe you were the Atesi's man, but no. Just an idiot in harm's way." She paused, taking several deep breaths. "But the insect ties you to all of this, aye? The locust will not allow you to walk away. Would that it was so simple as taking the amulet from you, but nay. You alone are the bearer. Such a shame the Atesi was here, and I failed. I'll confront him after I tend to this scratch." She then gave Hunt a weak shove. "Now, go. Go! You don't want to be here when the authorities arrive. Just go." O'Broin managed to lean on one elbow. "I'm alright, now leave."

Hunt rose, seeing that Brigid was now by his side. He shouted, "Anyone call an ambulance yet? Anyone?" And then he grabbed a colorful shawl from a table to cover his blood-stained hands and, motioning for Brigid to follow, moved into the still-stunned crowd. When Hunt turned back to glance at the scene, O'Broin was gone.

Chapter Seventeen

Thorpe didn't understand how they did it, but Collins' contacts at the Vatican repeatedly had new information that even Thorpe here at ground zero couldn't manage to acquire. Case in point, Collins had just learned that a Crimson Moon member had been shot at a marketplace and that Huntington had been involved. Apparently, not even law enforcement had such detailed information on the incident.

"Oh, Johnny, it's not as difficult as you'd think," said Collins. "The Catholic church has priests, monks, nuns, in every nook and cranny throughout the world. If they want information, all they need to do is to instruct these people to keep their ears open. Priests and nuns not only work in churches and convents but hospitals and other social service institutions throughout the community. People trust them and share freely. There's a lot of information floating around out there to be had. It's like the best spy network on the planet without ever employing a single spy."

"Brilliant," said Thorpe. "And I mean that quite literally. Now, re-mind me again of how you know this man we're meeting is the imam Maalouf implicated?"

"Connections, Johnny. It's all about connections."

Thorpe and Collins were seated in the insignificant office at the rear of a mosque. Thorpe was about to request a less ambiguous response when the imam entered. Thorpe sat on a tiny woven chair that was scarcely large enough to accommodate his bum and Collins had availed herself of the imam's desk chair. They had not been invited, but had broken in. Thorpe had argued that they were unlikely to gain the man's trust or cooperation with such an entrance, but Collins was certain the Muslim cleric would not agree to meet with them voluntarily. She never offered much of an explanation, but had simply said, "Trust me." Which Thorpe did not.

"Asalaamu alaikum," said Collins, offering a traditional Islamic greeting meaning, "Peace be upon you."

The Imam's gentle features hardened as he saw the intruders. "Oh. The Vatican troublemaker. You come to pester me again?"

Ah! So there had been a previous encounter. This explained Collins' insistence on breaking and entering. The man would not have granted her an audience voluntarily. Thorpe knew the feeling well.

Collins offered her sweetest grin. "Pester? No. We're just here to have a nice little chitchat."

Looking to Thorpe, the man said, "And who is this?"

"Just a simple thief," said Collins. "But don't worry. I have him on a leash."

Shooing a fly, Thorpe said, "Yes, well, an oversimplification, that. Jonathan Thorpe. Pleased to meet you and I apologize for the intrusion. Miss Collins here seemed to think you'd be averse to meeting with us voluntarily."

The imam nodded but did not step away from the door. He was a rather small man dressed in loose fitting traditional Muslim attire. He had a long full beard, wire-rimmed glasses, and a white kufi prayer cap. Thorpe had been curious about what the man might be like as his office was cluttered with Star Wars paraphernalia. There was a stuffed Chewbacca and a Han Solo Bobble-head on his desk, a model of the Millennium Falcon hanging from the ceiling fan, and a Lego Death star on the floor in a corner beside a long-haired cat lounging against the wall. Not traditional imam fare to be sure, but obviously it spoke to the man's personality. Thorpe had never had much use for clerics, but apparently, they had interests beyond their religions. He supposed this shouldn't be a surprise. People were still people despite their occupations or beliefs.

"Miss Collins," said the imam. "I am never averse to meeting with members of another faith. I am open to any constructive discourse. But you have proven yourself to be problematic. And now, breaking into a mosque? I can't imagine your employers at the Vatican would approve." And then, with a grin, he added, "I hope you haven't turned to the dark side."

"Oh, you have no idea," offered Thorpe.

Collins said, "I mean no disrespect, Imam Mohammed. In fact, the opposite. You are known to have your finger on the pulse of all religious activity in the area. I'm just a weary traveler hoping to tap into your vast store of knowledge."

The imam chuckled. Glancing at Thorpe he said, "The woman hopes to butter me up."

Collins grinned. "Oh, come now, Imam. No false modesty. Y'all know it's true."

Curious, thought Thorpe. The man was obviously not happy to see Collins, but they seemed to have an established rapport. Likely not all their previous interactions had been hostile.

Imam Mohammed smiled. "Tina, you are a treasure and a curse. Mostly the latter. Tell me what it is you want so that we may be done with this and I can send you on your way."

Collins cocked her head in that saucy way of hers. "I have a feeling you could guess."

The imam shrugged. "Make it easy for me. It's been a long day."

Here, Thorpe spoke up. "I believe what dear Tina is attempting to avoid saying is that we're in pursuit of Aaron's rod and we have reason to believe you might aid us in the quest."

Collins shot Thorpe a glare and the imam nodded. "I assumed as much. But I only became aware of its existence a few months ago, after it had been stolen."

"Oh, I know you don't have it," said Collins. "But I'm sure you can understand why the Vatican's concerned that such a significant relic might fall into the wrong hands."

"Of course," said the imam. "But what is it that I can do?"

Collins crossed one leg over the other and then laced her fingers over a knee. "It seems like there's a bit of a free for all. Multiple groups racing after the scepter and I'd like to know what you know about them and if you've heard anything indicating who might have the old stick."

Imam Mohammed smiled. "Brash as ever, I see. The old stick! You are horrible. Tell me, of which groups do you refer?"

Thorpe said, "Yes, well, how about we begin with Sons of Light? A man connected with them just lost his life to one of their grenades. Nearly brought us along for the ride." Thorpe failed to add that he was still stiff and fairly well bruised and Collins now walked with a slight limp, though she tried diligently to hide it.

The imam nodded. "I know little of Sons of Light beyond the fact that they believe certain relics have mystical powers and that they hope to somehow facilitate the apocalypse. They've been active for several decades, maybe longer, and claim to be the Sons of Light mentioned in the Dead Sea Scrolls. They are similar to another sect known as People of the Crimson Moon, though their beliefs and methods differ. My understanding is that both groups may be prone to violence."

"Lovely," said Thorpe.

"Have you heard any rumors about the rod, who might have it?" asked Collins.

"I know the Atesi desires it and he is the one you should truly fear."

"Great," said Collins. "Would y'all care to tell me who this Atesi fella is? That's a new name for my address book."

"Really?" said the imam. "I am surprised the Vatican has not kept you better informed." Apparently tired of standing, the imam crossed the

184

room and seated himself on the edge of his desk. Legs crossed casually and now holding his plush Chewbacca toy he said, "The Atesi is believed to be an ancient deity, Mongolian or Turkish, in origin."

"Hold on," said Thorpe. "I thought Muslims were monotheistic. Are you claiming there are more than one god?"

"Of course not. But Islam does acknowledge the existence of evil spirits or Shayatin. I believe the Atesi would fall into this classification."

"Wait," said Collins. "So, you're telling us there's a demon chasing after this artifact?"

The imam bobbed his head from side to side indicating some level of uncertainty. "Word has come to me that the Atesi has taken hold of a human host in order to pursue the scepter." Here he held up his hand staving the next question. "I am not claiming to either believe or discount this. I am simply relaying what I have heard. It has also come to me that the Atesi was recently responsible for the death of a university professor and the theft of an ancient tome."

Thorpe swallowed as his stomach tightened. "Calhoun." The word was barely a whisper.

"Pardon?"

"Dr. Calhoun. I'd left the book with her. She was to translate it. Apparently, she died soon after I left."

"Then," said the imam. "I suggest you proceed with utmost caution." Holding up the Chewbacca, he smiled and added, "Maybe hire a Wookie for protection."

Thorpe wasn't in the mood for humor and he found the man's attempt ill-timed and in poor taste.

"Well, that's cute and all," said Collins. "But is there anything useful, anything that can point us in the right direction?"

"As you say, I have my finger on the pulse of religious activity." He set the Wookie aside and said, "I've heard one other tidbit. Take it for whatever value it may offer. But I have been told that there is a man of learning that knows far more than he lets on."

Collins frowned and asked, "Any chance you have anything better than, 'a man of learning?' Maybe a name, an address?"

And, surprisingly, the imam told them.

Chapter Eighteen

Dana and Duck had just returned from the university campus when Hunt and Brigid arrived at the hotel. Hunt's narrowed gaze and Brigid's frazzled expression told Dana that something of significance had occurred. They all met in Hunt's room and compared notes. Dana had gotten relatively little from campus security. The area near Dr. Calhoun's office did not have security cameras and no one was much in the mood to be helpful.

Hunt and Brigid detailed their experience at the outdoor market which led to some discussion.

"What was O'Broin doing there?" asked Dana.

"Best guess, shadowing either me or Crimson Moon," said Hunt. "Everything went down too quickly. I didn't have a chance to question her properly."

"She said the Atesi was there," said Brigid. "I think she meant Brother Bruno."

"Yeah," said Hunt, pulling his yo-yo from his pocket and sending it into a twirl. "The last time I encountered O'Broin, she thought Qudsi was the Atesi. But the first Crimson Moon guy accused me of working for the fiery one. He said the Keepers were deceived by the Atesi. I don't think the Atesi and Crimson Moon are in the same camp."

"Which means O'Broin is wrong. Qudsi is not the Atesi," said Dana.

"Right. Strange though. When she first confronted me at the market, she said she was trying to protect me. But my gut says the violence was initiated by O'Broin. We had a tail, but he was a passive observer until O'Broin popped up. She was behind me when she shot, so I couldn't tell who pulled a gun first. Brigid, you weren't near enough to see the initial gun fight, but you were front and center when Qudsi shot O'Broin. What's your take on how that went down?"

"Qudsi had grabbed me and was accusing me of helping to steal the rod. Then you yelled my name. We both turned and saw O'Broin behind you with a gun. Qudsi pulled his gun and shot."

"Why did he think you were involved with the theft?" asked Dana.

"I'd visited the monastery a couple of weeks before the rod went missing. Hugo had asked me to go there for research." She paused, giggled, and added, "And to learn if rumors of the rod were true. I found nothing out about the rod, but I did meet Qudsi. Talk about a walking turd. No personality there. He seemed offended that I was there."

Dana met Brigid's gaze. "At the marketplace, did Qudsi say anything significant to you?"

Brigid scrunched a wadded red bandana between her hands. "No. It all happened quickly. Everything was chaos. After Qudsi shot O'Broin, he disappeared into the crowd."

"We've got a real mess here," said Hunt. "Sons of Light are in the hunt and, obviously, Crimson Moon hasn't reacquired the rod."

Brigid said, "Then who has it?"

"Take your pick: Sons of Light, the Atesi, someone we've yet to identify."

Dana shook her head. "No. We're missing something. If Sons of Light was following you—or Crimson Moon—that indicates they're still searching. The only reason they'd want us is if they haven't found the rod."

"That's not true," said Brigid. "Hunt was right. He has the amulet. They obviously know about the three elements: rod, insect, and codex. She's keeping Hunt in her sights until she can acquire all three."

"I agree with Brigid," said Duck as he offered the pretty archeologist a smile.

Dana said, "And so the question becomes, does she know we have the codex?"

"She hasn't copped to it," said Hunt. "But if she doesn't know yet, I'm guessing she will soon. She must wonder why Brigid was brought in. She probably knows about Professor Calhoun's death and the theft of the book. She'll put it together."

Dana looked at the group and said, "Let's not get distracted. Our goal is to return the rod to the Keepers. If neither Sons of Light nor Crimson Moon have it, then where are we with this?"

"Crimson Moon thinks the Keepers were tricked by the Atesi," said Hunt. "And by extension, that we're the Atesi's pawns."

"But O'Broin thinks Qudsi's the Atesi."

"Maybe the Atesi does have the rod," offered Brigid.

"No," said Hunt. "Everything that's happened seems to indicate the Atesi is still seeking the rod."

Dana shook her head. "The problem with all of these theories is that each of these factions appear to be searching for the rod. And none of them seem any closer to it than we are. There's got to be something we're missing." Dana then held up a finger. "A moment, if you will. A bit of brain calisthenics playing about the noggin."

She turned, pacing the room. Something nettled at her, something that had been said. Something of import. Qudsi had grabbed Brigid because he believed her to have a connection to the thief. Was there any truth to it? Dana didn't know Brigid, not really. The woman had, at first, been overly cautious, even insisting they wear blindfolds when traveling to meet Hugo Ghilardi. But aside from that single instance she'd been warm and apparently helpful. But what did Dana really know of Brigid Daniels? She'd done a basic background inspection and everything checked out as her being exactly as she presented herself. But she was an archeologist. By nature, she'd be predisposed to preserve an ancient artifact and keep it away from those who might misuse it.

Which was exactly what Ghilardi's group did.

Again, back to Ghilardi. He had been the one to send Brigid to the Keepers' monastery to learn about the rod.

He'd had her bring them to his home—blindfolded—so he could see Hunt's amulet.

He knew the significance of the codex and urged Brigid to offer her services as a translator.

Everything concerning Brigid pivoted with Ghilardi. She trusted him implicitly. His approval led to Brigid's approval. Suppose Brigid was as innocent as she presented herself to be.

But Ghilardi.

Bloody hell. That was it. Dana was sure of it.

"Brigid," said Dana. "I need you to tell me about Hugo Ghilardi."

Brigid looked to be confused. "What is it you want to know?"

"He said he and other academics had formed a group to help prevent artifacts from falling into the wrong hands," said Dana.

"Yes."

"You are a part of this group."

Brigid rolled her eyes. "Yes. I mean, it's not as if there's member-ship requirements or dues. It's nothing official, just likeminded individ-uals. There's a huge black market for antiquities. We keep an eye out for Biblical artifacts. As you've learned, there are those who would use them to their own ends."

"I see. And how exactly do you and your mates prevent these thefts or black-market dealings?"

Brigid offered a curious pout and twirled her earbud wires. "We keep our ears open. If we learn about a missing artifact being sold, we track it down." She cocked her head and grinned. "What are you getting at?"

Dana ignored the question. "Do you or Ghilardi ever attempt to secure the artifact yourselves in order to protect it from others?"

"From time to time, but it's not . . ." Brigid paused, the grin broadened, she pointed at Dana. "You think Hugo has the rod."

"You're bloody well right I do. Care to challenge me on that bit?"

Brigid shook her head and laughed. "God, no. I mean, he never mentioned it, but . . ." She trailed off, obviously thinking. "It could be. He has been overly cautious, nearly paranoid lately. But . . ." Again, she shook her head and laughed, this time throwing her hands up in exasperation. "God, I don't know. I love Hugo—as a friend and mentor, I mean. But he's always had this intense secretive side. I guess I never quite know what he's into."

"It's him," said Hunt. "Dana's right. I didn't get it at the time, just a weird anomaly. But my amulet was warm while we were at Ghilardi's. Noticeably warmer than usual. I don't know why I didn't pick up on it at the time, but I think it was somehow responding to a proximity to the rod."

Brigid said, "If you're correct, this is actually pretty awesome. It means we know where the rod's being hidden. It's safe."

"No," said Hunt. "It's anything but safe."

"What do you mean?"

Dana said, "Qudsi suspects him and knows the two of you are connected. That's why he accused you of helping to steal the rod. He knew about Ghilardi."

Brigid bit her lower lip. "Damn. Isn't that just a suck-fest?" She glanced from Hunt to Dana and then nodded. "I'll call him and let him know the rod's no longer safe. He'll know what to do."

"No," said Hunt. "He'll just go into hiding and then we're no closer than when we started."

"That doesn't matter," said Brigid. "The real issue is the rod's preservation, not who happens to be hiding it."

Dana said, "I understand your perspective, but the Keepers have held the rod for centuries. It's our mission to return it to them." Brigid was ready to respond, but Dana held up her hand, stopping her. "That said, the rod has become a very sought-after item. Once it's recovered, I believe it would be advisable for you and Ghilardi to help the Keepers to determine a better way to keep it safe. Obviously, the monastery is no longer a viable hideout."

Hunt said, "And neither is Ghilardi's place. We need to get to him before Crimson Moon or any of the others find him."

Dana suggested they move on this immediately. She could see that Brigid still had misgivings. Her loyalty was clearly with Ghilardi. But she seemed, for the moment, to go along with them. Dana turned toward where Duck had been standing near the door, but the young man was gone.

They soon found that he was not in his room, did not answer his phone, and that their rented jeep was no longer in the parking lot.

Chapter Nineteen

Jonathan Thorpe was conflicted. He'd stumbled into one of those rare morally ambiguous areas. Where he was almost always certain of his path and assured that his intellect placed him above the average person and therefore not subject to their laws and ethical restraints, he found himself confounded by guilt. He had no love for Tina Collins, perhaps a mild affection, or better, a professional respect, but they were not partners. There was no obligation to her. And so, he'd felt no guilt when, after learning from Imam Mohammed that a university professor by the name of Hugo Ghilardi held the rod of Aaron and, after some digging, learned of a remote home purchased under an assumed name and located on the outskirts of Luxor, Thorpe slipped away from Collins telling her that he was making a private call. He'd quickly disabled her vehicle and taken his own rented car with the intent of acquiring the prize for himself.

No guilt. Not in that moment at least.

But now . . .

Collins had at various times been both companion and nemesis. Their relationship was complicated. And it had been her contacts that had led them to Imam Mohamed.

But why should Thorpe help Collins recover the prize only to hand it over to the Vatican? What possible motivation was there in that? People had died while pursuing this bloody rod, Thorpe was risking his quite remarkable self in this search, why on earth should he do that with no hope of reward? Collins was pragmatic to a fault. Certainly, she would understand this.

Eventually.

And hopefully before she chose to put a bullet through his skull. The woman was rarely subtle.

And then there was Dana. He'd felt conflicted about cutting her out. But she would only turn the rod over to the Keepers. No. He'd recover the rod alone and receive the promised remuneration alone, everyone else be damned.

Thorpe had to assume that if this Ghilardi had gone to the trouble of dropping from sight that he likely wasn't too keen on visitors, and so Thorpe felt it better to be obvious in his approach. Stealth would cause immediate mistrust.

Upon pulling close to the secluded residence, Thorpe had written on his iPad in the largest font possible, "Others know you have the rod. We must talk!" He'd then stepped from the car, held the iPad toward the home like a gleaming sign while simultaneously reaching into the car and honking the horn repeatedly. No stealth or subtlety here. The man would know Thorpe intended to be seen.

He honked the horn again. He'd seen no movement in the home. There was a single light shining through draperies in what Thorpe assumed to be the living room, but he'd seen no shadow of a man moving about.

He waited another minute and then tooted the horn for a third time, this time in three prolonged bursts. Still holding the iPad high, he cursed under his breath. Was the man even here? Perhaps he'd switched locations, or maybe he'd gone out for supplies—or even gone to a bloody cinema. What would happen if Ghilardi returned home to see Thorpe's car in the drive, would he just continue past never to return? Thorpe couldn't wait out here forever. Collins certainly wouldn't be far behind him. She was an industrious sort; she'd find transportation quickly enough.

Thorpe was just about to walk up to the door and knock when he felt the gun pressed against the back of his head. "Who are you and what do you want?" The voice was a breathy hiss, the accent French.

"Yes, well, hello. The name's Jonathan Thorpe. As I'm sure you know from my little iPad note, I'm here to speak with you concerning a certain rod."

The gun was pressed harder against Thorpe's head. "I know nothing of any rod."

"Yes. Of course, you would say that. But you see, The People of the Crimson Moon, the Vatican, and a nasty fellow known as the Atesi have all learned that you have the rod of Aaron. I'm quite certain you'd prefer to talk with me than with any of them."

"Who are you? I don't mean your name."

"I'm an independent attempting to reclaim the rod for a group calling themselves the Keepers. Now, will you please take that gun away from my head and invite me inside before someone much nastier than I comes by and starts blasting away at us both?"

There was a pause and then Ghilardi started patting Thorpe down, searching for weapons. Thorpe did occasionally carry a firearm, but knew Ghilardi would be suspicious and so, even though he was walking into a potentially volatile situation, had decided against it.

Finding no weapons, Ghilardi gave Thorpe a push between the shoulder blades. "Move forward—slowly. I still have the gun trained on you."

"Understood," said Thorpe as he tossed the iPad onto the front seat of the car and slammed the door.

They made their way slowly to the small home. Ghilardi handed Thorpe the key and instructed him to unlock the door. Once inside, he ordered Thorpe to sit in a wooden ladder-backed chair that was backed against the front wall of the small living space. Ghilardi remained standing, gun still aimed at Thorpe. "How did you find me?" asked Ghilardi.

"From a Muslim cleric who shares information with a Vatican contact of mine."

"And how did this cleric learn that I possess the rod?"

"That, I do not know. But my Vatican contact is likely close behind. I was hoping to talk with you first."

Ghilardi nodded. "And what is your interest in the rod?"

"Profit, pure and simple. The Keepers have offered a substantial sum for its return."

Ghilardi scoffed. "Then this means nothing to you."

Thorpe offered his best winning grin and shrugged. "Quite true. But consider this. You've now been found out by at least two parties. There are some very dangerous people interested in this relic. If you're concerned for the rod's safety—and, I might add, your own safety—then you cannot keep it any longer. I'm offering to return it to those who have guarded it for centuries. If your goal truly is to protect this artifact, I am likely your best option."

Ghilardi glared at Thorpe, obviously contemplating all that had been said.

"Listen," said Thorpe. "You may not care for my motivations, but I'm offering you the best result. You must see that."

Ghilardi lowered his weapon, shoving it into his pants at the small of his back. "You're right. I don't care for your motivations. Too many people seek to become rich off history's treasures. But I will consider what you've said."

"Best not consider too long. The clock is most definitely ticking."

"Ah, but it is not," came a voice from a hallway to Thorpe's right. "The time has most definitely arrived."

A young man, mid to late twenties, dark complexioned, rather wiry, appeared from the hallway. Thorpe knew the man.

Ghilardi turned toward the intruder, drawing his gun. "Durukan, is it not? You were with the Huntington couple."

This was interesting. Ghilardi had obviously already encountered the Huntingtons but they had not determined that he had the rod. Shoddy work, that.

The young man angled his head, eliciting a sharp cracking sound. His movements were awkward, nearly strained, as if he wasn't quite sure how to operate the limbs. When he spoke, his voice was rich and leathery with the texture of advanced age but with the vigor of a world class athlete. His eyes were wide and fluttering and of a peculiar yellowish tint. The man's entire demeanor was unnatural and quite disturbing. Not at all the young man that had driven them to the monastery.

"You may call me Durukan if you wish. But I am quite another entity entirely."

Ghilardi stared for perhaps a full thirty seconds before he gasped, "The Atesi."

The young man's left arm jerked up and then, as if released from a marionette's string, fell limply to his side. A greenish substance slipped from his lips. "Quite perceptive of you. I give you credit for not feigning disbelief. That becomes so terribly tiresome." Another jerk of the arm, this one from the right arm—the gun arm. Thorpe feared the man might inadvertently discharge the weapon.

But it was Ghilardi who fired. The two men were no more than ten feet distant from one another, but in some impossible way the bullet missed.

The young man Ghilardi had called Atesi chuckled. It was a hideous sound.

The professor fired again, missing a second time. How could that be? A child could have made those shots.

Or was he really missing? Could it be something else?

Ghilardi was the larger of the two, more athletic in bearing, but the Atesi was upon him in an instant, the gun now in his hand, and Ghilardi on the floor some five feet back. Thorpe wasn't quite sure what he'd just witnessed. It was almost as if time had skipped several seconds, the two men in their first positions and then instantly in the next. None of this seemed right, or even believable.

"Now," said the Atesi in his leathery voice of the ages. "You are a sly devil. Very deceptive. And clever. I'll grant you that. Why, I stood in this very room and entirely missed the fact that you had hidden the scepter . . . Right. Beneath. My. Feet." With this, he stomped three times on the floorboard to his right, easily breaking it to bits. Kneeling, he reached into the newly made gap and withdrew a long narrow staff wrapped in a coarse white fabric.

"Yes, yes. You are quite clever," said the Atesi. He twisted his head to an extreme angle and laughed heartily as if amused at his own statement.

Thorpe felt as if he must do something, to intercede in some way. He was currently ignored, but near both men. Why was it, though, that his limbs felt a great burning weight? As if the very effort of movement would be both impossible and excruciatingly painful. What exactly was happening here?

Rising to face his adversary, Ghilardi said, "You are a devil on a devil's mission. You cannot be allowed the scepter."

The Atesi chuckled deep and throaty. "A devil? Of course, you would think me a devil. Tell me, O' learned professor, O' great scholar, what do you truly know of Ates Iyesi, the spirit you so casually call the Atesi? You have read that the Turks and Mongols claim I bring fire from the air. Oh, I am certain you have read these myths, perhaps even believed them at some level. But you, O' learned one, you have dug deeper beyond the surface, beyond that which is known to the masses. You have bridged the gap—however imperfectly—and recognized that I play a role in the most dreaded and anticipated event in human history. But, despite your years of research, your long months digging through the dirt, pulling from the earth this trinket and that, you still rely on the knowledge of men, and that, professor, will never suffice." The Atesi held up his hands as if to prevent Ghilardi from speaking. "Oh, I know, I know. I've witnessed the arrogance of men. You find a bobble here and a scrap of text there and suddenly you believe you've put it all together. You actually believe that you can outmaneuver a god!" He clapped his hands, one sharp slap. "Ha! Can you even begin to comprehend the impudence of it?"

"Enough!" shouted Ghilardi. "Enough already. You have the rod. What more do you want?"

The Atesi's arm spasmed, jerking up and then down three times in quick succession. "Ah! Ah-ha! Yes, yes, what indeed? Well, the Achaemenid Codex of course, which will be easily acquired. And the troublesome amulet, the insect if you will. Oh, I've been in close proximity to both of these for days now, only missing the rod. But there is a complication. You see the insect is connected to its intended vessel. Well, I certainly could have taken it from Huntington at any point, but it wouldn't be of much use then, would it?" He paused as if pondering, allowing mucus to dribble from his lips and onto his chest. "Well, perhaps even I lack all of the answers. What a travesty. You'd think a spirit of the ages would be all knowing, but . . . Ah. That is a tale for another day. It was clear that in the vessel's presence the insect would present a way to the scepter. All that was needed of me was patience. And behold, the insect was true to its nature. When Huntington was here, in this very room, the amulet became warm. Oh, he thought nothing of it at the time and said nothing. But it was a beacon, a sign. Once I learned of this, well, there was no need to wait. Huntington had served his purpose."

And suddenly, it all came together in Thorpe's mind. "All of those deaths," blurted Thorpe. "Dr. Calhoun, the man at the café, the priest— all of it was you. You were preventing anyone from distracting Hunting-ton. You needed him to lead you to the bleeding rod."

The Atesi twitched and jerked as he chuckled. "Oh-ho! The thief finds his voice. Yes, yes, needed him, that might be a bit strong. But I do require the insect. And for a time, the man and the bug needed to remain together. Peculiar the workings of mystic currents, don't you agree?"

Ghilardi rumbled, "And so you are nothing but a parasite. You fol-low a human about and pick up the crumbs. You're no god. You're not omniscient. You may be spirit, but you're confined to one place and one time just like humans. You have no enlightened view of the future; you just react and leech upon others."

Wisps of smoke appeared from atop the Atesi's head. "Ah! Oh, listen to this! Listen to this! See, see, the human arrogance. Ha! No, I am not the leech, but the one to set Huntington on his course. Have you not yet realized; do you not see the master's stroke? It was I that coerced the Keepers to bring Huntington to us. It was I that manipulated the scenario to bring the insect and the rod into proximity, for I knew that the time was at hand. Oh, I was not the leech, but the puppet master, you arrogant unknowing fool!" He spit on the floor and the substance hissed and bubbled, burning a hole in the wood.

Throughout the dialogue, Thorpe watched, both enthralled and horri-fied by the exchange. He'd encountered possession before, in the form of Marc Huntington's occupation by a spirit known as Anascoreth, but he never believed he'd encounter such a thing again. And the worst of it was, he was at a loss. This being, this Atesi, was obviously powerful and had means at his disposal beyond those of a human. What possibly could Thorpe do other than to allow the bloody devil to take the rod? Dear God, he could barely move his arms much less attack the devil. The Atesi must have placed some sort of bloody hex on him to render him immobile.

The Atesi glanced to Thorpe, a queer expression on his features. Had he somehow read Thorpe's thoughts? Thorpe scowled. The Atesi chuckled.

"Well," said the Atesi. "I suppose we are at a crossroads. Huntington will be here soon and I will acquire the amulet. And, yes, the stage will then be set for the grand finale, the final curtain, the event to end all events." He grinned, shook his head with stuttering cracks and pops. "But you—the both of you—are complications. I suppose I could eliminate you as I have others. I am, after all a fire god. A fiery death is, shall we say, my signature. But in this instance, I believe more mundane deaths are in order. I have expended far too much energy already and will need what remains in the coming hours. I'm sure you'll under-stand."

He then put two bullets into each man.

***

Tina Collins arrived some fifteen minutes later, or so it seemed to Thorpe. Time had become quite elastic. Ghilardi was dead. He was certain of this. And he was equally certain that he had only moments remaining.

Collins surveyed the area and then rushed to Thorpe. Kneeling, she said, "Oh, Johnny, you fool. Why couldn't you be smart, just this once?"

She surveyed his wounds, obviously hoping there was something she could do. Was that a tear he saw? Was Tina Collins actually crying over him? Bloody hell!

"Tina, dear . . ." His voice was weak, trailing off. He needed to tell her that the Atesi was still here. Thorpe was uncertain where the demon had gotten off to, but he was certain that he had not left the premises. "Tina," he said again. "The Ates . . ." He couldn't quite complete the word.

He so wished it had been Dana that found him. He truly desired to see her one last time. But it was appropriate that it was Collins, he supposed. They had more in common than he cared to admit. And now, too late for it ever to matter, he realized that maybe, just maybe, there actually had been something rather special between them.

"Tina," he gasped again. He needed to warn her of the danger. "Tina . . ."

"Yes, Johnny. I'm here. Just you hang on, you hear me? Just hang on." She was pressing on his chest, attempting to stay the bleeding. The tears were now obvious, her cheeks wet with them.

"Tina . . . so sorry . . ."

And then he was gone.

Chapter Twenty

It had taken the Huntingtons nearly an hour to secure another rental vehicle and to get on the road toward Ghilardi's home. They'd tried to call Duck repeatedly, but he'd not responded. Dana asked Brigid if Duck had indicated in any way that he had plans beyond remaining with them until the rod was recovered.

"No. Nothing," said Brigid from the back seat of the sedan. "He seemed mostly content, just going along with it all. He's rather sweet in an awkward way."

Dana said, "Well, sweet or not, it's fairly obvious the nutter's gone after the rod by himself. He disappeared as soon as we determined that Ghilardi had the relic."

"I'm with Dana," said Hunt. "But I don't get the why of it. Has he been playing us all along?"

The speculation continued until they navigated the narrow twisting road leading to the secluded residence and arrived at Ghilardi's home. Their rented jeep was there along with two additional vehicles. The front door was ajar.

"Something's wrong," said Brigid with some anxiety. "Hugo would never leave the door open, especially now. He's always very cautious."

The scene inside the room caught Dana's breath, stilling her lungs and constricting her throat. Hugo Ghilardi lay in a pool of his own blood, obviously dead and . . .

No, no, no, no, dear Lord, no.

. . . only a few feet to Ghilardi's right lay Jonathan Thorpe, also quite dead, his mouth agape, eyes staring sightless, his chest stained with blood.

My God, this can't be!

Hunt moved into the room, gun drawn, Dana directly behind him, Brigid hanging back but crying nearly hysterically as she called Ghilardi's name. If the perpetrator was still here, Brigid's cries had alerted him.

But Dana had difficulty focusing on the potential threat. What had Jonathan been doing here? He shouldn't have been here. Shouldn't have even been in this country. He was supposed to be gone.

He was supposed to be gone!

Pistol held before her, eyes on the scene, Dana knelt to beside Jonathan, pressing two fingers to his jugular. My God, his skin was already cool to the touch. Dana hicked, suppressing a cry. A single tear traversed her cheek. This couldn't be. This just couldn't be. He shouldn't be here. He was supposed to be gone.

Dana heard something. Movement from the hallway. Bringing her mind back into the situation at hand, Dana rose, gun extended in a two-hand hold as Hunt barked, "Stop right there. Come forward slowly, hands above your head."

"Huntington, is that you?" The voice was female. American south. A moment later a slender black woman appeared, hands held high, pistol held loosely in her right hand. "I'm not the bad guy, darlin'. You don't need to aim that thing at me."

Dana knew her. It had been a couple of years, but yes. "Collins?"

"There you go. Now you're onto it."

The last time Dana had seen her, Collins had been undercover for the CIA as hired muscle for a very bad man. Dana couldn't fathom why the woman was here? Had she been with Jonathan? They'd worked together before.

Gun trained on the woman, Hunt said, "You're CIA, right? What are you doing here?"

"Former CIA. I'm with the Vatican now. Sent to track down the rod of Aaron, just like you. Obviously, we all got here too late."

"Keep going," said Hunt.

Collins slowly placed her weapon on a nearby bookshelf. "That better?"

Both Dana and Hunt remained still, guns in hand.

"Alright. I get it. I know how this looks. Here's what happened. I came across Johnny a few days back. He was also after the rod and so I teamed up with him. A contact of mine pointed us to Ghilardi. Johnny doubled-crossed me, got here first, and got himself and Ghilardi killed." She pointed to a damaged section of floor about five feet in front of her. "My guess is that's where Ghilardi hid the rod."

"Did you see anything?" asked Dana. She nearly had to shout over Brigid's sobs. The woman hadn't moved from Ghilardi's side.

"I got here no more than five minutes before you. This is how I found the place." She glanced past Hunt to Dana and added, "Dana, I'm very sorry for your loss. I know you've moved on, but I should tell you Johnny still loved you very much."

Dana didn't know what she was supposed to do with the sentiment, could barely begin to keep her emotions in check. And so, ignoring the comment, she said, "You know I can't trust you."

"Well, that's your decision to make. But the longer we stand around playing games the further away the perpetrator gets."

"Oh, no, no. That is entirely wrong," came a voice from behind.

Dana whirled to see Duck standing just beyond Ghilardi's body and before Brigid. How had he entered the room unseen by anyone? "Duck, what's happened here?"

Duck stepped forward. His movements were all wrong: jerky, uneven. He had a peculiar pallor to his eyes. His mouth wore a twisted grimace. "Ah! There we go again. Mistaken identity."

Something was quite curious here. Duck's voice was entirely wrong. Deeper, richer, older. And the accent wasn't right. Dana couldn't place it, but it wasn't Duck's Turkish accent.

It was Brigid who said the word. "Atesi. He's possessed by the Atesi."

Dana glared at Duck in dawning realization. This clearly was not the young man Dana had spent the past several days with. The voice, the mannerisms, even the skin tone was wrong, having taken on a somewhat reddish hue.

"Alright," said Hunt, obviously accepting the nearly unbelievable truth of it. "So, you're the Atesi. Care to find out if you're bullet proof?"

The Atesi chuckled. His head tilted to an unnatural angle. "Oh! See here. See here. I like that. Most people have trouble coming to grips with spiritual beings. Very good, Huntington. I'm impressed." He then cocked his head sharply in the opposite direction and whispered something in an unknown tongue. Dana's gun was suddenly so hot that she was forced to drop it. She noticed Hunt and Collins—who had retrieved her gun from the shelf—also drop their weapons as well, each with a bit of a shriek.

Dana was at a loss. Her palm was beginning to blister where it had touched the hot metal of the pistol. They outnumbered the Atesi, but Dana wasn't confident they could be effective against this thing that had once been Duck. Still, what other choice was there? With no further thought, Dana launched herself at the Atesi hoping that Hunt and Collins would follow. Maybe, if he was overwhelmed . . .

But, unbelievably fast, the Atesi's left hand found Dana's throat. Squeezing, putting an uncomfortably warm pressure on her flesh.

"Really, Dana? Really. I was certain you were smarter than that." His breath was hot, dry, and smelled of spoiled meat.

Dana couldn't reply. Her throat felt to be on fire. She heard Hunt shout warnings to the Atesi. But her mind was already becoming foggy. Consciousness threatened to ebb away. What was he doing to her? It was more than just the hand at the neck. There was some other force in play, slithering through her thoughts, muddling her brain.

Surprisingly, it was Brigid who next attacked. She came from the Atesi's right, screaming something about Ghilardi. The Atesi smacked her away with a flick of the arm and then shot her. Where had the weapon come from? Dana hadn't noticed it before. Was this beast simply that quick that he could pull the gun with such finesse that the movement was nearly indiscernible?

With a startled yelp, Brigid took a stumbling step backward and then crumbled to the floor. Collins immediately moved forward dropping to beside Brigid, attempting to tend to the wound. Hunt cursed the Atesi but remained still. He had sense enough to know that a frontal assault was useless.

Smiling, the Atesi said, "Ah, and so it goes. But now that we've dispensed with the dramatics, shall we conclude our business?"

Dana could have asked what business that might be, but she was barely holding onto consciousness, couldn't even garner the strength to lift an arm. But she didn't need to ask. She knew exactly what it was the Atesi desired.

Maintaining his grip on Dana, the spirit man stepped forward and ripped the locust amulet free of Hunt's neck. Hunt made a move to come to Dana's aid, but the Atesi held up a finger. "No, no, no. She lives. I'm sure you prefer her to remain that way."

Hunt hissed, "You bastard," but remained still. She saw his hands jitter, his jaw clench, his eyes tear as he stared at the stolen amulet.

"Really, Marc. Such language. And in the presence of a deity. Have you no manners?" The Atesi glanced down to Collins, who was tending to Brigid's wound and then back to Hunt. "Good, good. Sensible people. That's what this world needs. More sensible people. Now, to be clear, you're going to allow me to leave, for it seems I have a preordained appointment at the Temple of the Perpetual Flame." He cocked his head, and licked Dana on the cheek. His tongue was rough like sandpaper, hot and dry. Dana nearly retched. "I have a soft spot for dear Dana. She will not be harmed unless you give me cause to react violently. I'm sure neither of you want that."

Dana saw Hunt work his jaw and clench his fists, but he remained as he was, allowing the Atesi to lead Dana to the doorway. What else could he do? She was in the hands of a ruthless monster and he was entirely incapable of defeating it.

Chapter Twenty-One

Hunt paced Ghilardi's living room nearly flinging his yo-yo about as Collins tended to Brigid's wound with field first aid supplies she'd retrieved from her rental car. The bullet had passed straight through, just below the left shoulder. It had hit no vital organs and broken no bones. Brigid had lost some blood, but not a serious amount. Hunt had argued that Collins take her to a hospital while he went after the Atesi to rescue Dana, but both women had argued against this.

Collins said, "Darlin', you have no idea where that bad boy got off to and no way of stopping him by your lonesome. Let's just take a breath and think this through before you run off and get yourself and your lady killed. And be careful with that toy. You nearly knocked me in the face with that thing."

Hunt grunted. She was right about the Atesi, of course, but it didn't make Hunt any more inclined to agree with her. "The longer we wait, the harder he'll be to find." And the longer before he reacquired the amulet.

"Maybe," said Collins. "Or, if we use our gray matter, maybe we can figure out just where he might go." To Brigid, she said, "This is going to hurt, sweetie. Grit your teeth." Collins was stitching the wound.

Hunt snorted and flung the yo-yo nearly knocking over a lamp. Again, Collins was right. He knew this. He tracked people for a living. But this monster had Dana—and the amulet, that damned all-consuming amulet! He couldn't just sit back and do nothing. "Fine," said Hunt in a near bark. "Fine. So, what do we know? Where would this crazy demon take Dana?"

Collins fed the needle through and pulled as Brigid clutched the arm of her chair. "Wrong question, Huntington. Where would he take the rod and the amulet? Dana's just along for the ride."

Hunt plopped onto the couch and then immediately rose. The inaction was killing him. He should have done something—anything—while they were still here. Why hadn't he acted? How had he let the Atesi take the amulet and Dana so easily?

And why was he as concerned about the amulet as he was Dana? Damn, he wished he'd never seen the thing. It had some crazy hold on him, screwed with his perceptions.

Collins was tying off the stitches as Brigid said, "Temple of the Perpetual Flame." Her voice was weak and she was panting heavily. "He mentioned the Temple of the Perpetual Flame. It's often believed that certain locales possess a spiritual energy or perhaps a window into the spirit realm. This temple's probably such a site."

"Okay," said Hunt. "Where's the Temple of the Perpetual Flame?"

Brigid squinted, whether from pain or concentration, Hunt couldn't tell. "I'm unsure. In Zoroastrianism, the religion based on the teachings of Zarathustra, the author of the Achaemenid Codex, there are fire temples."

"Fine. Where's that?"

Brigid shook her head. "There are dozens, well over one hundred."

Hunt cursed. "No wonder he was willing to say the name of the place. He was taunting us."

Collins said, "Maybe. But he didn't call it a fire temple. He called it the Temple of the Perpetual Flame. I'm thinking it's a particular site, maybe one of these fire temples, maybe not."

"Great. But that still puts us back to square one."

"Fine," said Collins. "We're at square one. What do we know? What clues do we have?"

Brigid said, "The Atesi is not mentioned in Christian or Judeo writings, but obviously he believes himself to be an instrument in Armageddon. It's likely he'd be considered a demon in those traditions, not a god since both faiths are monotheistic."

"I'm not following," said Hunt.

"In Christianity, the spirit beings that are loyal to God are angels. Those that rebelled against God are demons. There are no other deities in that tradition. One God with all other beings occupying a lower status. This is true in Christianity, Judaism, and Islam."

"So, are there other non-Biblical writings that might give us a clue?" asked Collins as she applied a gauze to the repaired wound. "Maybe something mentioning the Temple of the Perpetual Flame?"

Brigid squinted, obviously focusing. "The Achaemenid Codex. I've only translated a small portion. I didn't see reference to fire temples or the Temple of the Perpetual Flame specifically, but there was mention of a temple in the sand. The reference was vague. But it was in the same passage that mentioned the staff and the insect."

"A temple in the sand," said Hunt. "Any idea what that means?"

Collins chuckled. "Well, I don't know if ya'll have looked outside lately, but there's plenty of sand to be found around here."

Brigid straightened herself, tentatively touching her shoulder. "It would be a specific locale."

Hunt pressed his palms to his forehead. This was Egypt. There were temples and sand everywhere. How was he to identify the proper place? He had nothing solid to go on.

"Tell me about your investigation," said Collins. "What have you learned?"

Hunt turned toward her. His first inclination was to bark in anger. He had to find the amulet! He had to find . . .

Dana.

Dana first. Screw the amulet. He understood Ghilardi's explanation that there was a spiritual bond to the insect created when it entered his mind to drive the demon from him, but it still angered him that he was so focused on that damned thing.

"Huntington!" said Collins. "Are you with us here?"

"Yeah. Yeah, sorry. That crazy amulet screwed with my head. I don't know how to describe it but . . . It doesn't matter. What was the question?"

"Your investigation. What did you learn? Maybe we can piece this thing together."

"Yeah, okay. Bruno. We were focused on Bruno Qudsi. We learned of his connection to People of the Crimson Moon, that he's likely high ranking. Another group, Sons of Light, was also after the rod."

"What did you learn about Qudsi?"

"Well, obviously, he did steal the rod before Ghilardi came along and swiped it from him. He has radical views about the end times. It sounds like he joined The Keepers specifically to gain access to the rod." Hunt paused, stared at Collins. "Land. He purchased land. Out in the desert."

"Where? Do you have a location?"

"Yeah. We looked it up. There's nothing there. Just desert. No structures, nothing. It didn't make any sense. We speculated about ruins beneath."

Brigid straightened in her seat and said, "Lidar."

"What?"

"Lidar. It stands for Light Detection and Ranging. It's like radar, only it uses pulsed laser light to map buried structures in three dimensions. It's used in archeology. Perhaps there is something buried on Bruno's land." She paused, and, despite her pain, grinned. "Say, maybe the Temple of the Perpetual Flame? Just a guess."

"Now just push the pause button for a second," said Collins. "This is Qudsi we're talking about, not the Atesi. Why would he have interest in this temple?"

"No. I get it," said Hunt. "The Atesi was hiding within Duck all of this time because he thought we could lead him to the rod. He doesn't know or have everything. He's following our lead."

"Because you had the amulet," said Brigid. "He believed the amulet would lead you to the rod."

"Yeah. But he was with us when we learned of Qudsi's land. Maybe that was part of the puzzle too. Crimson Moon also wanted to bring about the Apocalypse. Maybe the Atesi and the Moonies both knew that this temple was crucial to their goal."

Brigid said, "That would make sense. There are certain sites thought to bridge the gap to the spiritual realm. If this temple is such a place, both the Atesi and the Crimson Moon might seek to utilize it. The fire spirit may have been collecting all of the pertinent information through-out your investigation, just storing it up for the right time." She paused, pondered, and then added, "The right time! Yes! The week of the holy convergence is upon us. It is believed by many to be a time when the stars align for preordained means."

"Like prophecies, Armageddon, all of that rigmarole?" asked Collins.

"Yes, yes. It started earlier this week. There are only two more days until the stars move out of alignment."

"Well, isn't that special?"

"That means all these factions are on a ticking timetable," said Hunt. "Brigid, can you get us this Lidar thing? The Atesi's not going to waste any more time than he has to."

She nodded. "It's costly. But yes. I have access."

"Don't worry about the cost. My gut tells me we're on the right track here." He didn't add that he felt it might be the locust pointing him in that direction. Hunt frequently went with his gut. But this was different. It was almost a physical sensation. The moment he'd landed on the idea of Qudsi's land a near electrical sensation raced through his form.

***

The damned codex had been stolen from Brigid's hotel room. It had to be the Atesi. He knew where to find all the pieces to the apocalyptic puzzle and had simply been waiting for it to fall into place. Hunt cursed, slammed his hand against a couple of walls, and paced about like a caged tiger, but in the end, it changed nothing. The plan was still the same. Find the temple on Qudsi's property and pretend like they had a clue once they encountered the Atesi.

Brigid went right to work making the arrangements. She chartered a plane and made several calls to acquire the Lidar equipment on such short notice. She remained on task, ignoring whatever pain she felt from the wound. Her only complaint was that Ghilardi had not revealed to her that he'd possessed the rod of Aaron. They had been close, she respected him greatly, and now, at the time of his death, she learned he'd been keeping something significant from her. This obviously troubled her deeply and likely made her grief more difficult.

Hunt was agitated and jumpy, unable to remain still. He felt that if something didn't happen soon, he might just slug someone. Collins noticed his mood—which, to be honest, was not well disguised—and approached him. "You okay, Huntington? I've seen you under pressure before. This isn't that same guy."

Hunt simply grunted. He didn't need a listening ear right now.

Collins smiled and said, "I know you're worried about Dana. But she's a big girl. She can take care of herself."

Hunt shouted, "It's not Dana! I wish to God it was—it should be. But it's the damn amulet. That's all I can think about. It's like I'm going through some crazy withdrawal."

Collins appraised him as he marched away from her, pivoted, and returned. With a gentle shrug, she said, "Johnny told me about what happened with the amulet in Botma. It really is what they claim, isn't it?"

Hunt nodded. His tone softened as he said, "Yeah. It is. And I want to hate the thing, but I wouldn't be alive right now if not for that damned locust." He huffed, took a step right and then reversed. "I feel nearly incapacitated. I'm all jittery and unfocused. How am I supposed to help Dana like this?"

"Well, right now your only job is to let your archeologist buddy do her thing. Once we find the hidden temple we'll deal with your issues."

"Sounds like it'll be too late by that time."

Collins grinned. "The Atesi has Dana. What else does he have?"

"The amulet."

"You bet your ass he does. I'm guessing the closer you get to that rock the more you'll feel like yourself. You weren't like this when you wore that bad boy. It could be a proximity thing."

"You'd better be right on that. We're going to need me on task when the time comes."

Fifteen minutes later, Brigid informed them that arrangements had been finalized. Five minutes later they were on their way to the airport.

The plane was a twin-engine Cessna. The journey took about three and a half hours, and this just to get to the general locale. Once there, the Lidar was to be engaged and the true search begun.

Hunt was impressed with Brigid. She'd taken some run-of-the-mill pain meds, nothing that would make her loopy, and soldiered on without a word about her bullet wound. He knew she was in pain. He saw her wince every time she lifted her left arm, and her South African accent was slightly more clipped than her normal carefree tone. But otherwise, she was an archeologist on task.

The Lidar machine was a box-like apparatus that sent out laser pulses at an astonishing rate to map the area below. Brigid had the data fed directly to her laptop computer and studied the findings as they arrived, stabbing at the keys, zooming in on certain images, scrolling left and then right. She was totally focused even as the small plane bobbed this way and that in the turbulence. As always, guitar music could be heard wafting from her earbuds.

After about an hour and a half of this Brigid said softly, "Cool, cool, I've got it." And then nearly shouted. "Here! I've got it. Here."

Hunt and Collins unbuckled their seatbelts and moved to where they could see her laptop. The Lidar image filled the screen with bright florescent reds, greens, and yellows.

"See here," said Brigid, pointing. "These straight lines. Nature doesn't make straight lines. Not like that." She moved her finger slightly to the right. "And here, that's a connecting wall. And here's another. There's a ruin buried beneath that sand."

Hunt glanced through the window to the seemingly endless desert below. "Okay. There's a ruin down there. But all I see is sand. So, how do we get into the structure? And for that matter, how did the Atesi get in there? Assuming he did. I'm not seeing any entranceway."

Brigid gazed out over the desert. "Nor do I. But the Atesi is in a physical form. If he's there, then there's a way in. We just can't see it from the air."

***

They brought the plane down about a half mile from the target locale as they didn't want to eliminate the element of surprise by noisily announcing their arrival. As anticipated, the landing was fairly rough. The pilot—an affable Egyptian named Khalid—was experienced in sand landings and takeoffs, but loose sand is not an ideal surface for aircraft and comes with inherent difficulties.

Even the relatively short half mile hike to the site was wearing as sand shifted beneath their feet and sun beat down from above. The one saving grace to the adventure was that the entrance to the ruins was not difficult to find from ground level. There was a simple tan colored canopy positioned above a trough dug into the sand and lined with sandstone bricks, leading to a stone opening some fifty feet down. The canopy was likely sufficient to keep anyone away who was not specifically looking for the site. There was essentially no foot traffic this far out into the desert and absent equipment such as Lidar, the canopy made the entrance invisible from the air.

The area leading to the trough was pristine, but Hunt did notice evidence of footfall as they entered the ruin itself. Brigid immediately identified it as a temple, noting the symbols on the two pillars framing the entrance. There were several rows of zigzagging lines crowned with what appeared to be a representation of the moon. As with most ruins of the region, the stone was tan, but the moon image offered a hint of scarlet.

The initial passageway was quite narrow and low, causing Hunt to crouch as he moved forward. The steps were of uneven stone, some of which was crumbled. Two steps were missing entirely causing each person to hop to the next available stair with hopes that it wouldn't break in the process. Cobwebs littered the corners and Hunt heard scurrying from above and behind. He wasn't certain what creatures inhabited this area of the desert but wasn't in any hurry to meet them. They used flashlights to light the way, though there were periodic skylights, small circular things that allowed the sun to creep through. Hunt noted that there was some sort of mirror system allowing the light access. Brigid explained that these couldn't be something inherent to a structure of this age. The temple would have been on the surface when first constructed and not needing such a system. Likely, Bruno Qudsi or some other latecomer had installed this means of illumination.

Brigid was amazed at the symbols carved along the walls, claiming they represented a progression in the complexity of the script. I.e., the earliest inscriptions were likely written centuries before the most recent entries, with each addition showing the evolution of the written language.

Hunt was certain that all of this was quite fascinating and he would have been interested at another time, but at this moment, he had to stay on task. Dana might be here. She could be in significant danger. And while Brigid's insights might give some clue as to what this place had been, or what the Atesi and People of the Crimson Moon had planned, this was first and foremost a rescue operation—at least until they had Dana back.

Hunt grinned at the thought. Dana. He was once again focused on Dana. Collins had likely been correct. He was presumably in proximity to the amulet and thus able to think clearly. Was this to be his life now? Forever tied to that damned bug.

The air became stale, thick with dust. In this section, the skylights were absent leaving only the narrow flashlight beams to illumine the path. Collins had been strangely quite through most of the trek but whispered, "I'm not liking this much. Feels like something that might end up a one-way trip."

Hunt couldn't disagree and so remained silent.

Brigid shined her light on an image on the ceiling above them. "Do you see?" she asked.

"Yeah," said Hunt. "A burning man."

Collins whispered. "Is that the Atesi?"

Brigid nodded. "In all likelihood yes. And do you see what he's holding?"

Hunt said, "I'm guessing that's a staff."

Brigid was about to reply when the floor beneath her shifted and crumbled. Hunt turned as her eyes went wide.

And then the floor beneath Brigid gave way completely and she was gone. Collins was between Hunt and Brigid and so made her way to the now gaping hole first, flashing her light into the gap and hollering Brigid's name. The passage was narrow, but still Hunt squeezed alongside Collins.

"Hang on, darlin'. Just hang on," called Collins. "Let me get some light down there."

And then they heard Brigid scream.

Chapter Twenty-Two

Somewhere in the Sahara

Dana was unsure of many things, but there was one thing she knew with certainty. She was not a victim. In the past few years, she'd been abducted, beaten, raped, taken hostage, but she'd always prevailed. And though she was now held by someone who might not even be human, she refused to roll over and cower. Defeat simply wasn't an option.

She'd spent the past several hours in what she could only describe as a mind fog. Duck . . . No. Not Duck. This person was the Atesi. The Atesi had transported her someplace via airplane. She was now in a small, dimly lit room with a guard standing just inside the door. Dana had been momentarily surprised to find that the Atesi didn't operate alone. She'd wrongfully assumed that a spirit being wouldn't need human assistance. But he was currently occupying the physical world and likely therefore subject to physical laws—at least to some extent. And the Atesi was considered a god by some and so it would follow that he had some base of loyal followers. She hadn't determined how many were in this locale—or even what this locale might be—but she knew he planned some sort of ritual and likely soon. He'd been furious earlier, when he found that the Achaemenid Codex was missing from Brigid's hotel room. Apparently, he'd needed this for his scheme but had determined to proceed, nonetheless. He seemed confident that it would turn up. Dana was quite foggy at the time and understood little of this. All she could be certain of was that this insane spirit thing was planning something perfectly awful.

The mind fog had begun to subside as soon as she'd been confined to this room. Likely, the Atesi felt she was secured and allowed his hex to evaporate. As lucidity returned, she realized that she was now in some sort of ancient structure. The walls were of coarse sandstone and were damaged in several areas. Likewise, the floor was crumbled in many places. This was a ruin of some sort.

Her guard was a slightly heavyset male, likely in his early twenties: acne, splotchy beard, wire-rimmed glasses. He didn't appear to be armed, but Dana couldn't be sure that there was nothing hidden within the folds of his loose-fitting garment. She calculated that she could reach him in five steps. Her hands were bound behind her back, but she'd already loosened them some. Another minute or two and she'd be free.

She considered engaging the man in conversation, to maybe try to learn something of the Atesi's plans, but the guard already seemed preoccupied, perhaps letting his mind wander as he watched the prisoner. Better to avoid drawing his attention. Most likely, the man had little or no military training and was unaccustomed to guarding someone or having a need to remain alert. He was a religious fanatic not a trained combatant.

Well, too bloody bad for him.

Dana was in movement nearly as soon as her hands were free. Five bounding steps, a twist, a chop, a pull, and she slipped the fabric that had bound her only moments before over the man's head and around his neck. He struggled, pulling at the impromptu noose, shifting his weight, stepping backward to squeeze Dana against the jagged and uneven stones of the wall. But Dana was determined, pulling tighter, tighter, refusing to release despite the pain she now felt at her spine.

Finally, the man's hands loosened, his arms dropped, and then he slumped to the floor.

Dana knelt, feeling for a pulse. Good. The man lived. Her intent hadn't been to kill, but simply to gain freedom. Quickly, she took the fabric and tied the man's hands behind his back and then frisked him for weapons. None. What kind of bleeding guard didn't carry a weapon? Leaving the guard where he lay, Dana rose. She wasn't sure how long he'd be out and so cautiously moved into the dark hallway beyond.

There was no artificial light, but sporadic sunlight beams crept in from somewhere above, offering just enough illumination to allow her to traverse the narrow corridor. She turned right for no other reason than that there appeared to be slightly more light in that direction. She was unarmed and soon found that she was lost in a maze of connecting corridors. The only thing she could do was to keep moving.

Eventually, she came to a small alcove with two staircases, one leading up, the other down. As this was obviously some sort of ancient ruin, and therefore likely below ground level, she assumed freedom would be up and so chose the upward staircase. The ancient steps were in disrepair. Several threatened to crumble as she gingerly put her weight on them, yet she somehow managed to climb the twelve steps to the next level.

But she hadn't found freedom. Not yet. From what she could see in the near complete darkness, this level was similar to the one below. Again, turning right, she moved through yet another dark, uneven corridor. Spider webs crisscrossed the way. There was an odor of decay, as if something had died here recently. She moved cautiously around a gap in the floor, glanced back to confirm she wasn't being followed, and then four arms reached out and grabbed her.

***

Hunt's flashlight beam penetrated the darkness to reveal Brigid lying on a rocky surface perhaps fifteen feet below. She appeared to be uninjured but was not likely to remain so as a large snake, more than four times the young woman's length, slithered forward. Brigid scurry-crawled backward but ran into a wall. The snake was making its way up her form as she screamed and beat at its head with her flashlight.

Hunt considered shooting the beast but feared hitting Brigid. Even if his aim was true, the bullet might pass through the snake and into her. Pulling his five-inch carbon boot knife from its sheath at his right ankle, Hunt launched himself through the hole in the crumbling floor and onto the snake. He heard Collins call after him, but she wasn't his present concern.

The snake had to be at least five feet in diameter, black, with a bizarre red swirl pattern weaving across its form. There was some sort of gemstone imbedded in its forehead. The thing was too thick. Hunt couldn't get his arms around it. Slashing furiously with his blade, he penetrated the cool scaly flesh three times before the creature responded. The head whipped around, long prehistoric fangs gnashed as Hunt rolled left, avoiding the first lunge.

Instead of retreating, he scrambled forward, stabbing about two feet down from the snake's head. He'd been aiming higher, but the creature was in constant motion. The beast thrashed, knocking Hunt onto his back. The knife remained imbedded in the cool flesh as the tail wrapped around Hunt's torso. He attempted to wriggle free, but the creature was both incredibly strong and quick. What was this thing? He'd never heard of snakes this size inhabiting the desert. Didn't this beast belong in someplace like the Amazon?

Hunt attempted to reach the Browning holstered at his tailbone, but the coils of reptilian flesh were in the way. He was being pulled further and further into the snake's grasp as it continued to wrap itself around him.

Brigid hammered at the thing with a large stone she'd picked up off the ground, but the snake ignored her entirely. Hunt could only hope this remained the case. Brigid was not trained in combat and survival; she'd stand little chance against this monster.

As if Hunt's odds were any better.

Hunt gasped for breath as he tried to reach for his knife. But the serpent snapped and dodged. Hunt now had both hands clasped around the base of its neck, but it thrashed from side to side, thrusting forward, the insanely long teeth coming within inches of Hunt's face. God, this thing was strong.

The eyes were of a modulating red, dark folding into light into darker yet. In some ways it was like looking into dual lava lamps, though these eyes were far more hypnotic than melted wax in a glass tube could ever be. Hunt felt his strength waning and wasn't sure if it was a result of the coils tightening about his torso or the weirdly compelling eyes.

Beautiful. They were beautiful.

And deep. An infinite depth swirling into eternity.

The sound of four rapid gunshots pulled Hunt back to reality.

That and the creature's head exploding onto his face.

Hunt tumbled away, gagging as he wiped brain matter from his flesh.

"Huntington, are you okay? Did it bite you?" It was Collins. She stood maybe ten feet distant, her Glock in a two-handed hold.

Hunt spit. "Yeah, yeah. Fine. God, that's horrible."

"Yeah, well it's better than being that thing's dinner." She moved to Brigid who was on palms and knees, gasping for breath. "Are you alright, Dr. Daniels?"

"As well as can be expected. My God, that was . . . Vasuki. A Hindu snake god. It was actually Vasuki. I'm sure of it. The eyes, so intelligent. So . . ." Brigid shook her head, still dazed.

Hunt rolled to a sitting position, saying, "Snake god or not, I suggest we move along. I'd like to find Dana, the amulet, and the rod before we run into any of that beast's buddies."

***

Dana felt the arms grab her and pull her from the main corridor. Immediately, she jabbed an elbow back and kicked. She heard a grunt, an exhalation of breath, and the loosening of a grip. She whirled to see that she faced two men. One held up a finger. "Shh, shh. We do not want to be heard by the Atesi or his followers." Neither appeared to be armed, nor did they make any further aggressive moves.

Keeping her voice low, she asked, "How do I know you're not with the Atesi?"

One of the men pulled back his sleeve revealing a blood red moon tattooed on his wrist.

"Crimson Moon? You're no better."

The second man, tall, balding, with a dour expression, shook his head. "You may believe that, but it's untrue. The Atesi's goal is to use the sacred scepter to bring destruction across the earth. We want no such thing but believe the rod of Aaron is meant to be the scepter Christ carries upon his return. By reuniting the rod and the locust we can beckon Christ to His return."

"Well, that sounds lovely and sweet, but why would Christ need anyone to beckon him? Wouldn't he come in his own good time?"

The man scowled. "Our Lord has always relied on the faith of his followers when performing great deeds. It is how he operates."

The other man, shorter, with subservient eyes, and narrow lips glanced to his companion and then said, "I understand that you may doubt us, but you've just escaped the Atesi. He or his people will be searching for you. We must get you to safety."

Dana looked from one man and then to the other and nodded. She sensed no immediate danger from them and felt they might even aid her in acquiring the rod—at which point all bets were off and she'd do what she'd been hired to do, gain the rod and return it to the Keepers.

The two men led her through several narrow corridors and down crumbling staircases. There were bizarre images carved into the sandstone and her escorts warned her not to focus on any of these for many were imbued with mystic powers and she might become transfixed. Dana knew such powers existed but wasn't prepared to take their word that random etchings in the ancient walls contained such influence. That said, she kept her gaze squarely on the floor before her.

Perhaps ten minutes later Dana was led into a small torch-lit chamber where six men, all in scarlet robes, but of varying ethnicities and ages, were huddled over a table. Catching a glance at the table, Dana saw that they were studying some sort of blueprint, likely of this very ruin.

All six men turned as they entered and Dana recognized Bruno Qudsi as one of them. With a near scowl, he said, "Oh, the Huntington woman. You are quite tenacious, though misguided."

Dana cocked her head and grinned. "Brother Bruno. You've sent us on quite the chase, haven't you?"

Qudsi scoffed. "I have been evasive out of necessity. You sought the rod. I was not interested in relinquishing it."

Dana was about to respond, but there was a sudden commotion at the doorway. Everyone turned as Hunt, Collins, and Brigid entered. Hunt and Collins had weapons drawn. Hunt barked, "Hands up—everyone! Or I'll blow your heads off."

There was a moment of utter silence and then Dana said, "It's alright, Marc. They're not a threat. At least not currently." He gazed at her, likely looking for some sort of sign that she was being coerced. The concern was evident on his face, in the clenched jaw, the slight quiver to the lips. He was terrified for her. And what was that all over his shirt and flesh? Blood? It didn't appear to be his own as he showed no sign of injury, but what had happened? Forcing a grin, she said, "It's alright, Hunt." And then, without a thought to what she was doing, she walked to him and wrapped her arms about him. What had he endured to find her?

Obviously startled at the unexpected intimacy, he could do nothing but return the hug.

Lowering her weapon, Collins said, "Okay, y'all are cozy. But do you mind bringing us latecomers up to speed?"

Qudsi stepped forward saying, "Our goal is to prevent the Atesi from using the sacred scepter to his own destructive ends." Moving to directly before Hunt, who now stood side-by-side with Dana, he said, "Do you understand your significance and how you are clearly meant to be here? The amulet, thousands of years old, woke only for you." His voice was stern, his tone commanding.

"Nah," said Hunt. "It only woke once and that was for a very specific circumstance. It's just been a lifeless hunk of stone since."

Qudsi narrowed his gaze. "Really? Are you certain of that? Has there been nothing recently? No hints to its intent?"

Dana saw Hunt hesitate before speaking. "When the Atesi took it, when it was far from me, I couldn't get it out of my mind. Like some insane addiction. And when we were first at Ghilardi's place. I didn't think about it then, but it was warm, probably because the rod was near."

Qudsi patted him on the shoulder. "And there you confirm my statement. You may not like it, you certainly have tried to deny it, but you are a part of this grand drama that unfolds before us."

"And what about your part in this great drama?" asked Brigid. "Obviously, you consider yourself to be significant."

Qudsi turned toward the young woman. "Yes, the People of the Crimson Moon are destined to play a role. It is our honor to rescue the holy scepter from the evil ones and present it to Christ upon his return."

Brigid stepped to within a foot of the man, twirling her earbuds, and cocking her head. "Really? That's your excuse for stealing a sacred artifact? That you're egotistical enough to think you're destined to play a role?"

Qudsi said nothing.

Brigid smirked. "Not to burst your pretty little ego, but I've yet to come across any writings that mention the scepter being delivered to the Messiah. For that matter, nothing in mythology connects your little gang in any way to Christ's return or to the apocalypse." She paused, put a hand on her hip, and added, "Huh! You might just be a common low life after all."

Dana couldn't help but grin. The seemingly free-spirited archeologist had some venom.

Seemingly nonplused, Qudsi said, "Any scripture, Christian or otherwise, is never complete in every detail of all that has or will transpire. There is much left to interpretation."

"So, you chose to interpret that you and Christ will have a comfy little face-to-face where you give him his scepter. Does the term egomaniac mean anything to you?" said Brigid.

Obviously wishing to get the conversation back on track, Hunt said, "Any thoughts on our buddy Duck being possessed by this ancient god,

Atesi? Seems we're going to have to face a wannabe deity to get the rod."

Qudsi turned to him saying, "It would appear the Atesi inhabits that form. It is a spiritual being we combat. And that being the case, this battle might be fought more on the spiritual plane than on the earthly. That said, your young friend hosts the demonic spirit. His safety is not our primary concern."

Chapter Twenty-Three

The Huntington's group and the People of the Crimson Moon discussed strategy, studying the diagram of the temple and debating on how best to attack the Atesi. But in the end, there were few options. Hunt found Qudsi to be very stiff, or perhaps rigid was a better word. The man showed very little capacity for warmth and seemed to have a perpetual glower about him. His accent was thick, his body box-like, seemingly well-muscled. His hands appeared knobby and weathered, though he was likely not much older than thirty-five or forty.

Both Brigid and Qudsi's people agreed that the Atesi would likely perform his rite in the ceremonial chamber. And since they were the ones with spiritual knowledge, Hunt felt he had to follow their lead on this. The chamber was situated deep within the temple at its lowest level and there was really no way to enter unseen. At best, they might manage a very short element of surprise. Somehow, they needed to subdue the Atesi and however many of his followers were in that chamber.

If this were simply about returning the rod to its rightful owners, Hunt probably would have aborted the operation. There was too great of a risk and too little hope of success. But this was bigger now—much bigger. Hunt had seen enough to concede that this might just be what these people claimed, that the Atesi could possibly summon some sort of Biblical-level catastrophe with the potential to kill millions. His rational mind would love to dismiss such a seemingly fanciful notion, but life experience had taught him that things weren't as simple as the rational world would like him to believe.

The Atesi could not be allowed to fulfill his plan. Period.

The party included the two Huntingtons, Brigid, Collins, and four Crimson Moon members. It was determined that a larger contingent might be cumbersome in a confined battle. They made their way through the narrow corridors, deeper and deeper into the bowels of the temple. The temperature dropped noticeably with each level they traversed and Hunt found himself wishing for a jacket. The skylight system was still in play and offered periodic illumination, but mostly they relied on flashlights.

"What was that?" asked Collins. "Did you see that?"

"What?" asked Hunt.

"I see them," said Dana. "They're like some sort of wisps."

Hunt wasn't entirely sure what she meant by wisps, but squinted his eyes attempting to focus on whatever it was they saw. There. Mist-like apparitions. The apparently immaterial forms were floating amongst them. And then one passed before him, just lazily floating by. At first it seemed like steam, a formless mist, but then it rolled, slowly, and Hunt recognized humanlike features within the dissipating cloud. A gaunt face staring, grinning.

"Oh!" said Dana with a start. "One touched me."

It didn't linger on her, but simply passed close by touching her briefly, but the effect was immediately obvious as Dana's hair slowly rose to stand on end.

"Dana!" called Hunt. "Are you alright?"

Dana shook her head as if trying to clear her thoughts. Her hair was already beginning to lower back to its normal state. "Fine . . . I think. It felt . . . I suppose . . . quite peculiar."

Qudsi said, "There are many forces at work here. Be cautious."

Collins quipped, "Well, the man might never win Mr. Congeniality, but he certainly is spot on in stating the obvious."

The wisps remained, hovering about the perimeters of the corridor, but made no further contact. It felt to Hunt like they were silent observers.

Or possibly spies.

Could these things be notifying the Atesi of their position? If so, there was nothing he or any of them could do about it. It wasn't as if they could shoot these vaporous wisps or restrain them in any way. It would be like trying to catch steam.

They moved deeper and deeper down winding stairs. There were whispering voices and whooshes of tingling air. But even these eventually quieted and the wisps eventually melted away. This was almost as unnerving as their presence. What could their absence signal? Fear on their part, or perhaps the end of the journey?

Brigid noted inscriptions etched into the walls in an ancient text. Moving to these, she touched the characters lightly with her fingertips. "It talks of great fire and of unnatural plagues. These are apocalyptic writings."

Dana asked. "Is there mention of the Atesi?"

"Not as such, but Atesi means flame. So 'great fires' could be a reference."

The party continued, now finding that the corridor was changing. Where they had been in a manmade ruin, they moved into what appeared to be a cave. The transition was subtle, the masonry ending and the natural stone continuing with no deviation in direction. They were now on a slope and could see flickering lights ahead.

"If I'm not mistaken," said Collins. "We're about to face that burning bastard that killed Johnny. Don't anybody be fooled by him, he's lethal." She held her Glock firmly before her.

The uneven stone corridor opened into a vast torch-lit chamber, roughly circular, and filled with stalagmites and stalactites. But these seemed peculiar and Hunt narrowed his vision, trying to make out the contours in the flickering light. There were human forms within the formations. Maybe they'd been carved into these natural protrusions, but if so, they were amazingly lifelike. It was as if living human beings had been infused into the stalagmites and stalactites. Each face expressed horror and agony, it seemed they clawed at some unseen barrier, their clothing in tatters, their hands bloodied. Yet, as grotesque as these were, Hunt had difficulty pulling his gaze free. Had those been living persons at one time? And if so, how had they become trapped in such a gruesome fashion?

A group of robed individuals stood in a circle around an elevated platform. They were an odd assortment. Mostly young, they gave the impression more of misfits than of dedicated fanatics. It was in their baring, the downturned eyes, the shifting of one foot to the other, the uneasy chuckles. Duck, or rather, the Atesi, stood at the center of the platform, slightly elevated above his devotees. The man looked simultaneously the same as the person Hunt had spent several days with and yet entirely different. His skin had a rich reddish hue, his hair had thickened, his body mass increased ever so slightly. And there were the mannerisms, the jittery movements, the random jerks of an arm or leg. It appeared that since the Atesi was now taking control of the body for a longer duration as opposed to hiding in Duck's subconscious, it was impacting the physical form in a more dramatic fashion.

The Atesi turned and offered an expansive smile that Duck never could have achieved. "Ah! Oh! Come! Come! Welcome. I've been expecting you." He paused, leaned forward, examining the party with yellowed eyes. "Is that the lovely Brigid? Oh, my host Durukan is quite fond of you. Quite fond indeed. One might even call it love, or at least the first inklings of such great affection. And my, you are much sturdier than I had imagined. You received a bullet wound and yet here you stand, side by side with a band of fools. Oh, dear Brigid, I do applaud your gumption." He glanced from Brigid to Hunt then to Dana and then Collins. "Oh, and speaking of gunshot wounds, let's avoid those, shall

233

we? Immediately, the guns flew from the hands of Hunt, Dana, and Collins, landing only inches before the Atesi's feet.

"Ah! Much better." The Atesi clapped in uncoordinated syncopation. "It really is much more fun this way, don't you agree?" His tongue popped out, fluttering and spraying shots of steaming liquid before him.

Qudsi stepped forward to the front of the small group, his square jaw set firm, his knobby fingers balled in fists. "We're here for the sacred scepter."

The Atesi laughed a dry parched chortle. "Oh! It's the incompetent. You, my friend, had us all running about in circles. Do you have any notion of the commotion you've caused? And all for nothing! Nothing! Just as we located you, you lost the scepter. Bungling fool!" He held the scepter in his left hand. "But here it is. Forever beyond your reach. Stunning, isn't it?"

Hunt hadn't really known what to expect. There were rumors that the rod was made of sapphire, others said silver, but it appeared to be nothing so regal. This was simply a long, polished staff of wood, perhaps five feet in length and slightly gnarled. It was difficult to see from where Hunt stood, but there appeared to be writing along the side, perhaps some precursor to Hebrew, but nothing within Hunt's language toolbox.

"Yeah," said Hunt. "All of this for one simple staff. What do you plan to do with it?"

"Oh-ho! That's right! That's right! You're the direct one. No subtlety there. Oh no." The Atesi spread his arms wide and cocked his head with a stuttering crack to gaze toward the ceiling. "With this great scepter, I will spread purifying fires across the world and usher in a new age."

Collins quipped, "Can anyone here tell me why everyone's so jazzed about the end of the world?"

Dana said to the Atesi, "Certainly, you don't expect us to be impressed. I, for one, have seen nothing to indicate you have any level of apocalyptic authority."

The Atesi laughed. "There! There! Do you hear that? Ah! You, my dear, are magnificent. Magnificent! Oh, you're entirely wrong, misguided in all things, but you are resourceful! You escaped my men, have overcome numerous horrific events in your life, and yet here you are! And resourcefulness, now that is always entertaining. You, young lady, are entertaining." He paused, smiled, appraised the group. "But enough of this. We—and I mean all of us—are here for a purpose. Might we get on with the drama?"

With this, he withdrew the locust amulet from his pocket, holding it up as if on display. Hunt immediately felt an unnatural compulsion to race to the thing. It was all he could do to remain where he stood. Dana seemed to sense this and grabbed his hand, more of a warning or restraint than a sign of affection. Hunt felt his heart pound. It almost seemed the organ might leap from his chest. He had to regain the amulet. He had to!

The Atesi grinned at Hunt. "Oh! Look at this. Look at this. Do you see it in his eyes? Look at the sweat on his brow. He can't help himself. He longs for it like a mongrel for a T-bone, don't you Huntington?"

Hunt remained silent, but clenched his teeth and balled his fists, it was a miracle he didn't break Dana's hand. My God, the urge was impossible.

"Yes," said the Atesi. "It's calling to you. You hear it don't you? Oh, of course you do. Look at that desire."

Hunt began to step forward but Dana, Collins, and two men from Qudsi's group all held him back.

"Oh, look at this," leered the Atesi. "How very touching. I would love to allow you to keep your pathetic husband by your side, dear Dana, but I've found that the locust simply refuses to cooperate without his touch. So very inconvenient." The Atesi hacked, coughing sizzling matter onto the floor. Wiping his lips with a jittering hand, he said, "But that being the case, let us dispense with any nonsense. Allow me to demonstrate what shall befall any who seek to challenge me." Here, he pointed to the Crimson Moon member that held Hunt's left bicep. A man by the name of Michael. He was slender and quiet, but Hunt had found him to be friendly enough. "You! Yes, you. You seem a rather thick-headed fellow. No great loss, I should think. Allow me to use you as an example."

The Atesi focused on the young man, his eyes nearly flaming. His lips twitched ever so slightly. He nodded as he raised his hand, palm up before his face, and then blew across his palm as if blowing dust from his flesh. Michael released his grip on Hunt with a shout and then tumbled to the ground screaming. Hunt turned, seeing that the man was batting at his body as if he were on fire. And then there was smoke, small wisps of it at first, but soon, dark crimson puffs. And then the first flame appeared, and another, and another. Within seconds Michael was ablaze, his entire body covered in consuming flames.

Qudsi pulled his robe over his head and dropped to the man's side attempting to smother the flames with his garment, but it was already too late. The entire process had taken less than thirty seconds, but Michael was already dead.

Dana shouted, "You bloody bastard!"

The Atesi smiled. "Oh, yes. Let's just agree that I am that and more, shall we?" He then turned his attention to Hunt. "Now, Huntington. You desire the amulet. I offer it to you." The Atesi dangled the amber neck-lace before him. "Come, boy. Come. That's it. That's a good boy!"

Dana said, "No, Hunt. You can't give him what he wants."

Hunt could barely contain the urge to race forward and grab the amulet. Even if he saw another option, he likely wouldn't have the will to refuse the locust's call. He choked out words, his voice small and constricted. "I can't, Dana. You saw what he did. Besides, I . . ." He trailed off, unsure of how to articulate what was happening within him, the pull that was nearly dragging him forward. "Dana, just . . . Do whatever you can to stop him, but I . . ." He shook his head, breaking away from Dana and marching toward the all-important amulet.

Hunt nearly stumbled forward. It was as if his body was moving of its own accord, summoned by some magnetic pull.

"Good, good," said the Atesi. "Such a good boy." He slipped the amulet over Hunt's head and patted him like a dog. Hunt caught a glimpse of Dana; Collins was restraining her as she tried to race toward Hunt. He locked eyes with her, held the gaze for several seconds, and then slowly shook his head in a silent warning to stay put, before turning to face the Atesi.

"Well, well, well," said the Atesi. "Here we are at last. It is a shame, I suppose—a complication, really—that the Achaemenid Codex is absent. But these things have a way of correcting themselves. Let's say we proceed and see what comes of it, hmm?" He patted Hunt's head again as one might a dog.

***

Dana watched in horror as, holding the scepter high while grasping the amber that was still connected by a golden chain around Hunt's neck, the Atesi began chanting in an ancient tongue. His voice rose and then fell, the pace quickened, and then slowed as he then nearly whispered. It seemed he repeated the incantation, though Dana couldn't be sure.

Brigid tugged at Dana's arm. "It isn't working. The scepter's not responding to the summons. He needs the codex."

Collins whispered, "Somehow I get the feeling that's not good for us—as if what he intended was any better."

As if on que, the Atesi said, "Ah, well it seems we will need to take more drastic measures, won't we?" And before anyone could move to stop him, he drew a blade as if from nowhere and sliced across Hunt's forearm. "It's always blood, isn't it?" said the Atesi. "It always comes back to blood. In this case, it's Huntington's blood the locust desires." It seemed Hunt was transfixed, for he showed no sign of pain or even concern but allowed the Atesi to raise his arm above the amber where his blood poured over it, bathing the rock in his life fluids. The Atesi, then yanked the amber free of its chain, allowing Hunt to tumble to the ground. The amulet shimmered, it seemed there was movement from within, the locust wings in motion, even extending beyond the boundaries of its golden confines to flutter in a great rush.

Dana raced forward as the Atesi held the blood-soaked amber and the rod together above his head. He resumed the incantation as Dana dropped to Hunt's side. He was conscious, but barely.

"Hey, hon," he said. "World kinda went wonky there." His voice was groggy, the articulation slurred as if he was inebriated.

"Hang on, Marc. You'll be alright. Just let me tend to you." The wound was deep but didn't appear to have severed a major vein or artery. Thank God!

Collins was now beside her, slipping her backpack to the ground, unzipping it, and producing first aid materials. "Here. You can bandage him with this. You need to stop the bleeding."

Dana almost barked at her that of course she must stop the bleeding, she wasn't an idiot, but held back. The woman was offering aid, she meant no insult. Dana was simply overwrought. She had nearly completed wrapping the wound when she heard a mighty whoosh and a deafening clap of thunder. She looked up to see blue flames swirling from the rod of Aaron. The air sizzled with electricity. The grotesque forms within the stalagmites began to writhe and kick as if attempting to escape their eternal prison and it felt as if gravity shifted, like she might just float from the floor.

"Um, what was that about him needing the codex?" said Collins.

The Atesi laughed, shaking both sacred objects as if daring eternity to strike him down. He shouted in apparent jubilation, though Dana couldn't recognize the tongue.

Flashes of blue/green lightening zigzagged just below the cave ceiling. Ethereal voices, piercing in tone, echoed off the walls in a strange forlorn tongue.

Collins shouted over the commotion, "We've got to stop him!"

Dana glanced as she finished bandaging Hunt's arm. "I'm open to suggestions."

Collins produced a gun from an ankle holster. "You didn't think I carried only one weapon, did you?"

Rising, she took aim and fired three quick bursts.

To Dana's amazement, she was able to see the bullets slow to a near stop and melt as they drew near the Atesi and fell to the stone floor. "Well, damn," muttered Collins. "I didn't see that coming."

Three of the Atesi's men turned to charge Collins. She fired again. The Atesi's magic apparently didn't extend to his followers as the closest man was struck in the shoulder and tumbled backward. The next shot struck the second man in the lower chest, a kid really, no older than seventeen. The third man, shielded by his companions, dove onto Collins who was thrown back, the gun skittering from her grasp. Collins twisted and flipped, gaining the upper hand on the startled fanatic, but just as she was about to subdue the man, his head exploded.

Bruno Qudsi had retrieved Collin's weapon and, with stoic precision, eliminated the threat.

Staring up at the rogue monk, Dana said, "You know more about the rod than any of us. How do we stop him?"

"The rod has been awakened. It can now only be put back to slumber through spiritual means. Thus far our prayers have been ineffective." As if to punctuate his point, several streaks of lightening danced about the chamber as the Atesi continued with his incantation.

Hunt leaned up on one elbow and said, "So you're telling us were screwed." His expression was one of concern, his eyes were clear and aware. Whatever spell the Atesi had over him appeared to have dissipated. Despite the situation, Dana was encouraged to see that Hunt was coming back to himself. The injury hadn't been severe, but the obvious mental confusion had been a concern.

She didn't have time to contemplate this further for at this moment automatic gunfire erupted throughout the chamber. Dana and the others turned to see several people both men and women marching into the chamber firing weapons toward the Atesi and his followers. But where the fire god remained standing, seemingly unperturbed, his ragtag followers fell screaming and bleeding to the floor.

"Who in the hell's that?" muttered Collins as she scrambled to behind a stalagmite.

"Sons of Light," shouted Hunt as he rolled behind an adjacent stalagmite. The human form within the formation writhed and clawed as if attempting to reach through the barrier to snatch Hunt. Two of the Atesi's men fell dead less than ten feet from where he'd just stood. One was nearly decapitated by the automatic weapon fire. Ignoring the grotesque form beside him, Hunt shouted, "That's O'Broin at the back."

The red-haired woman was indeed following the pack, but she wasn't carrying a weapon, but rather a book.

"The Achaemenid Codex," muttered Dana as she scampered to be-side Hunt as gunfire shattered a nearby stalactite. "So, she's the one who stole it."

"No surprise," said Hunt. "We had a feeling they knew we had it."

The Sons of Light were firing indiscriminately, Hunt knew they needed to make a move soon. It was only a matter of time before bullets found them.

Hunched low, Brigid joined Collins as Qudsi and his men scattered for cover. Sons of Light had brought an arsenal. Yet, while his followers fled and died, the Atesi stood, unaffected, reciting his incantation, seemingly oblivious to the carnage about him. If anything, he seemed overjoyed. Likely thrilled that he'd been right. The codex had made its way here.

O'Broin stood amidst her group, holding the codex before her and reciting a passage in an ancient tongue. All the Atesi's men were now either dead, injured, or in hiding and so O'Broin stepped forward, separating from her group, and marching toward the Atesi.

Blue/green lightening shimmered from above, striking a stalactite and causing it to fall only five feet to her left. Still, she continued forward, reading from the codex, her voice rising to match that of the Atesi. Soon, she was thirty feet from him, and then twenty. When she was only ten feet distant, the Atesi's voice faltered. He seemed to stutter and to nearly stumble. His voice held none of its previous vigor when he said, "Foul woman. This is not how it is meant to be. The seventeenth song of triumph. Recite the seventeenth and all will be put right."

O'Broin smiled but continued reciting her verse.

"I said, the seventeenth!" shouted the Atesi. His body twitched, it seemed he was convulsing. "We can initiate magnificence this very moment. Do you not see? Simply speak the seventeenth."

O'Broin stopped before him, grinning. "Nay. I will not aide you in usurping our Lord. You are an interloper and a fraud. And must be dispensed with properly." She then continued with her recitation.

The Atesi emitted a low growl that may have disguised a pained gasp. Through gritted teeth he said, "The codex. Give it to me."

"Why? So you may claim a victory that was never yours to claim? You are nothing but a troublesome spirit who has never known his true position in the scheme of eternity."

The Atesi rose a hand, glaring at O'Broin as she resumed her reading of the passage. Wisps of smoke curled from his fingers, but there were no flames. O'Broin's hair waved as if in a heavy breeze and her cheeks reddened ever so slightly, but she did not appear to experience any discomfort. In truth, a crisp grin creased her lips.

"Woman! You slay me!" cried the Atesi as the rod and amulet fell from his hands, clattering on the stone floor. He opened his mouth as if to speak but found no voice. The Atesi fell to his knees and then tumbled sideways quivering and twitching. O'Broin's grin grew into a full smile as she tucked the Codex under her left arm and retrieved the fallen rod and amulet from beside the now-still Atesi. Rising, she gazed toward the Huntingtons. "Don't try to follow me. My people will fire upon you, for ours is a holy cause and any who oppose us have declared war against the light." And then, focusing on Collins, she added, "Perhaps I'll see you at home."

She, turned and strolled from the room as her followers kept their guns trained on those remaining.

Turning to Collins, Hunt asked, "What did she mean by 'see you at home?'"

Collins shook her head, "Huntington, I wish to God I knew."

Chapter Twenty-Four

There were several moments of near silence as everyone gazed toward the exit, watching to confirm that the Sons of Light had truly left and wouldn't reappear to gun them down as soon as someone moved from cover. The air was heavy with the smell of weapons fire and the Atesi lay at the center of the room amidst the lifeless bodies of his followers. It seemed the assault had been intended for only the Atesi and his followers as no others had been shot. Peculiar, Dana supposed. But obviously O'Broin and her crowd had their specific motivations, whatever they may be.

Finally, one by one, the survivors rose and moved from cover, gazing about at the carnage, moving from body to body seeking signs of life. My God, what a waste. The Atesi's men may have been fanatics and fools, but they'd been defenseless against the assault. Not a one remained breathing. No one deserved this.

Dana was about to move toward Hunt when she heard a low moan and turned toward the sound. Movement, only slight, but movement.

The Atesi!

The rage came upon her without warning. It had been festering since they'd first arrived at Ghilardi's hideaway home and found Jonathan slain. And now, without warning, it was fully upon her. Marching to the fallen Atesi, Dana screamed "Murderer! Foul stinking bloody murderer!" She didn't even realize that she'd begun kicking the dazed and nearly dead form until Hunt gripped her by the biceps and tried to pull her away. "No! Let me go! He killed Jonathan! He killed Jonathan!"

"I know, sweetie. I know," he whispered. "Just calm down. Bring it down."

"No! He's a murdering bastard!" Dana pulled against him, but Hunt held firm, cradling her close into a hug.

Collins stepped forward as Hunt did his best to calm Dana. She knew he was right. She was allowing her emotions to get the better of her, but damn it, this thing, this demon deserved everything she could dish out and so very much more.

Collins stared down at the Atesi and smirked. "You're not looking too god-like, darlin'."

The Atesi offered a choked chuckle. "Ah. And the gloating begins. So be it. Though, I must note, you did nothing to bring about this circumstance." He coughed and wheezed.

"Where will Sons of Light take the rod?" asked Collins.

"Heh? You think I know? They have their agenda, I have mine." The voice was weak. The Atesi was blinking as if struggling to remain conscious.

Dana and Hunt moved closer. "What did O'Broin do to you?" asked Hunt.

"And I need to answer your questions why?" Again, the Atesi coughed. Blood seeped from his lips.

"Let's just say you're returning a favor. You took my blood for your spell, how about you answer a couple of our questions?"

Dana couldn't believe they were standing here having a conversation with this monster.

The Atesi shrugged, coughed, wiped the blood from his mouth with a quivering hand, and said, "Fair enough. It's not as if I'm in any shape to chase after her myself." He closed his eyes and for a moment Dana thought he had died, but then he said, "I'm not sure of the incantation she used. Something from Zarathustra's codex. But whatever the case, it was obviously effective. Apparently, I'm trapped within this dying form. Such an ignoble end."

The Atesi allowed his head to lull right, apparently gazing at the Crimson Moon group as they began to cluster.

Glaring at the beast, Dana said, "What will Sons of Light do with Aaron's rod?"

A hacking chuckle. "You kick me when I'm down and now you want to chat? Dear lady, you really are too much."

"Just answer the question or I'll kick you in that smug face."

The Atesi offered a weak smile through quivering lips. "Ah. But this face, it isn't mine, is it?"

"Just answer the question." Dana had no patience for this prat.

"Yes, yes. In a hurry to race off and get yourselves killed, I suppose." He paused, again wiped blood from his lips, and said, "Sons of Light see themselves as guardians of the one true faith as well as escorts to the long-awaited messiah or some such nonsense. Their plan is to release the Biblical plagues simultaneously on significant sites of all major religions. The goal is to bring all people under one unified faith. As if that's ever been an option."

"By killing thousands?" gasped Dana.

"Really, Dana. This surprises you? Religion has always been spread through bloodshed. The Christian crusades, the Muslim conquests, the Buddhist uprising, etcetera, etcetera. Fear and death are the great evangelists. Ah, but my reign. Well, my way would have been a less deadly use of the power. You shouldn't have opposed me. My kingdom would have been glorious."

Dana was about to counter, but the Atesi coughed. Harshly. Blood spewed from his lips. His voice went raw as he barked several syllables in a foreign tongue. He shook his head left and right as if fighting off a hoard of flies. With a mighty shudder, he hacked, wheezed, and went still. A red/orange mist seeped from the still form and then dissipated in the subtle breeze.

After several moments, Collins kneeled beside him, checking for a pulse. She glanced up, shaking her head.

"Well, isn't this perfect?" It was one of Qudsi's men, tall, bald, and perpetually stern-faced. So why was he grinning now? He angled his head as if in greeting and then turned, strolling toward were Qudsi and his peers stood. "Just absolutely perfect. All three elements gone and only hours left in the week of holy convergence."

Hunt turned to Dana. "This is insane. All three factions want to usher in some different version of Armageddon. As far as I can tell, all of them are violent."

Collins stood. "I think that's why they call it Armageddon."

Dana glanced to Qudsi who stood several feet away conferring with the remaining Crimson Moon members. "It's all ballocks to me, but you saw what Sons of Light did here. We can't exactly let them have their way."

"No," said Hunt. "The trick's going to be tracking them quickly. We need to get to them before they go all hell and brimstone on the planet."

Collins asked, "Do you really think they can do that?"

"You were here. You saw what the Atesi was doing, you saw what O'Broin was able to do with the codex. I don't think we have the luxury to sit back to wait and see."

Brigid squeezed between Dana and Collins, staring down at the still form of the Atesi. Dana had almost forgotten that she was present. "Do something!" shouted the young archeologist.

Dana stared at her, not understanding.

Brigid dropped to the floor and despite her bullet wound, started chest compressions on the Atesi. "Don't you get it?" said Brigid. "O'Broin's spell was designed to eliminate the Atesi not the human host. This is still Duck's body. We need to bring him back."

Dana said, "What if it's the Atesi we bring back?"

Brigid shot, "What if it's not? Are you willing to risk Duck's life on a what-if? Not cool, Dana."

Hunt said, "She's right, hon. I was possessed by Anascoreth, but the demon was driven from me."

Dana stared at Hunt for a moment, at the shadowy remnant of Anascoreth still evident on his forehead, nodded, and dropped to beside Brigid. "Let me do it. You're injured." She scooted over, taking over the CPR.

Collins said, "The Atesi said he was trapped in this dying body. He may still be in there. Are you sure you want to do this?"

Dana ignored her. Collins was right. There was at least a fifty percent chance that if she was successful, it would be the demon that awakened, not Duck.

But then there was the other fifty percent. Could she really sit back and allow Duck—an innocent—die for the sins of another?

Dana focused on her task. Pressing, pressing. Was there even a hope of reviving him? She had no concept of what O'Broin's spell had done to Duck's body—or what the Atesi's possession had done to him for that matter. How long had he been dead? A minute? Two? She wasn't sure. Certainly, not any longer. Under normal circumstances there would be hope, but this was something mystical, she had no idea what she was dealing with.

Dana leaned in, press, press, press. The young man's body felt hard, rigid. Rigor mortis couldn't have set in so quickly, could it? "Breathe, you bleeding plonker. Breathe!" shouted Dana.

And he did.

A subtle gasp at first. And then a cough. His eyes fluttered.

And Dana held her breath.

Who was it that stared up at her, Duck or the Atesi?

He blinked again. His eyes narrowed.

"Mrs. Huntington?"

"Yes."

"What are you doing?" The accent was Turkish, the voice young, rather small.

Duck's voice. Duck's facial expressions. The reddish hue was gone from his skin.

"Duck?"

"I certainly hope so. Who else were you expecting?" He paused. "Why do I feel so . . . unusual?"

Dana straightened, staring down on Duck. "You feel unusual? Really? That's all?"

Collins whispered, "Be careful, darlin'. We still don't know what we're dealing with."

Duck sat up gradually, seeming a bit unsteady. "Not entirely well. I feel fatigued, very sore. Did I fall down?" He scanned the chamber. "Where are we? This place is . . . How did I . . .?" And then, looking to his right, he saw Qudsi and his men. "I may have missed something."

Hunt stepped forward. "Yeah. Something like that. Good to see you, kid."

Collins said, "Do you remember anything of the Atesi?"

"I don't remember anything of you. Who are you?"

Dana said, "This is Tina Collins. She's with the Vatican. Her question is valid. What do you remember of the Atesi?"

Duck seemed to contemplate for a moment. "His name has come up several times. A Turkish god of fire. He's been seeking Aaron's rod."

"And you remember nothing else of him?" This from Collins.

Duck shook his head. "Should I?"

And then he saw Brigid. She'd been standing slightly behind Dana, a broad smile on her face. "Brigid. Hi. I hope I didn't do anything to embarrass myself in front of . . ." He paused. His mouth dropped open.

He stared at Brigid. She wore a loose-fitting collarless top. The bandage covering the bullet wound was clearly visible. Apparently, the wound had reopened during the fight as blood seeped through the fabric. "You're bandaged. Are you alright?"

Brigid nodded. "I am. And I'm glad you are as well." There seemed to be a little extra something in her voice. Was she suddenly taken by Duck?

Hunt said, "Listen, sorry to break up this little whatever-it-is, but Sons of Light have the rod, the amulet, and the codex. We need to learn where they're going to strike and figure out a way to stop them before all hell breaks loose—literally."

Brigid turned from Duck and said, "I think there may be a clue on the corridor wall."

Dana said, "The writings you were looking at?"

"Yes. There were some interesting glyphs. I'll show you." She turned, moving toward the exit the Sons of Light had passed through only minutes before. Hunt glanced at Dana, shrugged, and followed Brigid from the chamber. Dana and Collins helped Duck to his feet and walked beside him as he was a bit unsteadily. Rather remarkable considering he'd been dead only a couple of minutes prior. It would be interesting to learn more about the spell O'Broin had used. Dana had to presume that the primary effect was on the Atesi himself and not the human body he occupied. Otherwise, Duck's mobility and seeming relatively sufficient health would make little sense.

Brigid led them to a spot perhaps thirty yards up the corridor and, directing her flashlight beam, pointed to a series of images painted on the uneven stone surface.

Collins said, "Alright, darlin', care to tell us what we're looking at?

"The Atesi said Sons of Light would initiate plagues on significant sites of all major religions. I believe these to be representations of those sites. See the apparent flames and pestilence as the backdrop?"

Dana asked, "How do we identify the sites?"

Brigid offered a smile and said, "It's really not that difficult if you look at the symbols. See here, this is likely Mahabodhi Temple. See the Buddha-like image? And the backdrop fits Mahabodhi." She pointed at an image of a rather rotund man seated in a relaxed posture. "And this would be Kashi Vishwanath Temple in India. Note the golden spires. The design is clearly Hindu and quite specific to that site." She pointed at another. "This would be Mecca in Saudi Arabia."

"Islam," nodded Dana.

"What's this? Satanism?" asked Hunt pointing at the furthest image to the left. "This inverted cross?"

"No," said Brigid. "That's Christianity, most likely Catholicism specifically."

"I don't get it. Why's the cross inverted?"

Brigid offered a mischievous grin. "It's not just a cross. See, there's a figure on it. Christ was crucified upright, but tradition states that Saint Peter claimed he wasn't worthy to be crucified in the same manner as his lord and requested to be crucified upside down. Rather sweet, in a deathly gross sort of way."

"Saint Peter's Basilica," said Collins. "At the Vatican. She's going to do it at the Vatican."

"How do you know that's the proper location?" asked Dana. "It could be any of these."

"No," said Hunt. "O'Broin said she'd see Collins at home. Tina works for the Vatican. She's right. It'll be the Vatican."

"Very well," came a voice from behind. "We shall travel to Rome."

"Bruno!" said Brigid in a near growl. None of them had noticed the rogue monk and his men approach. "Nope. You're not invited. You already stole the rod once. Just chill and stay out of the way."

Qudsi shook his head and addressed the scowling archeologist. "Young woman, I understand your position. But we now have the same information as you. Therefore, we are going to the Vatican. The only question is, shall we join forces or get in each other's way, likely causing us both to fail in our most urgent quest?"

Brigid scowled and said, "You suck," before returning her earbuds to her ears and walking from the onetime monk.

***

Hunt and Dana stood apart from the others as the pilot prepared for the return trip to Luxor where they would then take a commercial flight to Rome.

"What do you think about Duck?" asked Hunt as he repressed a shudder. He was no longer in proximity to the amulet and so had begun to feel the withdrawal-like symptoms. "Do you think the Atesi's really gone from him?"

Dana shook her head. "How could we possibly know? The evil spirit was apparently hiding in him all along and none of us—including Duck—had the faintest notion."

"For that matter, how do we know Anascoreth is truly gone from me?" This was something that had plagued Hunt ever since the horrible events in Botma Africa. How could he ever really know for sure? What if some small fragment was still crawling around his subconscious somewhere?

Dana offered a conciliatory grin. "Marc, it's been months. There's been no evidence of reoccurrence. Has there?"

Hunt pulled his yo-yo from his pocket and attempted a basic maneuver, but his hand was shaking and the yo-yo refused to comply. "No. None." And this was true. Hunt hadn't had any indication whatsoever that there was still something malevolent inside of him. But he'd had the amulet throughout that entire span. The amulet which had driven out the evil spirit—or spirits, truthfully it seemed there were hundreds. But now the amulet was gone and he felt naked and exposed.

"I think you're safe, Hunt. I know this still troubles you. But I know you. And you're the same wonderful man I fell in love with."

Hunt stared at her, at her beautiful round face and bright gorgeous eyes. And the moment extended into an awkward silence. He didn't know where they stood, didn't know what she still felt. But he did know that they were at that crucial point where they would need to either begin the healing process or free each other to move on alone. When finally, the silence was broken, it was by both simultaneously.

"When you were taken by the Atesi . . ." said Hunt.

"When the Atesi slit your arm . . ." said Dana.

They both paused mid-sentence, laughed awkwardly and, again, simultaneously, said, "You first."

More laughter. Hunt gestured to Dana. "Ladies first."

"Oh, you know what I was going to say. I was worried for you. I thought this time you might be gone for good."

Hunt offered a weak smile. "I felt the same. When you were taken, I mean."

Dana nodded.

The silence returned. God, they were like two high school kids on their first date. This was his wife for God sake, why couldn't he just talk to her? "Listen, there's something I need to ask you. It's touchy. But it's been eating at me, so I guess I've got to get it out there before it makes me crazy."

"Go ahead."

Hunt sent his yo-yo into a couple of simple release and returns. His hands were shaky, but he managed. "Thorpe. When he . . . When you learned the Atesi had killed him, you . . ."

"Oh, blimey, Hunt. Are you really going to tell me you're jealous?"

"No. Just, he'd been your husband and you've spent a lot of time with him since we separated. Your reaction when he died . . ."

"Was bloody well appropriate," snapped Dana. "Yes, he'd been my husband. And after that he became my friend. And some mythical demon-god went and killed him for no reason other than . . . Well, I don't even know why. So, yes. I'm upset. Does that damage your self-esteem? I thought you were bigger than that."

Hunt should have known better than to have said anything. But it was on his mind and so needed to be said. Ugly or not, it was better to lay things on the table. Allowing it to fester would only make matters worse when finally, it emerged. Hunt shrugged, attempting a grin. "Yeah, well, Thorpe always called me a simian. Just chalk it up to cave man syndrome."

She glared at him for a moment, sighed, and then said, "Listen, we're both under a fair bit of stress. Off to stop bleeding Armageddon and all that rot. Let's just leave it, shall we? For now, I mean. Till this is over."

Hunt nodded, attempted to clear his muddled thoughts, and then said, "Qudsi and his men. I'm not happy about their involvement."

Dana cocked her head with what may have been a well-disguised wounded expression and said, "Alright then. Emotions stashed away, back to business just like that. No. I'm not at all happy about that particular development, but Qudsi was right in one aspect, he's going after the rod one way or another and its better we don't trip over each other as we go about it." And then she turned and marched away without another word. Yeah, Hunt had played that well.

Chapter Twenty-Five

Rome, Italy

Hunt wasn't Catholic, had never given the Vatican much thought, but he couldn't help but to be impressed by it. The architecture alone and the magnificent art throughout the sprawling campus astonished him. The Sistine Chapel was spectacular and the sculptures, the museums, the sense of history and majesty was tangible. That said, their current location within the Vatican held little splendor. They were situated in a large unadorned office adjacent an uninspired corridor. Essentially, they were in a holding area. Collins was elsewhere, speaking with her superiors, informing them of the situation while Hunt and his companions were left waiting.

While en route, Hunt had informed Duck of all that had transpired. At first, the young man had argued against Hunt's tale, claiming it was impossible. He would have been aware if he'd been carrying a spirit being with him for all that time. Hunt's response had been, "Then give me a better explanation for everything you did over the past couple of days, killing Thorpe and Ghilardi, shooting Brigid, using some crazy fire magic to roast one of Qudsi's men." Duck had none. He had no memory of any of it and was appalled that he'd injured Brigid.

The kid was obviously troubled by it all and Hunt could do little to console him. In truth, Hunt wasn't entirely convinced the Atesi was dead or gone. Duck seemed entirely himself again but Hunt now understood that he'd never actually known Duck absent the Atesi. The invading spirit had inhabited him and influenced him since before they'd ever met. In fact, it had been the Atesi, utilizing Duck's form, who had convinced the Keepers to hire Hunt in the first place. The Atesi who, even then, had been after Hunt's amulet. Hunt was certain that much of Duck's actions throughout their time together had been genuine, but not all. And so, going forward, how was Hunt to determine if his actions were inspired by something sinister? The most he could do was to keep an eye on the kid. He supposed they could have left Duck behind, but if he were still inhabited by the Atesi, this would have left the fire spirit free to act as he willed. At least this way the Atesi would be forced to lay low for a time. Maybe.

And right now, it seemed the young man was mostly interested in Brigid. The two stood in a corner of the room talking and sipping coffee. Qudsi and his three associates stood at the opposite side of the space, speaking in hushed whispers. Supposedly Crimson Moon's intent for the rod was simply to deliver it to the Christ—as if that were an everyday thing—while Sons of Light intended to initiate Biblical plagues throughout the globe. But Hunt trusted Qudsi's crew only marginally more than he did the Atesi. Dana sat beside Hunt. They'd discussed the mission but little else. Dana had become disturbingly quite after their conversation in the desert. Hunt tried to ignore it. This was crunch time, he didn't have the liberty to wallow in personal issues, but he was aware that things weren't well between them and that his fumbling comments of the day before might quite possibly have been the final nudge to cause Dana to walk away once and for all.

Hunt's contemplations were cut short as Tina Collins entered the room.

She wasn't smiling.

"Uh-oh," said Hunt. "That's not a happy face."

Collins replied with a scowl. "For people who've dedicated their lives to the spiritual, they sure don't want to accept that anything super-natural actually happens in the here and now."

Qudsi stepped toward the group, his block-like face rigid, his lips narrow with repressed anger. The guy was a real charmer. "Clarify, please."

Collins glanced toward Qudsi but addressed Hunt and Dana. "They see no reason to believe anything extraordinary will occur. In their minds the scepter has value only for historical and ritualistic purposes. It's a holy relic, nothing more. Dramatic supernatural events were relegated to an earlier dispensation, which basically means different supernatural activity is delegated to different time periods. A bunch of hogwash if you ask me."

Moving to join the conversation, Brigid asked, "Did you tell them about what occurred in the Temple of the Perpetual Flame? Hello. Lightning bolts shooting from the scepter."

"Of course. They explained it away as clever illusions."

"That was no illusion."

"Oh, darlin', of that I'm sure."

Dana asked, "So, where does that leave us?"

Collins shrugged. "My mission hasn't changed—get the scepter. As for the rest of you, you're guests of the Vatican, but have no official authority."

Brigid said, "How can they deny the supernatural potential? This is the tool used in the Bible to initiate plagues."

"Some people are of small minds," said Qudsi.

Brigid offered an icy stare. "Shut up, Bruno." Obviously, she was not a fan of the man who had stolen the rod and, by doing so, had set all of this in motion.

Collins moved to a corner of the room to a desktop computer. "Well, darlins', I saw what went down in the Temple of the Perpetual Flame. I'm not about to sit by and let bureaucratic mindsets usher us into

Armageddon." Sitting before the computer, she entered her password and within a minute's time had pulled up what appeared to be blueprints.

"What are we looking at?" asked Hunt.

"Blueprints of Saint Peter's Basilica."

Hunt nodded. That made sense based on what they'd seen in the temple. He said, "I saw what the Atesi was doing in the Temple of the Perpetual Flame. I'm not exactly sure what was going on beyond a spectacular light show. Can anyone tell me what we should expect out of the Sons of Light?"

Qudsi said, "If I may, I should be able to shed some light on the subject."

Hunt shrugged and nodded.

"The Sons of Light desire for the biblical plagues to revisit the earth in order to cleanse the world of the Sons of Darkness."

"Who apparently are any people that don't agree with them," mused Dana.

"Exactly," said Qudsi. "In their eyes, we are the Sons of Darkness. If they're successful we could see water turned to blood, great hordes of frogs and biting insects, wild animals on the rampage, livestock devastated by disease, boils, fiery hail, locusts, darkness, death of the firstborn. They truly hope to cleanse the earth of the unworthy."

All were quiet for several moments. The picture portrayed was devastating. Hunt wondered if all of this was even possible. He'd confronted the supernatural before, but this wasn't a troublesome spirit or some mystical mind control. This was world changing, catastrophic. Did that kind of power truly exist? And if so, could O'Broin and her crew access it? The Atesi was a spiritual being. It made some sort of crazy sense that he could tap into otherworldly power. But O'Broin was human. Yes, she'd used the codex to cast a spell or hex, or whatever you want to call it on the Atesi, she was obviously schooled in some sort of mystic arts, but this was a whole different level.

"Listen," said Hunt. "I don't know if the Sons of Light can really pull this off, but we've got to go with the assumption that they can. They've got the rod, the amulet, and the codex. I don't know how it all fits together, but we can't sit by and take the risk that they might slaughter thousands or maybe even millions of people. It doesn't sound like there's going to be any help from the Vatican, so I guess it's all on us. But this is going to be intense. You all saw what happened in the underground temple. O'Broin was able to take out the Atesi with an incantation and that was before she had the rod and the amulet. I can't guarantee that all of us—or even any of us—will come out of this thing alive. So, if anyone wants to back out, there's no shame. I just need to know who's with me. Because the week of holy convergence is nearly over. O'Broin's window of opportunity is growing short."

He glanced about the room. All eyes were on him. No one spoke.

"Okay," said Hunt. "Anyone leaving?"

Silence.

More silence.

And then Duck said, "Maybe we'll get lucky and they'll go somewhere else to end the world."

Hunt shook his head. "No. They're here. My head's clear. No shakes from being far from the locust. That means I'm in proximity. So, again, last chance to walk."

Duck shrugged. "I suppose dying an unimaginably horrible death isn't the worst thing that could happen to a person."

Everyone turned to look at him.

"Um, I'm in," he added with a nervous grin.

Hunt allowed several more moments before nodding and saying, "That's it then. We're all in." Turning to Collins, he said, "Tina, you've got blueprints up. What are you thinking?"

"Brigid pointed out that the graphic on the temple wall was of Saint Peter. Not just of Christianity or Catholicism in general. It was very specific to Peter. We all agreed this meant the target is probably Saint Peter's Basilica. I've accessed the blueprints. There are tunnels and chambers throughout the Vatican. Among them, there's a necropolis beneath the Basilica containing the tombs of several early popes, supposedly including Saint Peter himself. I'm going to take a wild guess that that's where they're headed."

Dana said, "Brilliant that. How do we get down there?"

"There are passageways. They give tours of the necropolis, but O'Broin would wait until late evening when no one's there. We'll need to be discrete. I'm a Vatican employee, but none of you have any special privileges. Not to mention, I made a pretty big stink with Cardinal Cancio just now. My share of grace might be running a little thin."

Qudsi said, "We will fight our way through if we must."

Hunt glared at the stone-faced man. "Yeah, that's not happening. There's no use in harming innocents and we're a small group. We can be subtle about this. There'll be plenty of time for fighting once we catch up with O'Broin and company."

Dana moved to beside Collins. "Show me the layout on the blueprints."

They spent the next hour huddled together, arguing, plotting, strategizing. In the end, they had a plan, which was when the People of the Crimson Moon drew their weapons.

***

It took less than fifteen minutes for the Huntingtons, Collins, Brigid, and Duck to free themselves from the duct tape Qudsi had bound them with but that still gave Crimson Moon a head start. It was past nine P.M. and there was little pedestrian traffic as they hurried to the basilica where they found the fresh corpse of a guard just inside the necropolis entrance. Dana heard Hunt swear under his breath as he checked for a pulse, confirming the man was dead.

The necropolis struck Dana with its stark contrast between old and new. The entranceway was pristine with cream, nearly white, colored walls and marble floors and subtly arched ceilings. Guardrails were in place to prevent tourists from proceeding down into the ancient tombs themselves. They each slipped beneath these and quietly moved below to where the stone was roughhewn with the appearance of ruins. The rock was of a rusty yellow, the walkways narrow and mazelike. Images of human figures were carved on many of the walls. Arched openings purportedly held the remains of over one hundred early popes, one of which was said to hold the inscription, "Peter is here." The remains within had been carbon dated to the first century A.D. and declared by the church to be the bones of Simon Peter the apostle.

Moving quietly amidst the tombs, Dana was the first to catch a glimpse of light ahead. "Around the corner," she whispered.

Hunt, who was beside her, nodded and moved toward the corner, peeking around. O'Broin was reading aloud from the codex. The rod and amulet lay side-by-side on what appeared to be a stone alter. There were six men with her, but the area was segmented. It was possible there were more who were obscured.

"Where's Qudsi?" whispered Dana.

Hunt shrugged. "No sign of him or his goon squad. O'Broin's doing her thing as if she had all the time in the world."

There was a subtle beep from behind and Dana turned toward Brigid who was withdrawing her phone from a pocket. "Brigid, quiet that," hissed Dana.

Brigid nodded, gasped, and then whispered. "It's a news alert." She paused, studied the screen, and said, "Oh my God. It's started."

"What?" asked Dana.

"News reports. Strange phenomenon. Planes knocked from the sky by fiery hail in Israel. Water turning to blood in the Nile. Insects swarming over Mecca. It's the plagues."

And then a shot rang out.

One of the Sons of Light fell dead. Another shot. Another man spun to his left, falling to the stony floor clutching a bleeding shoulder.

"Up there," said Collins pointing across the way to behind a partially crumbed wall. "It's Qudsi."

Dana followed Collins' gaze and saw Qudsi and his men across the way, on the tourist level, shooting down on the group as the Sons of Light began to return fire. Returning her gaze to O'Broin, Dana noted that the woman was continuing with her incantation. If the news reports were correct, she needed to be stopped immediately.

The People of the Crimson Moon had confiscated their weapons and so the Huntingtons and company were largely powerless while the gunfight continued. They could only hope that O'Broin was stopped before she could complete her invocation.

Hunt turned to Dana saying, "We can't just sit here."

But before he could continue, it happened. The area was suddenly flooded with frogs. They appeared as from nowhere. Pouring from the tombs like green and brown waterfalls, hopping this way and that, raining from the ceiling. The sound was deafening, thousands of croaking amphibians mixed with the slippery smacking sound of their movement.

Everyone stopped what they were doing.

That is, except O'Broin, who was unaffected. No frogs fell within a five-foot circumference of her and she continued with her evil rite. Her men were protected by no such magic and began screaming as they were overrun by the hopping horde.

Seeing this, Hunt bolted toward O'Broin, diving at her and knocking her free of the codex. One of her men was upon him immediately, but Dana and Collins were already in motion, knocking weapons free and disabling a man each before being toppled by the squirming mass of amphibian flesh.

Dana was pressed to the floor by the weight of hundreds of frogs and rolled first left then right, attempting to free herself from the swarm. She gasped for breath and a frog wriggled into her mouth, and toward her throat blocking her airway. Panic welled up from within. She was going to die here. Right now. In these moments. She was going to suffocate on a bleeding frog!

***

Hunt saw Dana go down but there was nothing he could do. He called her name, over and over. But saw no sign of her. O'Broin had clawed her way free of Hunt and was making her way back to the codex as the frogs parted like the red Sea, allowing her to pass. Hunt knew he should follow, that the most important goal was to prevent further catastrophes, but he needed to find Dana first. She could be suffocating beneath a sea of frogs. But if the hopping darting horde was aiding O'Broin it was anything but gracious to Hunt, bounding on him from all sides and preventing him from moving. There were thousands of them, all seemingly clamoring over each person. Hunt turned toward where he'd last seen Dana. It was as if she'd been swallowed whole by the sea of cool slippery flesh. Still, he repeatedly called her name. He had to find her. He had to!

He saw Collins batting at the things while one of Qudsi's men, driven off by the frogs, fell from the balcony above to land heavily on a stone sarcophagus. He had no idea where Brigid or Duck might be. But couldn't concern himself with them just now. He had to find Dana; she was all that mattered in the moment.

Unable to remain standing on the wriggling floor of frogs, Hunt tumbled sideways, connecting with a large stone slab balanced on two square supports. Grabbing the slab by both sides, he pulled it sideways and managed to lift the weighty piece nearly to above his head. He then let it drop, smashing hundreds of frogs in the process. He lifted it again, balancing it on one end before pushing it forward smashing another batch of the endless enemy. This time, the slab broke into two pieces, but there was still a large enough segment to use for his purposes.

He tried to lift this larger segment but was overrun before he could do so. It was amazing to think of frogs as having any real weight, but hundreds scaled his back and onto his head and eventually his knees gave way. Hunt fell forward swinging wildly, still calling Dana's name.

***

Dana's vision became blurry. She forced air in through her nose and thus far had managed to remain conscious. Biting down hard, chomping really, she managed to kill the frog in her mouth, nearly chopping it in two. Spitting it out, she clamped her mouth shut, leaving all her breathing, both inhaling and exhaling, to her nose.

Swinging her arms, wildly, she clawed her way to possible salvation. She'd spotted a fire extinguisher clamped to a wall on the level above, beyond the railing. She attempted to scale the coarse rock wall, but frogs were everywhere and every time she tried to get a hand or foothold, she would slip on the slimy green flesh. But she had to do this. She saw no other hope.

Swiping an arm left to right, she cleared an area of frogs and climbed upward until the swarm reacquired the space. She did it again and again, swiping the frogs away and inching into the cleared off space as they poured back onto the vacant spot. In this way she climbed the uneven wall to the base of the railing.

There was a new sound now. Rising above the croaking and slippery slapping of the frogs. A buzzing. It came in waves, softer, louder, softer, louder yet. And then they were upon her. Insects swarmed through the necropolis in jet black clouds that nearly obscured Dana's vision.

Grabbing the metal railing she heaved herself onto the upper deck as frogs poured over her and insects assaulted her flesh. Shouting and batting at insects and amphibians she continued forward, making her way to the wall mounted fire extinguisher.

Ripping the cylinder from the wall, Dana turned and sprayed her tiny assailants with the gray/white mist. The CO_2 did its job as several frogs flipped and squirmed, dying almost immediately. The insects, as well, were affected, dropping to the floor in spiraling stutters to accumulate in dying heaps. Still spraying in sweeping bursts, Dana surveyed the area below. She saw Duck wading through the sea of frogs toward an out-stretched arm. He clasped the extended hand and pulled the gasping Brigid above the frogs and into a cloud of insects. Collins was moving along the balcony area opposite Dana, making a beeline for Qudsi who now appeared to be alone. O'Broin had recovered the codex and re-sumed chanting in a foreign tongue.

But there was no sign of Hunt.

Still clinging to the fire extinguisher, Dana slipped under the railing and slid down the rocky wall on a bed of slippery frog flesh. Reaching ground level, she used extinguisher bursts to clear her way as she moved toward the place where she'd last seen Hunt.

Frantically, she called his name, sweeping the extinguisher stream right and then left. He had to be here somewhere. He couldn't be gone.

Dana felt a painful and peculiar sensation on her left shoulder, then her belly, then face, hands, arms, legs. Examining her arms, she saw dozens of large puss-filled boils emerging. Screeching a horrified cry, she sprayed the fire extinguisher in a chaotic stream with no specific purpose beyond revulsion and anger.

A gunshot echoed through the chamber, bringing Dana back to clarity.

Turning toward the sound of the shot, Dana caught sight of a boil-pocked Tina Collins battling with a similarly blemished Qudsi on the upper level. His gun hand was raised with Collins clamping it at the wrist. Insects swirled about the battling duo as Collins first kneed him and then flipped him. And then they both disappeared beneath the frogs. A moment later there was another gunshot. This one muffled. Dana did not see either combatant rise from amidst the sea of frogs.

Ignoring the painful soars covering her form, Dana screamed Hunt's name, spraying the CO2 frantically as she spun in circles, covering as much area as possible.

Above the sound of croaking, slippery slapping, and buzzing insects, Dana heard loud coughing and hacking. She raced forward toward the sound, reached into the squirming mass of green and hauled Hunt upright.

"Hunt!" screamed Dana as she pulled him into a fervent hug.

He accepted her embrace but continued to hack. "God, that stuff's almost worse than the frogs."

Their reunion was short-lived as a howling scream echoed through the chamber.

***

Hunt turned to see one of Qudsi's men, tall, bald, and perpetually stern-faced, arch his back and emit a warbling cry. What appeared to be red gas with darting sparks of flame erupted from his mouth. Within moments the gas began to bulge and squirm, stretching into bulbous protrusions, gradually taking on a roughly human-like form.

"The Atesi!" gasped Hunt. "Dammit! I'd hoped he was really dead."

"He must have escaped Duck's dying body and jumped to Qudsi's man at the Temple of the Perpetual Flame."

"Good an explanation as any. And now he's free and heading for the rod!"

Hunt and Dana both turned toward O'Broin. There was no need for discussion. They had to get to her. Hunt didn't understand how the Atesi was visibly manifesting outside of a human host, but that was the least of his concerns in the moment.

Out of the corner of his eye, Hunt saw Brigid and Duck tackle one of O'Broin's men who was moving to intercept them. All three forms disappeared beneath the frogs, resurfacing several moments later, Duck now holding the man from behind, his arm locked around his neck.

A gurgling, splashing sound now echoed through the chamber. Hunt turned to see blood gushing from each tomb, splatting on the frogs and slowly flooding the necropolis. My God, were they going to experience every one of the plagues?

The Atesi was already upon O'Broin, swirling around, jabbing at her. With every touch, her skin sizzled, little wisps of smoke rising from her flesh. The Atesi's cackling laughter cascaded about the hall.

Dana reached O'Broin, ripping the codex from her hands as Hunt grabbed her by the shoulders. It was like touching hot coals. "How do we stop it? Dammit, tell me how to stop it!"

O'Broin shook her head, her face a grimace of pain. "Ah, Huntington. You're too late, ya do know that. Far too late. We've all lost now."

Setting the codex on the alter, Dana said, "Help us! We need to unite to fight the Atesi. We can still stop him with your help."

But the Atesi swooped down engulfing O'Broin in flames. "Is that what you think? Ah! Ah-ha! Not so, not so!"

Hunt stumbled back, batting flames from his hands even as O'Broin ignited into a fiery pyre. She fell to the floor, writhing and screaming before sinking from view into the sea of frogs. The Atesi giggled and twirled as Hunt gagged at the smell of burning flesh.

Gunshots rang out. Tina Collins was on the upper-level firing shots at the Atesi. Not surprisingly, these were ineffective. The Atesi laughed and flipped. "Ha! Oh-Ha! Marvelous! Just marvelous! Miss Collins, you are a treat!"

Dana turned to where Brigid and Duck, both covered in boils, were wading through the sea of blood and frogs, their captive in tow. Swatting at the swarming insects, she bellowed, "Brigid! You'd been translating the codex. Can you read it? Can you reverse what O'Broin's done and stop the Atesi?"

The young archeologist shook her head. "Um, not exactly schooled in supernatural spell casting. It could take hours—days—to find and translate the proper passage if it even exists."

The Atesi swooped down, gripping Hunt. He could feel the searing presence of the demon, pressing, attempting to penetrate his being. No! Not again! Not again! The thing was attempting to wriggle into his brain. Hunt was fighting it, holding it off, but for how long? The force of the

Atesi's will was like a vice on his soul. He couldn't endure another possession.

There was a sudden rush of cold air. No. Not air. Gas. CO_2.

It was Dana, the fire extinguisher in hand. She was blasting the Atesi with it, attempting to extinguish his flames. Amazingly, it had some sort of effect, diminishing the blazing spirit's fire. Hunt couldn't imagine this could damage the beast or even deter it for long, but it had distracted the Atesi. Hunt could feel the spirit lessening its pressure within. He shouted within his mind, with every fiber of his being, *GET OUT!*

The Atesi snapped free of Hunt leaving him to stagger as it streaked to Dana, knocking the fire extinguisher from her hands and dropping flaming balls on her flesh.

"Bloody hell, that wasn't quite what I was going for!" screamed Dana as she batted at spots of flames appearing on her arms. The Atesi was swirling about her, smacking her with flames, igniting her bit by bit.

How could they fight such a thing? How could they hope to . . .?

With sudden inspiration, Hunt turned and raced toward the altar which held the scepter and the amulet.

Gaining the altar, he studied both objects. The scepter held the true power. The locust in the amulet had originated in this rod. But Hunt had no connection to the rod of Aaron. It was as foreign to him as some hunk of rock from a distant galaxy.

But the amulet . . .

The amulet called to him. It beckoned. He could feel its pull even now, calling to him, drawing him nearer.

Hunt snatched the oblong piece of amber from the altar.

It was hot, nearly searing.

"No!" cried the Atesi as, leaving Dana, the fire spirit raced to Hunt, now engulfing him.

But despite the searing heat, Hunt held the amulet tight in his grasp. He could feel the frantic vibration of the locust's wings that somehow extended beyond the confines of the golden-hued fossil. Holding the amulet high above his head, Hunt shouted for this to stop, for this madness to cease. But the words that passed his lips were foreign to him. A lost tongue. Maybe the same language O'Broin had used in summoning the plagues, but Hunt couldn't know for sure. All he knew was that they were the amulet's words, not his own.

There was a hush followed by a deathly cold and a whoosh of air. And then the room was as devoid of oxygen as the vacuum of space. The Atesi spun, pulled away by the fleeing oxygen, his form shredded into dozens of small particles even as his flames extinguished, and the fire demon hissed a final cry before vanishing into eternity.

Hunt felt lightheaded as he gasped but received no air. He saw Dana stagger, also gasping for breath where there was none. He wheezed again, nearly faltering. Consciousness was fading. Making eye contact with Dana, he took a tentative step in her direction. He had to get to her. He couldn't die yet, not without holding her one last time.

And then there was a shudder from the amulet and air returned, rushing in like a tidal wave. Hunt saw Dana's hair blow back as he squinted into the sudden gust.

The air stilled.

Hunt nearly fell, still clutching the now-cool amulet, but Dana moved forward to steady him.

Silence.

Stillness.

At first it didn't register.

And then Brigid began to laugh. "The frogs! The insects!"

And Hunt realized the significance of the silence. There was no croaking, no more slippery smacking sounds of slimy flesh moving upon slimy flesh, no buzzing. The frogs, all of them, not one of them moved. Every one of them was dead. Likewise, the insects had all fallen, the blood had ceased to flow.

And the boils! Already the boils were diminishing to nearly nonexistent.

Hunt joined Brigid with a low building laughter.

But Dana wasn't ready to celebrate. Snatching the codex, she began ripping pages from it. Shredding them, hurling them aside like rubbish.

Panicked, Brigid waded through the dead frogs toward Dana. "What are you doing? That's a priceless piece of history?" Her voice nearly cracked with horror.

"It's a bloody nuclear bomb is what it is," said Dana. "And I don't want anyone to ever have access to this type of power again."

"But . . ."

"No buts, Brigid. The thing is treacherous." Dana continued ripping pages from the ancient text, glaring a warning at Brigid as she did so.

"Hey, anyone want to give a lady a hand?" It was Collins, still on the upper level. She was holding a gun on Qudsi, who appeared to have a bullet wound on his left shoulder. The other members of People of the Crimson Moon, and apparently most of O'Broin's compatriots, had either fled or, more likely, perished beneath the sea of frogs.

Hunt smiled up at her. "Looks to me like you've got the creep pretty much under control. But I've got zip cuffs. I'll be up in a minute to give you a hand." He glanced toward Duck who still held O'Broin's man in a neck hold. "Be with you in a sec too." He then slipped the amulet into his pocket, tapped Dana on the shoulder, and kissed her fervently on the lips.

"I thought I'd truly lost you," he said when they finally disengaged. "I can't let that happen. Ever."

Dana grinned up at him. "Well, I suppose you might have something there." She kissed him then, long and lingering.

"Um, that's sweet and all," came Collin's voice. "But could we maybe tend to business first?"

"Coming," shouted Hunt. "Just . . . Yeah." Grinning, he gave Dana a peck on the forehead, and moved toward Collins.

***

Collins alerted Vatican security. It took them some time to make their way to the necropolis as the entirety of Vatican City was covered with dead frogs, insects, and drying blood. It would take some time before they could uncover all the bodies buried beneath the lifeless amphibians and determine a death toll. Other significant religious sites had been hit as well with various plagues: The Mahabodhi Temple, Kashi Vishwanath Temple, Mecca. All the places Brigid had identified by the symbols on the wall in the Temple of the Perpetual Flame. The world was reeling with confusion, with various end times predictions, terrorist theories, or alien invasion claims. The people of earth were frightened. Something inexplicable had occurred and they were trying to make sense of it.

The Huntingtons and their companions were questioned at length by Vatican officials. They gave a true account of all that had happened, though their tale was looked at with severe skepticism. Even amidst all that had happened, even for the truly devout, it was difficult to admit that something overtly supernatural had occurred. Humans are strange creatures. They can see otherworldly origins in any number of relatively common occurrences, a cloud formation that looked like Jesus, tree branches that formed something resembling the star of David, but when something truly spectacular occurred, every conceivable "rational" explanation was given no matter how farfetched, anything to deny the reality of what had occurred.

Qudsi and the surviving Sons of Light member were arrested and taken away. The Vatican took possession of the rod of Aaron, but, though they frisked Hunt and the others, they could not find the amulet. Very interesting, for it was a rather large lump in Hunt's right pocket. Apparently, the locust didn't want to be found.

Later, when they were finally alone, Collins asked for the amulet, claiming that it was a powerful symbol of faith and could do a lot of good.

Hunt smiled and shook his head. "Nope, nope, nope. The Vatican's history is too full of conspiracy and power brokering. You think it's really a good idea to give them access to both the rod and the amulet?"

Collins grinned as she leaned forward and whispered, "Absolutely not, darlin'. But it is my job to ask. You go hide that thing and never let it see the light of day."

Noticing Duck and Brigid sitting somberly at the opposite side of the area, Hunt excused himself and made his way to them. "You guys okay?"

Brigid offered a subtle smile and gave her earbud wire a twirl. "I suppose you could say we're coming to grips with everything that occurred."

Hunt nodded. "Yeah. Aren't we all?" He paused and then asked, "What's next for you two?"

Brigid said, "Back to the dig site. There's still much to be done."

"And you?" he asked Duck.

"I'm unsure. I'm not comfortable returning to the Keepers after betraying them."

Brigid nudged him saying, "It wasn't you that betrayed them, it was the Atesi."

"It was the Atesi through me. This gives me much to contemplate."

Hunt placed a hand on the young man's shoulder. "Listen, Duck . . . Durukan. Several months ago, I was possessed. I get what you're feeling. And God's honest, I still haven't figured out how to deal with it. It's an indescribable violation. I don't think I'll ever get over it. But the one thing I do know, is you've got to move on. Don't let this be the defining event of your life. You're free of that beast now. The amulet slew the Atesi. We all saw it. Put this behind you. Move forward."

Duck smiled and nodded but said nothing.

Brigid glanced up at Hunt and said, "And what about you? Are you finally ready to move forward?"

Hunt narrowed his eyes, not quite sure what she meant.

Brigid grinned and then angled her head toward Dana, who was in deep conversation with Collins.

Hunt raised his eyebrows. "Ah. Yeah. Well, I guess I'm about to find out, aren't I?" Placing a palm on Duck's head and ruffling his hair, he said "In case you two haven't figured it out, you both like each other. You'd make a cute couple." He then turned and strolled toward Dana as Duck and Brigid stared at one another in search of a response.

Epilogue

Indiana, U.S.A.
Six weeks later

Carrying a cup of tea, Dana entered the garage, leaned against the doorframe, and grinned. Hunt stood hunched over his workbench staring at the amulet. "It's a bit chilly at night," said Dana. "I'm still not quite sure I'm suited for this Midwest weather."

Hunt offered a wry grin. "I know you liked our Vegas condo, but this is home to me. I need to feel grounded—at least for now." After a pause, he added, "Besides, London weather isn't any better. I don't know what you're complaining about."

"I fled London, remember? Hence Las Vegas—the desert. Warmth. Heat. Dry. Never muggy."

Dana smiled. They'd had some version of this conversation nearly every night since getting back together. In truth, Indiana wasn't horrible. The weather was unpredictable, true, and Hunt's place was on what she considered to be the border of civilization, just at the division between suburban and rural. But it was comfy. The people were friendly. And Chicago was only an hour distant. She had access to the metropolitan world whenever she was willing to take a drive. Fine dining, the theater, the bustle and excitement of thousands of persons.

She knew Hunt liked it here. And for now, that meant she would like it as well. They'd been through a lot, both encountering life changing events that, in truth, had nothing to do with the other, but, nonetheless, had pushed them apart. And now it was time for healing, for rediscovering just who they were both as individuals and as a newly reunited couple. Dana looked forward to the challenge.

But there was still one more thing between them. One huge obstacle to them resuming any type of normalcy in their lives. Coming closer to Hunt, she said, "You've got to make a decision."

Hunt continued to stare at the amber amulet.

"Hunt, really. This is obsessing you."

Hunt raked his short hair. "For some insane reason, this thing was meant for me. It literally calls to me." He paused, swallowed. And then added, "It saved my life. Our lives. All of us. It slew the Atesi, stopped the plagues." There was a quiver to his voice, moisture at the corners of his eyes.

Dana remained quiet. This was something he had to come to on his own.

"But . . ." he said, pausing as if he wasn't entirely sure what he'd meant to say. "But what if the wrong people get hold of it again? I don't know if it's done everything it's supposed to do for me, or if it has some other reason for me to keep it. But . . ." he paused again.

"That's alright, Marc. Tell me what you're feeling."

He exhaled audibly. His hands were shaking. "It's part of me now, alright? It's a part of me. But it's dangerous. Deadly dangerous. And I have no control over how it might be used." He swiped a tear away, likely hoping that Dana hadn't seen it.

Dana nodded, placing a palm on his back.

He looked at her, his eyes wide and liquid. He opened his mouth as if to speak but apparently thought better of it. He nodded, paused, nodded again. Leaning forward, palms on the work bench, he offered a guttural growl. And then, in one swift movement, Hunt picked up a large metal mallet and began pounding the amulet to dust.

Facts within the Fiction

Full disclosure time: As I'm sure you know, *Fires of the Atesi* is a work of fiction and should never be considered anything but. Sure, I've used actual locales and weaved many real-world details into my tall tale, many of which interact intimately with fictional parts. But all but a few elements came directly from my often-peculiar mind. As such, I thought it prudent to clarify several plot devices within the story in an effort to avoid confusing you, dear reader, as to where fiction ends and fact peeks its head out from amidst the gale of relentless fantasy.

I suppose it would make sense to begin with the title character, the Atesi. I based this character loosely on the myth of a Turkish and Mongolian fire god known by several names including Ates Iyesi, Od Iyesi, Od Kahn, among others. He is sometimes referred to as the king of fire or blazing spirit. Nowhere in the mythology is this deity referred to as the Atesi. This was purely my creation. I did this, one, to further separate my character from the deity of myth, securing him solidly in my fictional world, and two, simply because I thought "The Atesi" sounded cool. Think about it. *The Atesi!* It sounds sinister, maybe even other-worldly. It has pizazz. And let's be honest, it rolls off the tongue a lot easier than Ates Iyesi or Od Iyesi. And Od Kahn sounds like a weird version of a Star Trek villain. I take no credit for the name "Atesi" as the word "atesi" is Turkish for fire. While most of the historical background on Ates Iysei within this book is culled from actual myth, none of his present-day exploits are real. There are no references to Ates Iysei possessing a human host and, to my knowledge, there are no present-day followers of Ates Iysei. As well, there are no historical writings tying Ates Iysei to any end times prophecies or to the rod of Aaron. These connections are my own concoctions.

Let's move on to the rod of Aaron. The Biblical account tells us that Aaron was the brother of Moses. Both brothers had staffs (or rods) that were used to perform miracles. Most spectacularly, they were used to usher in the Biblical plagues on Egypt. Tradition holds that Aaron's rod was eventually stored within the Ark of the Covenant (along with the tablets of the Ten Commandments and some mana) and has not been seen since the Ark was stolen by the Philistines and was lost around 586 B.C.E. Unlike my fictional account, there is no record of the rod ever being recovered. Obviously, this means The Keepers are entirely fictional. There are some non-Biblical theologies asserting that Aaron's rod will be the scepter that Jesus holds upon his return. Another legend is that God created the rod on the sixth day of creation and gave it to Adam after which it was passed down from generation to generation eventually ending up with Aaron. I've used some of this apocryphal lore as a plot devise within this story.

Hunt's amulet first appeared in the previous Huntington novel, *A Savage Distance*, and is purely fictional. While locusts were one of the Biblical plagues, there is no myth of one of these locusts "returning to its nest" or of being encased in amber and granted mystical properties.

The section of Cairo known as Manshiyat Naser, or "Garbage City" is an actual place and I've done my best to represent it accurately.

People of the Crimson Moon are entirely fictional as is the scorpion god Anascoreth.

What about Zarathustra? He's brought up several times throughout the story. Yes, Zarathustra is a historical person born somewhere around six hundred B.C.E. and was one of the early religious leaders to promote a type of monotheism in the form of the god Ahura Mazda, meaning Wise god. As his culture was not ready to denounce all other deities, Zarathustra advocated Ahura Mazda as the greatest god among lesser immortals. His teachings are thought to have had a major impact on the emerging religion of Judaism. Present day followers of Zarathustra may attend a place of worship known as a fire temple, but the Temple of the Perpetual Flame is fictional. While, Zarathustra did live, the text called the Achaemenid Codex and credited to him in this novel is a fabrication, though the term "last turn of creation" is his terminology from other writings dealing with the end times. The word Achaemenid refers to the time of the Persian Dynasty 553-330 B.C.E.

Sons of Light is a group prophesied to battle an opposing force, the Sons of Darkness, in the end times. This prophecy is written in an ancient document known as the War Scroll, which is one of the documents comprising the Dead Sea Scrolls. For those unfamiliar with the Dead Sea Scrolls, these were first discovered in 1946 by some children exploring the Qumran caves on the northern shore of the Dead Sea. These scrolls include some of the oldest copies of most of the Hebrew Bible as well as many other religious writings. I've lifted the idea of the Sons of Light from the War Scroll but everything having to do with the present-day Sons of Light within my novel is purely fiction.

The serpent king, Vasuki, seen in the Temple of the Perpetual Flame, is from Hindu and Buddhist traditions.

I think that pretty much covers the major elements of the story. I hope you've enjoyed *Fires of the Atesi*. Keep reading. Keep imagining. Enjoy!

Thom

COMING SOON!

THE VOYAGE OF THE AMETHYST CASTLE
BY THOM REESE

**A mystical world filled with magic and
mystery in a castle floating on the sea!**

Teenaged cousins Echo Hernandez and Chettermelon Jones discover a peculiar castle made entirely of amethyst. Entering the structure, they discover a fantastic palace with whimsical residents and magical properties. Vines and bushes crawl about performing daily tasks, long-extinct creatures roam the corridors, meandering spirits offer dubious advice, and there's a heavy scent of peculiar in the air.

But all is not well in this mystical haven. The castle tumbles into the sea and is carried away, trapping the cousins aboard. Uncovering a plot to kill the king, Echo, Chettermelon, and a new band of friends are soon thrown into a world of conspiracy and intrigue. With only their ingenuity and their bond of trust in each other to guide them, they have mere hours to stop a brutal attack on innocent civilians, rescue the king, and expose the true culprit before hundreds die.

At once, whimsical, quirky, and action-packed, *The Voyage of the Amethyst Castle* is a manic romp through a unique and enchanted world that is guaranteed to capture the imaginations of all.

**For more information
visit:** www.SpeakingVolumes.us

On Sale Now!

MORE EXCITING THRILLERS
BY THOM REESE

**For more information
visit:** www.SpeakingVolumes.us

Sign up for free and bargain books

Join the Speaking Volumes mailing list

Text

ILOVEBOOKS
to 22828 to get started.